EPITAPH

ANITA WALLER

Print ISBN 978-1-913419-72-1

For everybody who has a Doris Lester
in their lives – and if you don't have one, get one!

I got you to look after me,
and you got me to look after you,
and that's why.
John Steinbeck, *Of Mice and Men*

Piglet sidled up to Pooh from behind.
"Pooh," he whispered.
"Yes, Piglet?"
"Nothing," said Piglet, taking Pooh's paw. "I just
wanted to be sure of you."
A A Milne, *The House at Pooh Corner*

1

'Don't forget to pack a swimming costume,' Doris Lester said, switching her phone from one ear to the other so she could tick that item off her to-do list with her right hand.

'I thought we were visiting cemeteries,' Wendy Lucas said. 'Why will I need a swimming costume? They've not had pools in any cemeteries I've ever been to.'

'Are you being deliberately obstructive, Lucas? A couple of the hotels I've booked for us have pools. So unless you plan on swimming in the nude, you'll need a costume.'

'I'm giddy.'

'I can tell.'

'Okay, got it. Swimming costume. Anything else?'

'Not yet. I'll ring if there is. What time are you getting here tomorrow?'

'If you're going to nag me, Lester, about ten minutes before bedtime.'

'Nag?' Doris tried not to laugh. 'I've never nagged in my life.'

There was a splutter from the other end of the phone. 'Yeah, right. I'll be there for about four. Shall we eat at the Bowling

I

Green? My treat to say thank you for doing so much of the organising.'

The eating place Wendy referred to was a seventeenth-century pub only a couple of hundred yards from Little Mouse Cottage, Doris's home for the past year.

'Great minds and all that,' Doris responded. 'Then an early night. I'd like to be on our way by nine on Monday morning. Belle is booked in at the cattery from tomorrow morning, so my first holiday in six years is actually happening.'

They disconnected, the two close friends both feeling buoyed by the thought of the strange holiday they had planned over many nights and phone calls, and they were sure adventures were waiting around the corner. Doris hoped for quiet adventures and an answer to a problem, Wendy slightly more rambunctious ones.

At first Wendy had laughed. *Let's go visit famous dead people's graves*, Doris had said, and five minutes later Doris's enthusiasm had spread to her friend. Subsequently they had a file full of spreadsheets, timetables, hotel bookings and a big fat journal each, for the sole purpose of recording their discoveries. They planned on having overworked pocket-sized Sprocket printers producing picture after picture after picture to stick in the journals, recording their travels over two weeks of some pretty intense driving. Wendy had laughed at her friend's meticulous preparations, saying other people made lists of clothes to take, trips to go on when they got there, eating stops on the journey – Doris had planned every footstep and every gravestone. A week earlier she had made a last-minute addition with several question marks on it, but it wasn't on Wendy's paperwork.

. . .

Doris settled down for the evening. She felt refreshed by the shower following her shortened daily run around the village, and she pushed her wavy silvery-grey hair around, hoping she could get away with it drying naturally. The small lines around her blue eyes crinkled as she smiled at the thought of the holiday to come.

It was the end of April, but England's temperatures hadn't reached any giddy heights so she lit the log burner. She could give it a good clean before leaving, she decided, then hopefully that would be it until early October.

She patted her knee and Belle obligingly jumped up. 'Good girl,' Doris said. 'I'm really going to miss you. I need you to be well behaved for two weeks. Think you can manage that? No shredding tea towels, clawing at furniture, and no demanding tuna. Dry food only for the next fortnight. Think you'll cope?'

'Miaow.'

'I'll take that as a yes then,' Doris said. The cat stood and kneaded with all four of her paws until she was convinced she had made her mistress's knee as comfortable as it could be, then the cat settled herself with a purr.

Doris too felt comfortable. Connection, the investigation business in which she was a partner alongside her granddaughter and her friend, was exceeding all their hopes and this holiday was at everyone's insistence. Connection will manage without you for two weeks, they had said, so bugger off, old woman.

Old woman. She smiled at their words, a reference to her recent seventieth birthday celebrations when she had declared herself to be a fully paid-up member of the Old Woman Society. An old woman with a black belt in karate and a phenomenal brain for absorbing facts and making computers sing.

. . .

Cat and mistress listened to a play on Radio Four in the absence of anything palatable on television, and Belle was finally put into her bed in the kitchen. Doris knew the beautifully slender animal would go in and out through the cat flap a couple of times during the night but would be waiting for her breakfast the next morning as soon as Doris entered the kitchen. A lovingly predictable animal.

Doris spent Sunday folding clothes neatly into her suitcase, checking things off against her list, and missing Belle. She had felt tears prick at her eyes when she had left through the main door of the cattery, but it came highly recommended and she knew Belle would be safe. The cat would probably be huffy with her when she returned, but she guessed she would be able to deal with that.

She placed a hot water bottle into the spare bed, knowing it hadn't been slept in for a while, and hoped Wendy would be comfortable. The room was pretty; white paintwork against small-flowered wallpaper gave it a cottagey feel, and Doris had enjoyed choosing antique furniture to help the ambience even more.

She sat in the armchair for a moment and looked around her. When the previous owner had lived here this had been the unused room, the one where everything went that didn't have a home elsewhere in the cottage. Now it was as it should be, and Doris loved it. She placed the little card welcoming Wendy to her home in front of the tiny vase of fresh flowers, took a last look around to make sure all was good, and went back downstairs.

Her guest would be here in an hour, so time for Doris to put up her feet and relax.

· · ·

4

Wendy sat down in the armchair with a sigh. 'I'm stuffed. That was a lovely meal.' She patted her stomach. 'I might have been nine stone when I left home earlier, but I've just added half a stone.' Her brown eyes twinkled as she spoke. 'I've been on a bit of a diet for this holiday, and had my hair cut.' She ran her hands through her hair. 'I've not had it coloured or anything for the last year, I've given in to old age.'

Doris laughed. 'Your hair is a lovely grey. It never needed colouring. And as for going on a diet, numpty, is this in preparation for overeating for the next two weeks?'

'Certainly is. And that holiday eating clearly started tonight at the Bowling Green.'

'You want a brandy?'

'That would be nice. Only one though, if we're setting off early. Why are we setting off at nine if we're only going as far as Chesterfield?'

'I'm taking you somewhere else first. I told you it would be an adventure, and an adventure it will be.'

Doris poured them both a drink, and then sat down in the armchair. 'You've brought your file of paperwork with you?' she asked Wendy, well known for being a little scatterbrained.

'Too right I have. I'm planning on having an hour or so every evening filling in my journal, printing off the little photographs, and keeping these dead bodies alive.'

'They're dead.'

'I know they're dead, but I'm never going to have another holiday like this one, am I? I want it recording, and besides, I like this little Sprocket thing. I've bought loads of papers so we don't run out.'

Doris smiled, remembering Luke's comments about the tiny printer. She had taken a selfie, printed it and stuck it to his computer in the Connection reception area.

'What's this?' he had asked. 'Why are you glaring at me?'

'I'm not good at selfies,' she had responded. 'And it's to let you know that I expect that new course to be finished and submitted by the time I come back to work; my eye is on you at all times.'

He had laughed uproariously, winked at her and said, 'As if I'd dare have you come back and that course be unfinished. Still, it's nice to have your picture, I might even frame it and sit it on my desk properly. It'll frighten all the baddies away, that's for sure.'

The two women sat almost without speaking, Doris going through her own file which she intended keeping in her laptop bag; she knew every step of the journey, and had toyed with the idea of maybe writing a small travel book about this particular holiday when she returned. It would fill the long winter nights of November through to March, but their journals, handwritten, decorated, ticket stubs stuck in with the glue sticks they had packed, would be her primary focus for the book, and a pleasurable end-of-day activity for them when they returned to their hotel.

'I went to see Bingo Jen last night. Thought I'd better tell her we were going away, because if I missed two sessions she'd have the police round at mine checking I wasn't dead.'

'You tell her where we're going?'

Wendy nodded. 'She asked. I said we were visiting dead bodies in cemeteries, famous dead people. I mentioned one or two of the names, but she looked a bit blank.'

'It's different people having different interests, isn't it? Take me, for instance, I couldn't call a game of bingo to save my life, but Bingo Jen can. And she's brilliant at it, it's why we have such a laugh when we go. But she couldn't kill a man with a precisely placed foot or hand.' Doris spoke in a matter-of-fact tone, and Wendy shivered.

'No, I don't suppose she can. I don't suppose I can, either. We're not going to have to kill people on this trip, are we?'

'Nah, shouldn't think so,' Doris said with a laugh. 'I'm not actually allowed to do it anyway. I just can. Did Bingo Jen make any further comments about our unusual holiday?'

'She did. She said two little ducks, twenty-two.'

'What?'

'I think she meant we're quackers.'

Alarms set for eight rang out in both bedrooms and twenty minutes later they were in the kitchen enjoying a cup of tea. They chatted quietly, neither lady being a morning person, and then washed and stashed away the cups and plates they had used.

Stowing everything away in the boot was an art form in itself, but finally they were ready to leave. Doris checked all lights were switched off and every door secure, then went out to join Wendy, patiently waiting in the passenger seat.

'Everything okay?' Wendy asked.

'All good. I've asked Luke to pop round a couple of times while we're away to make sure it stays that way, so we can go and not worry about anything. Ready, partner?'

'Ready, partner,' Wendy responded, and Doris drove down the hill towards the village outskirts.

They didn't speak much. Wendy lived in a Sheffield suburb, so didn't get to see Derbyshire in the way that Doris did; her eyes were glued to the scenery, envious of the beauty that Doris enjoyed every day.

Knowing that their first foray into grave spotting was Chesterfield, Wendy felt slightly puzzled by the route Doris was taking; she said nothing until they began the long drop down into Sheffield.

'This isn't the way to Chesterfield.'

'I know. We have another one to visit first. Indulge me.'

Wendy could sense an edge in Doris's voice and was wise enough to say nothing further, knowing an explanation would be there eventually.

Fifteen minutes later they turned into the entrance of City Road Cemetery, the largest one in Sheffield.

'We're here to visit Harry?'

'We are.' Doris no longer had an edge to her voice; it was grim. 'And tonight I'm going to show you some stuff that will explain why I'm here, because I think this is the final goodbye, not the one I said at his funeral.'

2

Doris stood by the graveside, and Wendy sensed anger flowing from her in waves. It hadn't been an easy marriage, that much she knew, but Harry had been dead a long time. She glanced at the headstone.

Harry James Lester
25.12.44 – 18.7.05
Much loved husband, dad and granddad
Rest in Peace

He'd been dead nearly fifteen years but clearly he'd managed to upset his wife from beyond the grave. And upset seemed a pretty mild word.

'What's wrong, Doris?' Wendy asked quietly.

'Possibly everything. Everything I thought was okay, and it wasn't. I've something to show you that I've only been aware of for less than a week, and I almost cancelled our holiday because of it, but then I decided we could make it part of the holiday. I don't want to say anything more until you see things for yourself, but I needed to come here this morning, get him off my mind for ever and do it without benefit of Connection. He was Mouse's granddad after all. She loved him.'

Wendy said nothing further; she waited by the side of the grave until Doris felt it was time to move.

They stood for a few minutes; Doris appearing lost in her thoughts. Suddenly she turned.

'Let's go.' She glanced around, moved a couple of steps and plucked a dandelion. She threw it on the grave, and walked away, heading towards the car. The action said more than any words, as far as Wendy was concerned, and she followed her friend, thinking it was going to be an interesting evening.

The sight of the Crooked Spire rising up into the heavens told them they were in the heart of Chesterfield, the satnav directed them straight to Holy Trinity Church and the remains of George Stephenson. A small plaque in the grounds informed them that he was buried in a vault inside the church, and further information added to that said he was under the altar.

Doris's foresight in emailing to ask that the church be unlocked for them had proved to be a smart move, and they were met at the door by the vicar, who told them his wife would make them a drink once they were ready for it.

They viewed George Stephenson's resting place together and they decided it made sense to split up and gather booklets to add to their journals, sharing everything between them each evening.

Doris switched off from her thoughts of Harry, and began her holiday in the beautiful church. She stood by the altar for some time. All her life she had been in awe of people who had contributed in some way to society; the only way to feel their presence, once they had died, was to stand by their gravesides and think. She did this in the welcoming church. Her father had given her a love of railways, and a love of George Stephenson. She felt honoured to be standing by the side of such a great man, even if it was only in death.

She didn't want to take photographs; she sat on a pew and did a quick sketch of his final resting place, then moved on to inspect the church properly. She met up with Wendy, and together they found the small room used for after-service drinks by the congregation.

The vicar's wife made them tea and scones, and then left them to talk.

As they left they dropped money into the donations box, and walked out into the sunshine.

A quick tour of the grounds, and they were back in the car, and heading out of Chesterfield towards their first stop for the night at Cromford.

'That was fab,' Wendy said. 'I thought you were crazy when you suggested this, but when you've done a bit of research and you feel you kinda know the chap, it makes a difference. Clever bloke, wasn't he?'

'Certainly was. You want to stop for lunch?'

'Not bothered if you're not. That scone was huge. I can wait till we have our evening meal, maybe have a mid-afternoon coffee at the hotel. Does that suit you?'

'It does, and I promise, after we've eaten tonight, I'll explain what all that was with Harry's grave. It's too complicated for me to have told you when we were there, and I couldn't tell you last night because I still wasn't sure I was going to do anything about anything. But around two this morning I knew I was.'

Wendy stared at Doris. She couldn't ever remember a time when Doris had been unsure of anything.

The two women settled into their hotel rooms, and after eating in the hotel rather than going out to find food, they headed back to Doris's room.

Doris pulled her file towards her and removed a letter. 'I need to talk to you about Harry.'

Wendy grinned at her. 'The dandelion said a lot.'

'He might have been dead fifteen years, but he's not taking it lying down, believe me. When I had Claire, things were definitely not good with us. I had to take leave of absence from work to have the baby, and as you know I was much higher than him in pay grade and it always rankled. I believe now that if we hadn't had Claire, our marriage wouldn't have lasted.'

'This was when you were in work and pensions?'

Doris gave a brief smile. 'Kind of. Work and pensions was my cover. I can't say much more about what I did because when you sign the Official Secrets Act it's a lifetime thing, but I know a little about work and pensions.'

Wendy's eyes widened slightly. 'And you were senior to Harry?'

'I was. I think he thought having a baby would stop me, but it didn't. I really only finally gave up my work when Mouse came to live with me. Even now my knowledge is still sought, but nobody at Connection knows that. However, that's irrelevant. I discovered he had been having an affair while I was pregnant. I wasn't good while I was carrying the baby, sick a lot, uncomfortable pain, that sort of thing, and I asked him to leave as soon as I found out.'

'You must have backtracked on that.'

'I did. I listened to him. I think he must have kissed the Blarney Stone or something because he persuaded me it was over, he had ended it because he didn't want to lose me or the baby I was carrying. He promised he would never stray again, it was a weak moment in his life... you know, the usual rubbish men come out with when they've been caught dallying. Anyway, I had Claire, went back to work when she was six months old and we lived a comfortable life. I never had any reason to doubt him again, until this week.' Doris stood. 'Shall we have a cuppa?'

'It's that serious? Shall I fetch my whiskey?'

'No need. I've brought mine.' Doris reached into her suitcase and took out the Jameson's. She made their drinks, and sat back down by her file, picking up the letter as she did so.

'When I bought Little Mouse Cottage I arranged for mail redirection, stating mail addressed to anybody with the surnames Lester or Walters should be forwarded to my new address. I paid for a two-year provision. I get maybe one a month now, usually junk mail, but last week I got an actual letter, and it was addressed to Harry.'

'Wow! Did it upset you?'

'Receiving a letter addressed to him? Not initially, I thought it was strange. Once I'd read it... I can't say I felt upset, but I felt bloody angry.' She passed the letter to Wendy. 'Read it and then we'll talk.'

Wendy took the A4 sheet of paper that had been folded into three and smoothed it open.

27 Long Lane,
Hucknall,
Notts.
NG23 7WY

Dear Harry Lester,

I'm sorry, I don't know how to address you. My name is Rosie Steer, although when I was born forty-six years ago (on the fourth September 1973) it was Rosie Chambers. My mother was Lily May Chambers.

My mother died two months ago and I am in the process of sorting out her papers and clearing her home. She never married anyone after you left, and has always said that you were a fly-by-night who couldn't commit to anything.

It now seems that was wrong, and that she had a long-term affair with you that lasted the best part of three years, and, according to her diary, she gave you up because I was growing older and she didn't want me to have memories of you. It seems you had another family and a wife, who you wouldn't leave to go to her. I know she told you lies, and it is important I set the record straight.

I would like to meet with you at some point. My mother became really bitter and I can only assume it was because of the hand she had been dealt in life.

I won't give you my email because the only one I have is connected to work, but I would like to hear from you. You can write to me at the above address.

Regards,
Your daughter,
Rosie

Wendy read it through a second time, then carefully refolded it. 'The bastard. The evil bastard.'

Doris gave a slight laugh. 'Don't hold back, will you? You're right though. So I need to make a decision. Do I go to see Rosie, or do I simply write to her and say her father is dead?'

'I think you have to see her. She's clearly not happy that she missed out on seeing her father, and it might soften the blow of finding out he's dead if that information doesn't arrive in a letter. And anyway, aren't you a little bit curious?'

'No, but you obviously are.'

'So when are we at the nearest point to her?'

'Tomorrow we're going to track down Sir Richard Arkwright's grave, spend the rest of the morning in his Masson Mill then on to Hucknall and Lord Byron straight after lunch. As you can see, Rosie lives in Hucknall. That's the day we stay at the Cockcliffe Country House. We're only there for one night. So if we can see Lord Byron in the early afternoon, we can also visit Rosie then. I don't have a phone number to warn her we're coming so...'

'Don't make me laugh, Doris Lester. Put your Connection head on and find something out about her, including her phone number.'

Doris shook her head. 'I don't feel I should. If she'd wanted Harry to have that number, she would have included it. Besides, a bit of a surprise might help things along.'

'Or she'll have a heart attack in front of us.'

'You think I shouldn't do this?' Doris was troubled.

'Of course you should do it. She deserves some answers just as much as you do. It's a pity bloody Harry isn't here to face the music though.'

'Have you worked it out that she's two years younger than Claire would have been?'

Wendy nodded. 'I have. He obviously lied, and simply carried on.'

'That's the bit that hurts. And going by this letter, it was actually Rosie's mother's decision to end the affair, not his. It cheapens our marriage, but I'll get over it. I'll never visit his grave again. You think it was his way of paying me back for being so much his superior at work? It never sat easy with him, but I had more skills that the Civil Service needed. And I'm not one to turn down challenges, as you know.'

'This is a bit of a challenge, Doris. You up for it?'

'I'm up for it.'

3

They put thoughts of a cheating Harry Lester to one side, and opened their journals for the first time. The little Sprockets churned out several photographs and the memories began. Doris's sketch of the last resting place of George Stephenson was photographed by Wendy so that she could have a phone and a Sprocket copy, and they cut out sections of information from the leaflets they had gathered. Even the receipt for the tea and scones in the church was placed in carefully, and when they had finished both of them sat back and smiled.

'If we write as much as this for every grave we visit, we'll need two journals each. I'm going to leave two pages between each day's entry, because I feel as though I'd like to know more,' Wendy said. 'And tomorrow's chap I know precious little about anyway, other than he invented the spinning jenny.'

'Sir Richard Arkwright,' Doris mused, 'began the industrial revolution. He did a lot of good, but the downside was he used a lot of child labour. I remember studying him at school, and I can vaguely recall a class trip to his grave and the mill, but not much else. I've deliberately not looked anything up in detail for any of these, it's much more fun doing the digging together. Don't forget we have the laptop if you want to look stuff up at any time.'

Wendy spluttered. 'As if I'd dare, Doris Lester. I've brought my iPad that works when it thinks it will; I'll manage with that. So, he's in a churchyard, isn't he?'

'He is. It seems he was buried in St Giles' Church in Matlock, but then his remains were moved to St Mary's in Cromford. Other than that, I only know snippets of his life, so I'm hoping we find out lots more when we get there. I need to go back to that office and dazzle Luke with my superpower knowledge.'

'Oh, I think you dazzle him anyway.' Wendy smiled. 'In his eyes, you're the boss, not Kat and Mouse.'

'You think?'

'I don't think, I know. Who does he turn to with queries? Who does the surveillance jobs these days? You and Luke.'

Doris smiled. 'He's a lovely lad. I've moved into Nan mode with him now, as easily as I did with Kat. But enough of work. Let's see what we can find out about Lord Byron, he's the next on our list.'

'And Rosie Steer,' Wendy said softly. 'You have to put this one to bed, Doris, because if you don't it will eat away at you. You're the strongest woman I know, so don't let this peccadillo get the better of you.'

Doris gave a slight shake of her head, as if clearing her thoughts. 'I won't, but I've no idea what to say to her. She's only recently lost her mother and I'm going to be saying she hasn't got a father either, she's fifteen years too late.'

'You'll think of something, and you'll get it right, little Miss Diplomacy.'

Doris poured them both a whiskey into their tooth glasses, and they returned to their journals, looking through the information already garnered.

'So, Richard Arkwright.'

'Sir Richard Arkwright,' Doris corrected.

'And George Stephenson wasn't a Sir?'

'Seems not. But our next one is, or was, a Lord.'

'Mmm, Lord Byron. I know his work but precious little about him. Every day's a school day on this holiday, isn't it?' Wendy laughed. 'So, anything I should know about Sir Richard before we get to the romance of Byron?'

'I don't know much, but the basics are that Arkwright was born in 1732 and died in 1792 and he was the youngest of seven surviving children of a marriage between Thomas and Sarah. In 1769 he patented the first spinning frame which revolutionised the cotton industry. Clever chap, yes?'

'Certainly was. I've all on threading a needle.'

'I know. I'm hoping to inspire you tomorrow. We'll go visit his grave, then have a couple of hours at Masson Mill. This mill was his pride and joy. It's on the banks of the Derwent, because it had so much more power than the water that fed the Cromford Mill. It's a museum with shops and cafés but there's still a working part of it. I think we'll have a good morning there, then after lunch we'll head over to Hucknall for a date with Lord Byron.'

Wendy downed her whiskey, gathered up her belongings and said goodnight. 'Breakfast at nine?' she asked.

'Yes, I think so. It will only be a brief visit to his grave, then down to the mill. I'd like us to be leaving by about half past one, then we can head over to the Cockcliffe Country House and get booked in before we look for Lord Byron. Is that okay?'

'Fine by me. See you in the morning.'

Doris found sleep difficult. She got out of bed a little after three and made a hot chocolate, opened up her Kindle once again, and settled down to read. Her thoughts were constantly drifting to Rosie's letter and Doris recognised she was still unsure about what actions to take.

The letter gave no clue as to Rosie's character; was she a nasty piece of work, or a pleasant, welcoming woman who would be sorry she hadn't met her genetic father and got on with her life? Doris dragged herself back to her book and tried to dismiss the unknown Rosie, but it was proving impossible.

Doris put the Kindle on the bedside table, slid down under the covers and forced her eyes closed. She had to sleep; she was doing the driving.

Doris was quiet during breakfast, partly due to lack of sleep and partly due to the impending Hucknall visit. Her eyes felt full of grit, and she blinked frequently to try to wake them up properly.

'You're quiet.' Wendy looked across the table at her friend. 'Didn't sleep too good, I presume.'

'No, I was still awake and making a hot drink at three. I'll be glad when today's over and I can put this peccadillo, as you call it, to one side and forget about Harry and his paramour.'

'Peccadillo, paramour – all the "p"s this morning. You read a dictionary during your waking hours, then?'

Finally Doris laughed. 'If I had, I'll leave you to imagine what other word beginning with p I could use in relation to Harry bloody Lester.'

Wendy thought for a moment and then grinned. 'Got it. Five letters, and means to stab with a needle.'

They high-fived, and the young girl who had served them breakfast came over with the cafetière to top up their coffee cups.

'Can I get you ladies anything else?'

'No thank you.' Doris smiled. 'We're incredibly fat and full after that delicious breakfast, and we've got a date with a grave.'

'You're here for Sir Richard?'

'We are. Do you get many people here for that?' Doris asked.

'Oh yes. They visit graves of famous people, it's the thing to do, it seems.'

'That's exactly what we're doing,' Wendy said. 'We're off to see Lord Byron's this afternoon.'

The waitress smiled and removed their plates. 'Have a good day, it's supposed to be sunny, but maybe that's after the rain's finished. It's bucketing down at the moment.'

'Great,' Wendy said and turned to look out of the window. 'Look at that.' The rain was river-like as it ran down the panes of the large bay window.

'Don't be a wimp, woman. We've got brollies and raincoats, haven't we?'

'Yes, but yours is bright yellow.'

'My brolly is black. And I love my yellow coat. Let's face it, when I've got that on, you won't lose me in a crowd.'

'You think there'll be a crowd at Sir Richard's grave?'

'No, but there might be at the mill. Then you'll be glad I've worn a yellow coat. And it's from Marks and Spencer.'

'Does that make a difference?'

'Certainly does. It means the yellow won't fade.'

'Oh dear gods.' Wendy dropped her head into her hands. 'I was counting on it fading.'

'I'll compromise,' Doris said, trying to keep her face straight. 'I'll not wear my yellow shoes with it.'

'What?' Wendy lifted her head. 'Yellow shoes?'

Doris pushed back her chair. 'Good Lord, Wendy, you're so easy to wind up. Of course I haven't got yellow shoes. They're boots. See you down here in ten minutes?' and she turned and walked towards the lift, a grin on her face.

Wendy watched her friend, her brain frantically trying to think of a way of repayment. Her time would come, she decided.

With Doris dressed in yellow and Wendy in bright red, they made a colourful sight in the grounds of St Mary's Church in Cromford, walking around between the graves, taking note of where the extended Arkwright family was buried before heading inside, through the beautiful triple-arched entrance.

Sir Richard was in the crypt, lying beneath the chancel and the nave, along with close members of his family, and the two ladies stood for a moment, their thoughts filled with the knowledge they had gleaned of his life, and the part he had played in history.

They collected the obligatory leaflets, dropped their donations into the collection box and came out in awe of the splendour of the church. The wonderful lighting had shown up the paintings hanging on the walls to perfection, and Doris was surprised to hear Wendy say, as they left the church, 'You could certainly feel the presence of God in there.'

Doris simply nodded in agreement and they headed back to the car, both lost in thought.

Masson Mill, Arkwright's most favoured mill, kept them fully entertained for a couple of hours, and they came away loaded with souvenirs, a book on Arkwright's life, and both feeling slightly sick after the coffee and cake they had enjoyed, despite already-full stomachs following the excellent breakfast.

The sun had returned by the time they left the building and walked around to the car park. Doris took off her yellow raincoat and placed it in the boot, slipping on a navy jacket to match her navy and white skirt.

'That's better,' Wendy said. 'You'll not frighten this woman to death now. She could easily have thought there was a giant wasp standing at her front door.'

'And you don't resemble a giant strawberry?'

'I'll put on a jacket when we get to the hotel. Don't worry, she'll think we're perfectly normal people.'

Doris laughed as she slipped behind the steering wheel. 'That'll be a first for the two of us.'

Following the advice on the website, Doris keyed in the address of the Cockcliffe Country House Hotel, knowing that to put the postcode in was likely to send her adrift.

The hotel, impressive in appearance, was welcoming and warm, and they were shown to their rooms without delay. They unpacked what they needed for the night, met up downstairs and had a coffee, then took collective deep breaths before heading back outside and to the car.

Tuesday afternoon would start with a visit to Byron's grave, and end with a visit into the unknown; Doris felt nervous, something she wasn't used to feeling, and Wendy was aware of her friend's disquiet. She had slipped a small hip flask of whiskey into her bag in case either of them required a little Dutch courage.

'You have everything you need? Wendy asked as she sank back into the comfort of the passenger seat.

'I do, but what could I possibly need? I'm there to tell her the father she never met is dead, and all I can give her is his grave location. What else can she ask of me?'

4

But there is that within me which shall live. Torture and time, and breathe when I expire.

Doris and Wendy stood by the stone dedicated to Lord Byron and drank in the words etched into it.

'This is overwhelming,' Wendy mumbled. 'Absolutely overwhelming. I thought the others we have seen tugged at the heart strings, but this is... Byron. My God, Doris, thank you so much for this. Without you and this crazy adventure, I would never have stood and felt like this. It's...'

'Overwhelming?' Doris took hold of Wendy's hand. 'I know exactly what you mean. A few years ago I stood at Elvis's grave in Memphis and felt like this. Maybe it's because they were young. Byron was only thirty-six when he died.'

They stood in silence for a few minutes, only moving when someone else came towards them, carrying a small bunch of flowers.

'Let's go find somewhere to have a coffee. We'll be busy tonight, I reckon, with these pictures and leaflets to get in the journals.' Doris stepped away and Wendy leaned down and gently touched the inscribed words. She said nothing, simply followed her friend out of the church grounds.

The coffee shop was small and they ordered two lattes, feeling somewhat mortified when the owner asked if they wanted skinny or ordinary.

'Do we look as if we should be having skinny lattes?' Wendy hissed as the pair sat at a nearby table.

'I didn't when we set off yesterday morning, but we've had plenty of cakes and stuff since then.' Doris laughed. 'We'll wait until September or so before we get back on any scales. In the meantime, we're on holiday and can have full-fat lattes if we want. Skinny lattes, indeed.'

The drinks were duly delivered, and Doris took out Rosie Steer's letter, smoothing it until it was flat.

She reread it, and passed it to Wendy. 'Hang on to this then read the postcode out to me when we're in the car. We'll let Susie Satnav take us to it.'

'Think she'll find it?'

'Has she ever let us down?'

'Yes. That show we went to in Leeds, she made us late.'

Doris laughed. 'Oh stop being so picky. She's getting on a bit, and she is rather overworked. She gets there in the end.'

Wendy slipped the letter into her bag and picked up her glass cup. 'This is nice. Glad we didn't go for skinny.'

Long Lane wasn't a long lane at all, and Susie Satnav found it with no difficulty.

You have reached your destination, the disembodied female voice told her two passengers.

'See, oh ye of little faith,' Doris said, smirking at Wendy as she pulled on the handbrake. 'Delivered right to the door.'

Number twenty-seven was a semi-detached stone-built cottage, with a long path leading up to the shiny black front door, complete with gleaming brass door furniture.

'Looks nice,' Wendy murmured, trying to peer around her friend, still sitting in the driver's seat. 'Her brass is shinier than yours.'

'Oy! Nothing wrong with my brass.'

'So,' Wendy continued, making no further reference to Doris's door furniture, 'how do you want to do this? You want me to go with you, or wait in the car?'

Doris turned a panicked face towards Wendy. 'Go with me of course. This is scary enough, and if I turn stroppy I need you to bring me down to earth. Harry's philandering ways aren't the fault of this poor woman.'

'Hmm, another p word we can attribute to your errant husband,' Wendy observed with a smile. 'Come on then, screw your courage to the sticking place, Doris Lester, and make Shakespeare proud of you for following his advice.'

She handed the letter back to Doris, and they opened the car doors simultaneously. 'Let's get this over with and enjoy the rest of our holiday,' Doris said, and pressed her key fob to lock the car.

The path seemed endless, and when they reached the door it was opened before they had the chance to lift the brass fox to knock.

'Yes?' The dark-haired woman with deep brown eyes standing in front of them looked to be around forty, a little harassed, and must have thought they were Jehovah's Witnesses; her attitude was slightly abrasive.

'Mrs Steer?'

'Yes. What do you want?'

'My name is Doris Lester.' Doris held out her business card, and the woman took it, then read it.

It seemed that the lightbulb suddenly switched on and she looked up. 'Doris Lester? As in Harry Lester?'

Doris nodded. 'This is my friend, Wendy Lucas. Can we come in for a moment?'

Rosie opened the door, and Wendy and Doris edged past her, then stood waiting while she made the door secure. 'Please... come into the kitchen. Can I make you a drink?'

Doris gave a half-smile. 'We're fine for drinks, but thanks. We've recently had coffees.'

They reached the kitchen, and as they did so another woman, smaller than Rosie and with shoulder-length dark-blonde hair, stood. She looked at the two newcomers, then turned to Rosie.

'Shirley, this is Doris Lester, and this lady is her friend, Wendy...?'

'Lucas,' Wendy said.

Rosie gave a brief nod as if she remembered, then turned to Doris. 'And this is my sister, Shirley Ledger.' The sisters shared the same dark brown eyes, and they turned them towards each other as if reaching for comfort.

Doris and Wendy extended their hands and she shook them.

'Please, sit down,' Shirley said.

All four of them did so, and Doris produced the letter from her bag. 'I received this,' she said.

Rosie inclined her head, and Shirley reached for her hand. 'I sent it to my father.'

'I'm sorry to have to tell you that Harry Lester died almost fifteen years ago.'

There was a prolonged pause, and then Shirley said, 'No...'

The two younger women turned to each other. 'We're too late,' Rosie said.

Wendy felt uncomfortable. The figure of speech was wrong. We're too late? Surely it should be I'm too late. She could tell that Doris had picked up on it also, by the stiffening of her spine.

'You said you were sisters.' Doris tried to keep her tone casual.

'We are,' Rosie said. 'Mum was pregnant with Shirley when she and Harry split up. She never saw him again, and it changed her. It was her decision to make him go, because he wouldn't leave you, but she never bothered with anyone else. I can't remember him, he's like a shadow to me, and of course Shirley never knew him.'

'You didn't mention Shirley in the letter.'

'No, I intended telling him to his face. According to my mother's diaries she told Harry that she lost the baby. As far as he was concerned he had one daughter with Lily, and that was me.'

Doris felt sick. Who was the man she had lived with for all those years? And had their employers been aware of his clandestine activities with this other family? She thought not, he would have lost his job as they would have considered it a massive security risk. A national security risk, given her own career.

And how could he have walked away from a three-year-old little girl who had presumably been a large part of his world until Lily had told him to go? He deserved an Oscar for his acting abilities, Doris would give him that. After he had said he would finish with the other woman when Doris had told him she wanted a divorce, he hadn't given her any reason to doubt his fidelity from that day until a week ago.

And now it appeared he had two daughters from that relationship, Rosie Steer and Shirley Ledger. They were presumably both married as neither was known by their birth name of Chambers, but Doris wasn't convinced that she wanted to know anything further about them. That direction could spell unease and catastrophic complications.

She stood and Wendy repeated her actions. 'I'm sorry it was bad news for you, but I didn't want to tell you in a letter. We'll be on our way now. My email address is on my card if you ever need to know anything, but really, with Harry being dead, I can't imagine I can be of much assistance.' Doris attempted a small smile but recognised it couldn't have looked more false if she had tried. She placed another business card on the table, pushing it towards Shirley. 'I've already given your sister one.'

They had almost reached the kitchen door when Rosie spoke. 'I have a twelve-year-old daughter.'

Doris halted, and Wendy bumped into her.

'And have you told her about her grandfather?'

'I have. Not that he's dead, of course, but I have explained he was with Mum for around three years before she made him leave her.'

Doris turned around slowly. 'Please don't make Harry Lester out to be something he wasn't. Let's not forget he cheated on me for every one of those three years, and I had a baby too. When he left your mother, my Claire was nearly five years old. He never said a word to me about the baby born to his bit on the side, because that's what she was. I was the mug married to him.'

Wendy could sense that things were getting out of control and she touched Doris's arm to indicate they should leave.

The front door banged and a child's voice called out, 'I'm home, Mum. Whose is that car outside?'

'We're in the kitchen, Megan,' Rosie answered, and Doris moved to one side, expecting the door to open with some force.

Megan Steer had Harry's eyes. Beautiful dark brown liquid pools. Her equally dark brown hair was pulled up into a ponytail and secured with a red gingham hair bobble. She stopped as she came through the door and put her hand to her mouth. 'Oops, sorry,' she said, and laughed infectiously. 'I didn't know Mum had visitors.'

Doris couldn't hold back the smile. 'We're leaving, Megan. It was nice to meet you. Have you had a good day at school?'

'So-so. Loads of maths homework, but it won't take me long. I'm good at maths.'

So like Harry, Doris thought.

'I'll walk you to the door,' Rosie said, and followed Doris and Wendy down the hallway. 'I'm going to be telling Megan tonight that her grandfather has died. I'll also explain who you are, we don't have secrets. I guess that's because my whole life felt like a secret, growing up with Mum. And please,' Rosie held out a scrap of paper, 'this is my phone number. Just in case...'

'Thank you. Does your sister have any children?' The words were out of Doris's mouth before she knew what was happening. She really didn't want to know anything about Harry's offspring, and here she was asking questions.

'Yes, but her husband insists they go to boarding school. She has twin boys, Adam and Seth, eleven now. She misses them so much, so comes round here a lot to kill the time. It's a good job we get on.'

Doris shook her hand and turned to walk down the path.

'Thank you,' Rosie called. 'For letting me know, I mean. There may be questions...'

'If I can answer, I will.' Doris didn't turn around to say the words. She carried on walking, climbed into the car, and waited for Wendy to fasten her seat belt.

'You settled?'

'I am. That was a strange carry-on. Bit emotionless, not sure what happened there, are you?'

Doris shook her head. 'I was ready to leave before they started asking questions. So he had two daughters...'

'Didn't do things by halves your late beloved, did he?'

'He certainly didn't. Let's go back to the hotel and get drunk,' Doris said.

'You hardly drink.'

'I can practise.'

She put the car into drive, and they left the cottage, with Rosie Steer still standing in the doorway, watching as the car disappeared, heading back towards Hucknall town centre.

5

Megan listened carefully to what her mother was saying, sipping slowly at her glass of milk. It had seemed strange that Aunty Shirley had left for home almost as soon as the two ladies had driven away, but now her mother had finished explaining the grandfather she had never met was actually dead, and had been for some time, she understood why Aunty Shirley had disappeared.

'Why did he die?'

'What do you mean?'

'Was it cancer? Heart attack? Accident? Didn't she say?'

'That's a pretty gruesome question, young lady. And no, she didn't say.'

'Can we get his death certificate?'

Rosie looked startled. She had accepted the words telling her of his death at face value, and hadn't thought to question Doris about it. 'The honest answer is, I don't know. I don't suppose it's anything to do with us, really.'

'Of course it is. Suppose he died from something like Huntington's disease. That's hereditary, isn't it? We'd need to know about that. Mum, I can't believe you didn't ask the lady!'

'Megan, my love, we're not all trainee doctors, or conversant with every disease known to man. Or twelve-year-old girls. Mrs Lester had just told me I would never get to meet my father. That was enough to take in at that time. I have her card, so when I have questions I'll email her, or ring her.'

Megan pulled her iPad towards her and typed in 'death certificate in UK'. Within seconds she had her answer. 'That's good,' she mused. 'We can get his death certificate. Will you order one for me, Mum?'

'Certainly not.' Rosie laughed. Sometimes she felt swept along by her daughter's sheer love of life and exuberance; she couldn't wait for anything, it had to be an immediate happening.

'Then will you ring her? Ask her to come for a cup of tea. Then I can ask her questions.'

'No, Megan, I can't. It's over. We have no familial link to Doris Lester, so she probably doesn't want to know us at all. Don't forget we're the results of her cheating husband. How would you feel if your dad did the same sort of thing?'

'I'd make sure it looked like manslaughter and not murder.' Once more Megan's mind went into overdrive. 'That's a funny word, manslaughter, isn't it? If you split it, it becomes man's laughter. Think that's significant, Mum?'

Rosie sighed. 'Probably, my love. Let's see this homework started, and I'll consider feeding you. Dad's not home tonight, so it's only the two of us. Pasta bake?'

'Ooh, that will be good. Will you ring Mrs Lester tonight?'

'For goodness sake, child, no I won't! I'll maybe have a chat with Aunty Shirley though, once you're in bed.'

Megan grinned and picked up her school bag. 'But you'll tell me all about it, won't you? It might be your dad, but he's my granddad. And I need to know everything for the family tree.'

'Family tree? We've never done a family tree.'

'We're about to now.' Megan gave a brief wave of her hand

and shortly afterwards Rosie heard her climbing the stairs to her room.

Rosie remembered back to a time when she had been full of enthusiasm for things, anything, but it had been physically knocked out of her by a mother who had withdrawn from everything once Harry Lester had left her world. When Megan was born, Rosie had vowed to be the type of mother she would have wanted, instead of the mother she had been given as a role model.

Megan would be given the freedom to be herself.

And because she had such an inquisitive, genuinely loving daughter, Rosie knew she would be speaking to Doris Lester shortly. Tonight's chat with Dan would be interesting; she often felt he was somewhat astounded by the daughter they had produced, and telling him Megan's thoughts on the situation would, she knew, lead to gales of laughter. He always said she completely rolled over them both. No matter what decisions they reached, if she didn't agree she would argue her side and they would end up giving in.

'You can't give in to her, you know,' Dan warned when he phoned that evening. 'This whole Harry Lester thing is for you and Shirley. He was your genetic father. Whatever is done, it has to be because you want to do it, not because Miss Megan Sherlock Holmes Steer wants it.'

'But that's the thing, isn't it? I do want to know more about him. I don't even know what he looks like. Mum kept no pictures of him, and I bet she'd forgotten about the diaries she left. She even stopped writing them after he went. If she'd had, say, a cancer diagnosis, I bet those diaries would have disappeared so fast... but dementia took her memory. She'd be devastated if she knew we'd found them. I wish you were here, Dan, I need you tonight.'

'I know, but I need to meet up with a client, with Northbrook's in Chester in the morning, so I can't come home. I'll be back tomorrow, most likely mid-afternoon. We'll have takeaway for our evening meal, as long as the daughter promises to curb her ideas.' He laughed.

'Fat chance. She'll want you on her side. I'm probably the evil witch at the moment because I won't send for a death certificate for her. She's not going to let this drop, you know.'

'What was she like, this Mrs Lester?'

'Very nice. She has an investigation company at Eyam, in Derbyshire.'

'And she knew nothing of you?'

'Not prior to getting my letter. And she knew nothing at all of Shirley. That must have been a massive shock to her. She knew of Harry's affair with Mum, but she apparently told him to choose, and he chose her. As far as she was aware until a week ago, he had ditched Mum, and she didn't know it carried on for three years and two babies. I can't approach her yet, she needs to assimilate everything she's found out, and I can't begin to imagine how she's feeling.'

Doris couldn't describe her thoughts. Her initial reaction had been relief that it was over and they could get on with the holiday, but the more she dwelt on the afternoon, the darker her mood became.

The letter had initially made her see that she hadn't really known her husband at all, but meeting up with both his daughters had thrown her. She could accept that he hadn't known about the second baby if Lily Chambers had told him she had lost it, but he had obviously completely disregarded Rosie. He couldn't possibly have paid anything towards her upbringing, because she was the one who balanced the books for their lives; both salaries went into a joint account, their savings were rarely touched, and she managed their investments. He had been happy to pass on that responsibility. In fact, thinking about him, he had been happy to pass on all responsibility for everything, including his two girls to Lily.

Wendy had disappeared early to her room, saying it had been a long day and she was tired; Doris had felt relieved. She too had needed time out, time to think, but she knew she could feel tears starting and emotions invading her brain.

She knew the Hucknall families would want to know more. They had seemed close, Rosie and Shirley, and she guessed once they had had chance to discuss her visit, they would realise they still knew nothing about their father. And what could she tell them? He worked for the Secret Service? The Official Secrets Act said no, she couldn't do that.

She would, out of necessity, have to leave a huge gap in their knowledge of him. She could simply say he was a civil servant, but even that would lead to questions she couldn't answer. Her thoughts went to her own daughter's questioning of her about what Mummy and Daddy did, after Claire heard her giving instructions to Harry. Harry had had to come to terms with his wife being his boss, but Claire had spent a lot of time trying to get them to say exactly what it was they did. In the end she had given up, but Doris suspected it was because she grew up and realised exactly what the term civil servant could entail. She stopped asking.

Doris was afraid that Rosie and Shirley, and even possibly Megan, would ask. Doris dabbed at her eyes, keeping tears at bay. The knock on the door surprised her, and she cautiously opened it.

Wendy was standing there with a whiskey in each hand. 'I figured there'd be tears around about now.'

Doris opened the door fully and Wendy walked in. She handed one of the glasses to Doris, and sat on the bed.

'Let's talk.'

'My brain is buzzing,' Doris said with a slight smile. 'I'm so sorry I made the decision to include this in our holiday...'

'You think I'm not a good enough friend to share this burden with you?' There was a challenge in Wendy's voice.

'Of course you are, but we're on holiday. I should have put it to one side and dealt with it after we got home.'

'That's what I've come to talk about. I think we should postpone the rest of the holiday. We can restart in a few weeks. I don't work now, you can take time out whenever you want, so we can wait. We know we've enjoyed doing it, and I'd be more than happy to carry on, but not at the moment. I think you have things to resolve, and you're going to be distracted and not enjoy our dead people as much. I think we forget Sylvia Plath for the time being, and start with her next time.'

'Are you serious?'

'I am. Never been more so. You're seventy, I'm seventy-two, and if we can't change plans at our time of life, then there's something wrong.'

Doris sat down in the chair with a thud, clinging to her toothbrush glass of whiskey. She said nothing for a minute.

'If I agree to this postponement,' Doris said finally, 'there's a condition.'

Wendy waited.

'Nobody is expecting you home until the weekend after next at the earliest, not even Bingo Jen, so if we go home, will you stay with me at Little Mouse Cottage? Let me show you Derbyshire, we can do that on odd days while I'm dealing with this and getting it out of my life.'

'Yes.'

'Yes?'

'Yes.'

'No discussion, no arguing?'

'Doris Lester, for crying out loud. Of course I'll stay with you. There may be things you need to discuss, and you know it will go no further. You can't guarantee Belle not running off to her feline friends and telling them your problems, can you?'

'You're a star, Wendy Lucas, an absolute star. You see, I can't help but feel they should have some knowledge of Harry, these girls, but equally I'm not sure that what I will be giving them will be totally accurate. It was the nature of the job to be secretive for both of us, and he certainly took secrecy to a whole new level.'

'So that's settled then. We'll cancel our bookings in the morning, check out of here and head off to Bradwell. Don't forget to let Luke know. He'll die of shock if he walks in to check everything's okay, and we're sitting there in our PJs.'

Doris laughed. 'I feel so much lighter now. It's like a massive worry has gone because I've not felt in control of what's happened. I'll have to let Kat and Mouse know also, but make sure they understand I'm still on holiday. I'll make up some excuse – you might have to have caught a heavy cold or something – because Mouse knows nothing about this secret in her granddad's life, and I'm not ready to share it yet, if ever.'

6

Mark Ledger straightened his tie slightly and turned to face his wife. 'We'll go next weekend instead,' he said. 'I can't miss this function on Saturday.'

'But the boys are expecting us to visit them on Saturday.'

'Shirley, it's Thursday tomorrow. Ring the school and ask them to pass the message on to them that it will be next Saturday and not this Saturday. That's plenty of time to get the information to them.'

'They're only eleven, Mark,' Shirley said quietly. 'You know I don't like them being away from us at this crucial point in their lives.'

Mark gave a short bark of laughter. 'Huh. You mean you don't like them being away from you. They couldn't care less about me. This school made a man of me, and it will do the same for them. I had to pull a lot of strings to get them in, you know.'

'They hate it,' she whispered.

'I did for the first year, but then you get used to it. They'll be fine. Stop worrying about them. Do I look okay?'

'Yes,' she said shortly, not prepared to tell him about the

chalk mark on the back of his jacket. Let others see it, and maybe tell him. 'Where are you going?'

'The Grand. I'm speaking on global warming and what this area can do to help the national effort.'

She gave a small nod. Another subject alongside schooling for eleven-year-old boys that he knew nothing about.

'And what time will you be home?'

'Don't wait up for me. Now, how do I look?'

She wanted to say revolting, but didn't. The truth was he was an almost-perfect specimen to look at, nearly six feet tall, dark hair that insisted on falling slightly forward on to his face, adding to the cavalier look he portrayed; his grey eyes exuded warmth to the people he wanted to impress. To her, they showed coldness.

She watched him walk out of the bedroom, ignoring the clothes he had scattered around the place, and she listened for the bang as the front door closed. Holding back tears of frustration, she put his clothes in the laundry basket, leaving his suit till last, remembering he had asked that it be dry-cleaned.

Maybe he would die. Maybe there would be an accident on the bypass and he wouldn't survive it. Then she could go to the school on Saturday, tell her boys that unfortunately their father was dead, and they could come home and go to a state school. Maybe.

Melanie Brookes, dainty, her short dark hair brushed until it gleamed, sat by the side of her partner, Patrick, at a large round table and listened to Patrick's brother speaking from the top table. Her blue eyes, perfectly complemented by the long blue silk dress she was wearing, were fixed on Mark.

Mark was an inspiring speaker, no matter what subject he was covering – she could almost believe he cared about global warming, cared about what the Nottingham area could do about it. Almost believe.

Patrick Ledger moved his hand along the table towards hers, and gave it a gentle squeeze. She responded with a smile that looked genuine but her mind was fixed on Mark Ledger, not Patrick. It was so wrong, how she felt about her potential future brother-in-law. He totally set her on fire every time he touched her, and several times during his speech he had glanced in her direction; she knew the smile was meant only for her.

She shuffled in her seat, uncomfortable with her thoughts, her feelings, and her disloyalty to Patrick, but hadn't a clue in hell how to change things. Walk away from Mark? That was the logical thing to do, but the sex was so bloody good...

'Thank you for your attention, ladies and gentleman, and I hope we can count on your help and support when we start to put these plans into operation.' Mark sat down with a smile, immediately glancing over towards the table where Patrick and Melanie were sitting.

Patrick, a slightly weightier copy of his brother and with the same grey eyes, was speaking with the waiter, so she gave a little wave in Mark's direction, and he inclined his head in acknowledgement.

Mark was beginning to worry about the foolishness of seeing Melanie. If Shirley ever found out... he shuddered at the thought. He would lose everything. The house, the boys, probably his job. Oh, and Shirley as well.

The house was owned by both of them, but he knew if they split up she would stay in the house; the boys would definitely not want to go with him. And he had got his current job through a friend of Shirley's at the WI, so there was half a chance he wouldn't get to keep that.

If anyone found out about him and Melanie, the consequences didn't bear thinking about; he guessed Patrick would be none too pleased as well. He'd ordered some flowers to be delivered to Mel's home for the following afternoon, wishing her luck for her York conference, softening her for the planned Monday evening together they hoped to enjoy. And the sex was so bloody good...

The room was emptying, and Patrick waved Mark over towards their table. 'We're going to get off now,' he said, and winked at his brother.

Mark knew exactly what the wink meant and wanted to punch Patrick in the face. Instead, he smiled. 'Okay, you two. Be good. I'm stuck here for a bit until a few more have gone home, then I'll be getting off. Patrick, you in or out Monday evening?'

'Out. We've a bridge tournament in Nottingham, and I can't cry off.'

'Okay, doesn't matter,' Mark replied, 'it wasn't anything important. We'll meet up some other time.' *I'll be meeting with Melanie on Monday, then.*

Patrick stood. 'I'll go and get your jacket, Mel. You got the ticket?'

Melanie fished around in her bag and handed over a cloakroom ticket. Patrick walked away and Mark sat down by her side.

'Are you okay for Monday?'

She nodded, feeling almost breathless at how close he was to her. 'I am. You coming to mine?' Melanie spent most of the week at Patrick's, but still maintained her own small flat – it had proved to be a smart move when she started seeing Mark.

'I will. Make an excuse for you being out somewhere, so if he does come back early it won't matter. He'll know there's no point going to yours, you won't be in.' He stroked her leg, then stood up as he saw Patrick heading towards them, holding Melanie's jacket.

'Let's go,' Patrick said. 'The chap on the door is getting us a taxi.' He high-fived Mark. 'Good talk tonight, bro, thanks for getting us the tickets. Pity Shirley couldn't come, but maybe next time.'

Mark smiled. 'Yeah, she was gutted at having to miss it, but she'd already booked something to do with the WI.' The lies came so easily.

He leaned forward and kissed Melanie on the cheek, then shook his brother's hand. 'Take care, speak to you soon.'

It was a warm evening and Mark checked his watch as he walked down the stone steps. He'd refused the doorman's offer to get him a taxi, saying he'd brought his car and would be driving home. By the time he'd reached the bottom of the steps, he knew he wasn't going to be driving anywhere. His head felt as if it was moving in a different direction to his feet, so he decided to walk home, clear his mind, have a good sleep and collect his car the following day.

He grinned to himself. Surely he'd have sobered up by noon the following day. God, he must have had a lot to drink.

The doorman watched Mark as he tried to walk along the pavement, and shook his head in disbelief. The bloke had said he was driving home, but he was struggling to walk, never mind drive. 'Changed your mind, pal, have you?' he said to himself.

.   .   .

Mark staggered along the road, occasionally using the light on his mobile phone when the going became a little tricky. Sometimes there was a pavement, sometimes there wasn't, and when there wasn't, he dug out his phone. The third time he did that, he saw the text.

Don't bother coming home. You won't get in.

A wave of anger washed over him and he threw the mobile phone with some force against a tree. The light disappeared, along with the phone. He staggered over to the tree and felt around at the base; there was nothing there.

'What the fuck!' he roared, and staggered back to the road, looking right and left, hoping against hope that there would be a red phone box. Any damn colour phone box. There wasn't. He went back to the tree and searched again, but in the end had to admit defeat. It must have bounced off the trunk and it could be anywhere, he finally realised.

He set off to walk again, and had gone a couple of hundred yards before remembering what had caused him to throw the phone – the text from his dearly beloved. 'You can't tell me not to come home,' he said through gritted teeth. 'Who the hell do you think you are, Shirley bloody Ledger?'

After half an hour of further walking and two bouts of vomiting, he sat himself against a large oak tree, closed his eyes and gave in to the overwhelming fatigue. He couldn't carry on; he'd have to sort his bloody wife out in the morning when he was sober.

The postman woke him. He took in the smart suit, the shiny shoes and silk tie, all covered in vomit, and helped Mark to stand.

'You stink, mate. Can you go somewhere and get a wash before you go home?'

Mark shook his head. He'd never felt so ill, and knew he wouldn't be going into work later. What the hell had he had to drink? He tried to remember how much, and was somewhat surprised to realise he'd not had an empty glass throughout the night, the drinks had kept coming. He groaned, knowing he must look as bad as he felt. 'You got a phone?'

The postman nodded.

'Can I ring for a taxi, please?'

The postman handed it over. 'You not got one?'

'Threw it at a tree,' Mark mumbled.

'Yeah, I can see you doing that. In a bit of a state, were you?'

Mark paused and looked at the man. 'If you'd had four glasses of wine, would you look like this?' The lie came out easily.

The postman shook his head. 'No, mate, you look as though you've had four bottles, not four glasses.'

Mark spoke to the taxi office, and handed the phone back. 'Thanks for your help. It'll be here in five minutes.'

'You'll be okay?'

'Yeah, I'll be home in no time, sort out the bloody wife, and ring in sick.'

The postman nodded again, wished him good luck, and resumed his walk to work.

Mark stepped nearer to the edge of the road and waited. He saw the blue Mondeo approaching slowly, obviously looking for him and he walked out and waved his hand. Quarter of an hour later he was home.

. . .

He was a little surprised to find that when he turned the key, the door actually opened. He had assumed that following Shirley's text she had put on every chain, every bolt and every lock, to keep him out. That was clearly not the case, and he shouted her name, once he was standing in the hall.

He had no idea why she had sent the text; was she pissed off with him for cancelling the school visit on Saturday, or had she found out about Melanie? She had been fine when he left the house, so what had happened in the meantime to make her think she could order him around?

'Shirley!' he shouted once again. 'Where the fuck are you?'

Silence. He kicked off his vomit-covered shoes, dropped his vomit-covered tie in the waste bin, and climbed the stairs. 'Shirley,' he called, this time not so loudly. He was starting to think maybe she wasn't in the house.

He checked every room. No Shirley. Sinking down onto the bed, he groaned. What was the silly cow playing at? Rosie. Shirley would have gone to her sister's. Thick as bloody thieves they were, that's where she'd be. He glanced at his watch, saw it was just after six and thought it was a bit early for her to have gone to Rosie's. Maybe she'd gone while he was doing his talk.

He forced his legs to take him to the bathroom, and he put the shower to its hottest setting.

Ten minutes later he hoped his skin wasn't peeling off; the smell of sick had gone, and he felt a little more alive. He might make it to the office by twelve if he continued to recover. All he had to do was find his wife, make sure she understood she couldn't send him texts like that without expecting there to be consequences, and mostly, make sure she knew she wasn't to bugger off to her sister's without asking his permission first.

7

There was a small bunch of flowers on the kitchen table along with a note saying *Welcome home, travellers. You want anything, you shout. Love Luke. X*

'He's a star, your lad,' Wendy said.

'You're not kidding. And he's not really a lad now. I'll send him a quick text to tell him we're home and thank him for the flowers, because he'll not relax until we've checked in.'

'And I'll put the kettle on,' Wendy said. 'I know my priorities.'

They decided to collect Belle at some point in the afternoon; there was nothing to be gained by leaving her at the cattery. Initially she was a little huffy, her owner had abandoned her and she was not to be forgiven, but she was quickly bribed with tuna and everything was good at Little Mouse Cottage.

· · ·

Rosie was startled to see Mark pull up outside her front gate. He stormed up the path and she reached the door at the same time as he did.

'Where's my fucking wife?' he growled, pushing past her. 'I've had to get a taxi to go and get my car because she wasn't there to run me down.'

I'd like to run you down, Rosie thought, but instead she said, 'Good morning, Mark. Please do come in.'

He looked at her and mumbled, 'Sorry,' before proceeding through to the kitchen. 'So where is she?'

'I have no idea. Have you tried ringing her phone?'

'Can't. I've lost my mobile.' His mind had a flashback to it smashing against the tree. 'And I can't ring her on the landline because I don't know the number.'

Rosie looked at him, trying to hide the loathing, and picked up her own phone. She rang her sister, listened to it ring then go to voicemail. 'She's not answering. Didn't she say where she was going?'

'I've not seen her since I went out last night. I thought she'd be here.'

'You had an argument?'

'Of course not.'

Rosie tried ringing Shirley once more. 'Nope, no answer. She was still in the house when you left last night?'

'She was. And she'll be in trouble when she comes crawling back, I can tell you. Anyway, I'm off to work. Give me a ring when you find her.' He turned to walk out of the kitchen and Rosie threw a saucepan at him.

'Don't speak to me like that,' she said, wanting to laugh at the shock on his face. 'I'm not Shirley, and if she's left I couldn't be happier. If I hear from her I'll decide whether to tell you or not, depending on what she says. Piss off to work, Mark, and don't come back here until you've had an attitude transplant.'

He slammed both the kitchen and front door, and Rosie heard the screech of his tyres as he pulled away from the kerb.

'Dickhead,' she muttered, but the unease she felt for Shirley overrode any thoughts of Mark. Where was she, and why had she disappeared without saying anything?

Doris and Wendy went supermarket shopping in the afternoon and by the evening were settled in, both of them reading. Wendy glanced up from her book to see Doris staring into space.

'Would a Ferrero Rocher help?' she asked gently.

'I don't think anything will help. I'll get over it, I always do, I was considering whether to tell Mouse or not. Eventually I suppose I'll have to, because I would hate her to find out sometime in the future when I'm dead and gone.'

'Oh dear.' Wendy laughed. 'Are we feeling our own mortality a little bit?'

'Not really.' The sigh was huge. 'But I really could have done without this. What a pathetic plonker I married.'

'It's all about the p words, isn't it? But you had good times with Harry, you know you did.'

'I know. That's what's so bloody annoying. He was a proper Jekyll and Hyde, wasn't he?'

'Seems like it. And I've decided I'm going to have to contact Rosie to get an email address where I can send copies of Harry's birth certificate, death certificate and suchlike. I know she doesn't want to use her work email, but it's not rocket science setting up a personal one.'

'It is to some people.' Wendy laughed again. 'You had to sort me out.'

. . .

Before they headed off to bed for the night, Doris had sorted out some photographs of Harry, his birth and death certificates, and had written a brief résumé of his life, taking care to put that he was a civil servant and nothing more.

'I'll ring her tomorrow and tell her what I have for her. If she doesn't want to give me an email address I'll copy them and post them. It's no big deal either way.'

'You think you'll sleep tonight now you've done this?'

'I hope so. Who would have thought I'd feel like this at my age. It's supposed to be the calm after the storms of earlier years, but it doesn't feel that way. If he wasn't already dead, I'd strangle him.'

Rosie couldn't sleep. There had been no word from Shirley all day, and she was sick of Mark ringing to check if his wife had been in touch. She had initially thought that wherever Shirley was, she would be back by Friday night because she was off to see her boys at school on Saturday, but now it appeared that wasn't the case. Mark had postponed the visit for a week.

She knew Shirley would have been horrified by that; visiting her boys was everything she lived for. What she couldn't understand was why Shirley hadn't said to her, *I've had enough, I'm leaving.* They couldn't be any closer, with a cold-hearted mother they had clung to each other all their lives, and it was unthinkable that Shirley would disappear without being in contact first.

Rosie got out of bed and went back downstairs. She opened the fridge, took out the milk and poured herself a glass.

'I'll have one of those please, Mum,' Megan said.

Rosie almost dropped her glass. 'Good grief, girl, what are you doing up? It's after midnight.'

'I heard you come down. You worrying about Aunty Shirley?'

They carried their drinks to the table and sat down. 'I am. It's not like her. I wish she'd ring. Drink that milk, and let's have you back in bed. School tomorrow.'

'I could stay home and help you look for Aunty Shirley.'

'Nice try, Megs, but I wouldn't know where to look anyway. The only thing she does is go to the WI, and I can't see her hiding away in the church hall, can you?'

'No, but I also can't see her going to a hotel either. Uncle Mark's not generous with her, is he? She'll not have much money.'

'She does. Mark doesn't know about it. Your nan's house was a rented one, and because she knew she would never buy one to leave to us, she took out a hefty insurance policy. The policy specified it was for both of us equally, and we have that. We took the cost of the funeral out of it, and we're left with a little over thirty thousand pounds each. So you don't need to worry about her not having money, she does. This is secret, though, Megan. She didn't want Mark to know, so she opened a new online bank account and her part of the money is in that. I have all the log in details and everything, because she says if anything happens to her, the money is for her boys. I checked it about ten minutes ago, funnily enough, and she hasn't touched it.'

'And does Dad know?'

'Yes, until I told you, only Shirley, Dad and I knew. Now there's four, but it really is secret, Megan. Uncle Mark must never know, he'd find some way to take it from her.'

'Honestly, Mum, I understand. I'm Team Shirley, anyway. Can't stand him.' She finished her drink and stood. 'You'll be okay?'

Rosie smiled at her daughter. 'Of course I will be. I'll be better when Shirley rings, but I'll sleep now, don't worry. Off to bed. You need your sleep.'

. . .

All became silent once more in the cottage in Hucknall, although it wasn't the silence of sleep. Rosie tried her best; she read, she tiptoed downstairs to make a hot drink, she sat and brushed her long brown hair thinking it might soothe her, and she pulled her diary from her bedside drawer and wrote down her feelings. This activity drove her thoughts back to a long-ago Christmas when she and Shirley had both received diaries, little books with locks on and fairies on the front. Every night they wrote about their day, heads under the bedclothes, a torch shining on to the pages. After that Christmas, a diary was always at the top of their wish list.

Now they made a special day of going to buy their diaries, usually at the end of November, bringing their current ones with them to decide who had the fattest diary. They stuck in photographs, recipes, articles from newspapers – anything that took their interest, and it was their 'thing', although Megan was making noises about joining in with them.

She wrote *Where are you, Shirley?* at the end of her thoughts, sighed and put away the diary. Perhaps Shirley's diary could throw some light on where she was, but Rosie had no idea where Shirley kept it. She stashed it away from Mark's prying eyes, wrote during the day while he was at work, but she had never actually revealed her hiding place. To stop Mark asking, because in the first flush of love she had told him of a shared activity of having a diary alongside her sister, she kept a second diary that was purely for appointments, and which she kept in her bedside drawer.

Rosie watched the digits on the bedside clock tick over to 04:00 and thumped her pillow. She'd be having strong words with Shirley when she eventually turned up, putting her through this. She closed her eyes and refused to open them.

· · ·

Megan woke her to say she was going.

'Going? Going where?' was Rosie's groggy answer.

'School, Mum. I left you to sleep as you'd clearly forgotten to set your alarm. I've had my breakfast, and I'm off now. Text me if you hear from Aunty Shirley, please. I'm worried too, you know.'

Rosie tried to sit up, prior to getting out of bed. 'You're a good girl. And of course I'll let you know. Your dad will be home by the time you get back from school.'

'Good. We need him. We've got to go and find her.'

'Don't spend all day worrying about this, Megan,' Rosie warned. 'You've exams next week, concentrate on your lessons.'

'Easy peasy,' Megan said and blew her mum a kiss. Before she left the bedroom, Megan said, 'Stay in bed, you've nothing to get up for.'

Rosie wished she believed that. She picked up her phone and once more rang Shirley's number. Voicemail. She left a short, sharp message for her sister. 'Ring me, idiot. You know I'm worrying. Where the hell are you?'

She disconnected, wobbled out of the bedroom towards the bathroom, and her day began, turning the warm shower to a cold one in an effort to wake her up properly. It did.

Weetabix and a cup of tea told her she was still alive, and she loaded the dishwasher with the odd bits of cutlery and crockery they had acquired since the previous afternoon, then set it going. That was enough chores for the day, she decided, if anybody was bothered by the dust around the television, she could hand them a duster. And really, if the ironing troubled anybody in her household, she would set up the ironing board for them. Today she had new priorities, she had to find her sister.

8

'Good morning.' Wendy smiled at Doris as she walked into the kitchen, hugging her dressing gown around her. 'Tea or coffee?'

'Don't be so... awake,' Doris said crossly. 'And you're dressed!'

'I am. I woke at six with sun streaming into my bedroom, so thought it best not to miss it. I've been sat outside under the gazebo with a drink and my book. I'd come in to fill up my coffee, so which do you want?'

'If coffee's done, I'll have that. You had breakfast?'

'No, thought I'd wait for you. We can discuss today's activities then, because you might be a bit more awake. Didn't sleep too good?'

'My brain's out of control. I need to ring Rosie Steer and get this stuff off to her, then I'll feel better.' Doris took the proffered coffee and moved towards the back door. 'Did the weatherman say it was going to be nice?'

'Yep. For the next three days apparently.'

'Okay. What day is it?'

'Friday. All day.'

'That's good.'

'Is it? Why?'

'I don't know. I always like Fridays. It's fish and chip day. I feel a bit woolly-headed, can you tell?'

Wendy laughed. 'I can, but you're always like this when you first get up. You'll be fine in ten minutes. Scrambled egg on toast good for you?'

'Oh, it is. I'll have a walk around the garden while you're doing it.'

'No problem. Belle's somewhere in the back garden, she's had her breakfast.'

'Thank you, you're a star,' Doris said, and stepped out into the warmth of that Friday morning.

Doris pulled the phone towards her, and Wendy gave her a thumbs up sign. The scrap of paper handed over by Rosie with her phone number written on it was lying on the table, and Doris tapped in the numbers.

It was answered immediately.

'Hello?'

'Hello. It's Doris Lester. I felt as though I should have a bit of a chat with you. I have some things that you may want, photos of Harry, birth certificate, death certificate, that sort of thing. I obviously can't send you the originals, but if I can email you with copies...'

'I do have a personal email address, Mrs Lester. I didn't want to make things easy for my father, I wanted to make him write a letter, buy a stamp and physically post it. I didn't want some anonymous email arriving. And thank you for finding the papers out. I'll email you within the next two minutes, so that all you have to do is click on reply, then–'

'I have a degree in Information Technology, Rosie.' Doris laughed. 'Email me and I'll respond immediately. The photos show Harry at various stages. The first one was taken about the time you were born, the second one he is about forty, and the third one was taken shortly after his cancer diagnosis, about a year before he died. Will you forward the email to Shirley, please?'

There was a pause from the other end of the phone. 'She's missing.'

'What?'

'Shirley. She left here about ten minutes after you went on Wednesday, and nobody has seen her since around seven o'clock that night.'

'Has she done this before?'

'No. Shirley is the cool, calm and collected one, level-headed, lives for her sons, but we don't know where she is. I'm sorry, we shouldn't be burdening you with this, it's not as though you know us. I'm so worried...'

'I can tell. Has her husband reported her as a missing person?' Doris felt herself going into Connection mode.

'Huh. Mark's far more concerned that she's left without doing a pile of ironing.'

'Then you report her. I'm guessing you've tried ringing her?'

'Yes we have. It goes to voicemail.'

'Maybe she simply doesn't want to be found yet. I'm sure that when she's had some time to think, she'll be in touch. And it will probably be with you, if Mark is the reason she's left. Hold that thought as a positive, and take it that she maybe only needs time out. I wouldn't wait much longer before reporting her as missing though. I'll get this email off to you, and I hope Shirley is soon back with you.' Doris's Connection brain resurfaced. 'Maybe check any hotels near the boys' school. Perhaps she simply needed to see them.'

There was a slight lift in Rosie's voice. 'Thank you, Mrs Lester. I hadn't thought of that, I'll get on to it straight away, after I've emailed you. And thank you for listening. I've been going out of my mind all night worrying about her.'

They disconnected and an email ping followed almost immediately. Doris took care of scanning and emailing the documents, then sat back with a sigh.

Wendy placed a second coffee in front of her. 'Trouble?'

'For Rosie, yes. It seems Shirley's gone missing. She was there up to about seven on the day we met her, but nobody has seen or had contact with her since. I've told her to report it. The husband, Mark he's called, sounds a bit iffy; he's not told the police she's disappeared. Apparently he simply wants his shirts ironed. No wonder she's gone.'

'You're not.'

Doris grinned at her friend, knowing exactly what she meant. 'No, I'm not getting involved. They're not my family, they're Harry's. I've advised them to go to the police as soon as possible, and that's as much as I can do. You saw me email their papers over, so let that be an end to it. Now, where shall we go today? What about a drive around, ending it by coming down Winnat's Pass and then lunch in Castleton. Once we've had lunch we'll decide whether to come home, or go somewhere else if we've got the energy.'

'Sounds lovely. Must be forty years since I last saw Winnats, and that was on the back of a motorbike.'

'It doesn't change. Still the most stunning view in Britain as far as I'm concerned.'

Although Doris didn't stop on the way down the Pass, she slowed down as much as she dared, given the convoy of traffic behind her. Wendy's second view in forty years of the outstanding vista before her stopped her speaking. She looked around, blown away by the beauty. She clicked away with her phone, recording the views she would spend some time printing on the Sprocket, until finally they reached Castleton village, enjoying a cooked lunch so they didn't have to cook at home later. The fish and chip Friday evening meal was cancelled.

They were laughing and chatting as they entered Little Mouse Cottage, and Wendy went straight through to the kitchen to put on the kettle. She didn't like to go much longer than a couple of hours without being watered; she had explained to Doris many years earlier that she would simply wilt and fade away into obscurity if she didn't get regular tea or coffee fixes.

'I'll have water, please, Wendy,' Doris called as she slipped her shoes and coat into the hall cupboard grandly known as the cloakroom.

'Okay,' Wendy responded. 'You're going into the reading room?'

Doris stood for a moment. 'You turned into a mind reader?'

Wendy appeared in the kitchen doorway and grinned at her friend. 'No, it's where your computer is, it's where your books are, and it's a TV-free zone. I know you, Doris Lester. And it's where the Ferrero Rocher are.'

'How could you possibly know that's where the chocolate stash is?' Doris was astounded. She thought it was carefully hidden.

'I didn't,' Wendy laughed and turned away to make her tea. 'But I do now.'

Wendy carried a tray with the two drinks and a small plate of biscuits into the reading room, and Doris was opening up her laptop.

'I was right,' Wendy said. 'You can't ignore it.'

'I thought I'd run a quick check on Shirley's husband. I'm hoping they've found her now, but it doesn't hurt to know a bit about him.'

Wendy placed Doris's water by the side of her laptop, and handed the plate of biscuits to her. Doris absently took one, said thank you, and began giving her computer a series of instructions. She leaned back for a moment staring at the screen and allowed the machine to do its work.

Wendy sat down with her book, but her mind drifted off in different directions. She had been friends with Doris for more years than she could remember, and yet there were aspects of her life she knew nothing about. It actually felt strange that she had opened up a little about the work she had done during her earlier life, work that Wendy suspected still went on, although to a limited degree. And she was sure it had only surfaced currently because of this situation arising through Harry's infidelity.

She'd liked Harry. He'd always seemed pleasant enough, adored Claire, and nothing was ever too much trouble for him. She remembered back to the time when she had had a leak and couldn't move the stop tap at all. She'd rung on the off chance that Harry was in, and within five minutes he had solved the problem. By the time her own waste of a space for a husband had returned home, the job had been sorted and tidied away. That had been husband number two, she mused, he didn't last long after that. The first two had merely paved the way for the love of her life, husband number three, Barry Lucas.

And her thoughts drifted away from Doris. Her time with Barry hadn't been long; five years and cancer had taken him so quickly. She had had no time to prepare for a life without him, and she missed him every day. She had been envious of Doris's life with Harry, but in view of the recent revelations maybe

Doris hadn't come out of the institution of marriage in such a good way.

She heard Doris say a quiet *yes*, and knew it meant she had found something.

'He's got convictions for fraud and GBH,' Doris said, 'although to be fair, they were some years ago. Nothing recently. Married for ten years to Shirley, nee Chambers, two children called Seth and Adam, aged eleven, so obviously they married after the birth of the twins.'

'Did he do time?'

Doris nodded. 'The fraud was a paying back type of thing, with community service and a fine, but the GBH got him three months in Strangeways. That must have felt like a life sentence to him, because he's been a good boy since. Maybe.'

Wendy laughed. 'We've never met the bloke, and already we don't like him.'

'I get the impression Rosie doesn't. And it seems as though Shirley doesn't either. She's ditched him, temporarily or otherwise. I wonder if they've heard from her.'

'Ring and ask, put your mind at rest.'

Doris closed down her laptop after telling it to print, and moved to sit on the sofa. 'I can't, I said no involvement. I'm going to leave it alone. I'm sure she'll be back by now anyway; she's got two boys. She's not going to abandon them, is she?'

Wendy shrugged. 'Depends how desperate she is. Maybe her plan is to get the boys and go. I still think you should ring Rosie.'

'That's because you're a nosy old bat, Wendy Lucas. I'll ring tomorrow. Will that satisfy you?'

'It will,' Wendy said, smiling. 'But I'm not convinced it'll satisfy you, Mrs Karate-Fifth-Dan-Give-Me-A-Mystery Lester.

You'll not be able to leave this alone; you know you won't. Fancy a glass of wine?'

'Has the sun gone over the yardarm?'

'Well over, in Hong Kong.' Wendy spoke seriously.

'I'll have a fruity little white then, please, my alcoholic friend. Cheers.'

9

Saturday morning at six showed no promise of the sun that the weatherman had said would be present all day. It wasn't particularly warm, and there were no dancing shadows of leaves on the path, or the whisper of a breeze in the trees. Apart from the occasional bark from Tyrone, the Jack Russell with attitude, there was complete silence. Even the birds didn't seem to have realised dawn was blending into day at a fair old rate.

As dog and master approached the area where the stream ran, the tinkling sound of water became a slight disturbance in the previously soundless existence, and Tyrone barked, this time a little louder.

'Shut up, Tyrone,' his elderly companion growled. 'I'm not happy at being out at this ungodly hour, so don't make things worse by barking at every damn thing.' He took the dog's lead out of his jacket pocket with the intention of it being a threat to the dog that he would be anchored to it if he didn't stop being noisy. The little black and white dog with a black moustache marking on his otherwise pure white face dashed off into the undergrowth, his answer to the old man's action.

Joseph Flint increased his pace as best he could, hampered

by a walking stick and a dog lead, and tried to follow Tyrone down the path. 'Bloody dog,' he grumbled, but he knew he wouldn't dare return home without the canine terror; he wouldn't be allowed back in the house.

He waved his stick as he shouted Tyrone's name, and was relieved when there was an answering bark. He'd not lost him – yet. Joseph carried on down the small incline, getting a whimpering bark each time he shouted the dog's name, until he eventually spotted him down by the stream. He was standing on the edge, and Joseph felt relieved that at least he hadn't ventured into the water.

Unlike the woman's body floating face down in the stream.

Joseph faltered, knowing what he was seeing but not wanting to believe it. He used his stick to balance himself as he edged closer to the body, and Tyrone lifted his face as if to ask him what they should do next.

She was floating towards the middle of the stream, about six feet away from Joseph and Tyrone, and Joseph could see that she was caught on something. She wasn't going anywhere and there was no doubt that life was extinct. She hadn't gone swimming at six in the morning.

He eased himself gently down onto the grass, knowing it wouldn't be easy getting back up again, and took out his mobile phone. He blessed his granddaughter for bringing it to him. Her words had been something along the lines of *you never know when you might need one, Grandy. What if you fall when you're out with Tyrone. We wouldn't know where you were, would we?*

He mentally acknowledged her foresight, and pressed three nines. It was answered within seconds and he quickly explained the situation. The operator kept chatting to him until the first police officers arrived; she asked him to put Tyrone on a lead to prevent scene contamination, and to make sure the little dog didn't try to bite the officers. She had said they would be there within ten minutes, and he was surprised when they arrived in eight. Their progress through the woods was noisy, and as they reached him he said goodbye to the nice lady at the other end of the phone.

He waved his stick to show where he was, and the first officer slid down to join him.

'Mr Flint? Thank you for this. My colleagues will be here any second now. You haven't been in the water?' He glanced down at Joseph's trousers, which were slightly damp around the bottom of the legs, and definitely damp around his rear end where he had sat on the grass. 'Good man, we can protect the scene knowing nobody's been near her. Your dog didn't go in the water?'

'No, he barked a fair bit, but he's dry, so I'm pretty sure he took the sensible decision to stay out of the stream.' There was a touch of sarcasm in his voice, which the young DC couldn't help but notice, and he laughed.

'Sorry, sir, I'm being an idiot. My boss, DCI Grace Stamford, will be here shortly, and she'll probably want to speak to you, so I can't let you go yet. Can we head back up the hill a bit, and find you a fallen tree or something, I'm sure it will be comfier than the ground.'

Joseph held on to the DC's arm and they walked about fifty yards from the stream before finding a tree stump.

'You'll be okay here?' The DC thought the elderly man looked a bit grey.

'I'll be fine. It's knocked me off kilter a bit. I've been doing an early morning walk with this dog for the past five years, and the most I've seen before is a dead hedgehog. Don't worry about me. Send your wee lassie to see me when she arrives, and I'll be on my way. I'm going to let the wife know where I am though, because if I'm not back in the next three and a half minutes she'll be ringing the police anyway, convinced I've dropped down dead somewhere.'

Wee lassie. DC Sam Ellis tried hard to keep the smile off his face and the laughter from his voice. DCI Grace Stamford was not his idea of a wee lassie. He left Joseph to make his phone call, Tyrone's lead firmly anchored around his master's wrist.

The peace was definitely shattered by the arrival of Grace Stamford. Statuesque at six feet, her piled-up curly brown hair adding several more inches to her height, she approached the elderly man sitting on the tree stump. Her smile extended to her green eyes.

'You've got her out then?' Joseph got his question in before she had even opened her mouth.

'Yes, we have. Forensics are setting up the tent any moment now. Thank you for waiting. You didn't touch anything at the scene?'

He shook his head. 'No, I could see there was no point me getting wet through going in to drag her out, that wouldn't have helped anybody.'

'Thank you.'

'There will be my footprints in the mud at the edge, but I don't think she went in here, anyway. I think she's drifted down from somewhere higher up. If the forensics want to take imprints of my shoes now, I'm happy to take them off.'

Grace Stamford halted for a moment. 'Thank you. You want to be SIO?'

He laughed. This was the most fun in years, he'd already decided. 'I'm sorry, I'm winding you up. Before I was Joseph Flint, I was DCI Joseph Flint. And if I'd thought there was any possibility of life in that young woman I'd have had her out of the water in a flash, but I knew it was too late for that. No, I'll leave you to carry on being SIO, and good luck with it. I'll hang around until somebody's talked to me, then I'll be off with Tyrone and get back home. My investigating days are over.'

Grace inclined her head. 'Now I can put a face to the name. Bit of a legend, sir, and it's an honour to meet you. The tent's up so I need to go and see what I can find, but I'll send somebody to take your details, and you can get off home. I imagine a cup of tea might be most welcome, so we'll not keep you hanging about. Thank you again for treating the scene with respect, but I do think you might be right, that she went in higher up. It's a bit of a trek through the woods to get to this point. It all depends on whether there's water in the lungs, really.' She leaned over and shook his hand. 'Would you like a lift home, sir?'

'No, it's not too far from here. And then I can get back to enjoying my retirement. Good luck, DCI Stamford.'

Grace Stamford sent Sam Ellis to the man sitting patiently on the tree stump, careful to tell him who he was, and then she reached the tent set up to hide and protect the body.

Pathologist Owen Bridger looked up. 'Grace. Yes, it's suspicious because she's young and she was found in water, but I can't tell you much yet. I think she's been in the stream at least twenty-four hours, but I need to get her back to the autopsy suite before I can expand on that. She's nothing on her to say who she is, so we'll check fingerprints as soon as we can. I would think she's in her twenties, maybe early thirties, but even that's a guess. She may be a fit forty-year-old. And before you ask, I don't know when she died, not yet. Or how, but I suspect asphyxiation.'

Grace smiled at him, aware his manner was a touch irascible. 'Too early for you, is it, Owen? Did you have to get out of bed?'

'I bloody did. I'd only been in it four hours. Late night, early morning, doesn't sit right with anybody.'

'I'll leave you to it, go and see what the troops have found, if anything, but there's nothing to say she went in the water at this spot. DCI Joseph Flint confirmed that.'

Owen's head shot up. 'Joseph? He's here? Why?'

'He found her. To be totally correct, his dog Tyrone did. DCI Flint rang it in. I've left him with one of the DCs, he'll be okay. It felt like I was in the presence of royalty.'

'You were.'

Grace walked over to the spot where the body had been lifted from the water. Two of her team were wearing thigh-high waders, and had gone back in to see if they could locate anything of use, but they were climbing out.

'Nothing obvious, boss,' one of them said. 'Maybe a diver could locate something by going under the water.'

'I'll organise it, but thanks for trying, you two.'

The area was taped off, and one or two early morning dog walkers were standing at the top of the incline watching the activities with interest. Joseph had finished giving his statement to Sam Ellis and was escorted under the tape.

'Thank you, sir,' Sam said.

'No problem, young man,' the ex-DCI said, 'come and find me if you need anything else. Although I don't think I can help in any way. I can't imagine I would know her, the age range of my acquaintances has increased exponentially with my own age, so she would definitely not be on my Christmas card list.'

Sam laughed. 'Probably not. Are you sure I can't give you a lift home? You may be a DCI but a dead body is still a shock even though you've probably seen a lot over the length of your career.'

'I'll be fine. I'll finish off Tyrone's walk, I'm not too far from home at this point.'

'Then I'll head back down to the stream. Take care, sir.'

And so the day began. It was a Saturday that shortly developed sunshine, the breeze lifted and leaves cast swirling shadows over the scene. An old man and a dog began their last half mile, and Mrs Flint made an immediate pot of tea as they arrived home.

'That was a bloody funny early morning walk,' Joseph said, and she took him in her arms and kissed him.

'Go and sit down, I'll bring your drink through. And try not to get in any more trouble, will you?' She smiled at him. 'I thought we'd done with all this suspicious death malarkey. Seems we haven't.'

10

Doris and Wendy made the decision to go to Bakewell as soon as the sun confirmed it would be in evidence, and it would be warm. They packed a picnic, judging it would be nice to sit in Bakewell Park for their lunch, after feeding the ducks and touring the shops.

'We will continue the holiday, won't we?'

'We will, and I promise to bury anything that arrives to distract me,' Doris said with a laugh. 'I'm really sorry we stopped it early, but I think your idea was right. In fact, when we get back, I'll get my diary and we'll set a definite date. I've a couple of things I can't miss, seminars and suchlike, so I'll work something out around appointments, and we'll start off with Sylvia Plath.'

'Good. I read her book because I knew we were going to see her grave. Fascinating writing, and with *The Bell Jar*, she came up with a brilliant title to go perfectly with the story. She was a disturbed young lady though. I'd like to go and tell her that.'

'We definitely will.' Doris pulled out of a junction, and they dropped down the hill into Bakewell.

The car park wasn't too full, although they knew that later it would be heaving. Doris collected the picnic basket from the boot, and Wendy carried a blanket. They headed for the river that ran parallel to the car park, and Doris pulled half a loaf of bread from her bag. She handed some to Wendy, and they fed the ducks. It seemed, like them, that everyone was ignoring the notices that asked for no duck-feeding. There were currently different thoughts on the subject, so once again the underweight ducks were coming back to their fat and full status.

The women spent a half hour by the side of the river, then headed to the shops.

The book shop benefitted because they both bought two books, before strolling around to the café and having coffees.

'Bakewell's my go-to place,' Doris said. 'If I'm feeling a bit hemmed in, or wanting some time out, I come here. Eyam is lovely, but I work there so it stops it being a place I can use for escape, and I love Bradwell, but it's my own village, so Bakewell is my refuge of choice. I like Mondays because it's market day, but it's also hectic, so to come on a Saturday is a real pleasure. I used to come here a lot with Harry and Claire...'

'Bugger Harry,' Wendy said. 'I bet Claire loved the ducks, though, didn't she?'

'She did. She used to squeal as we turned into the car park, because she knew what it meant.'

'Then those are the memories to treasure, Doris, not the retrospective horrible ones. Right, I want to pick up a couple of postcards, and maybe a Bakewell pudding for later. It'll go down nicely with a glass of vino.'

'Certainly will,' Doris said, her smile restored. 'But we'll buy the pudding on the way back to the car, or it may be a damaged Bakewell pudding.'

. . .

Wendy spread out the blanket on the bench, and Doris placed the picnic basket between them. Coffees were poured from the flask, and sandwiches sorted onto plates. They sat mostly in silence, watching a large family playing a game of rounders on the grass a short distance away.

Doris took out one of the books she had bought and read the blurb.

'*Rebecca*?' Wendy asked.

'It is. I love mingling a classic in occasionally with the more modern crime stuff I read, and I've been promising myself a copy of this for so long. I didn't want to get it on my Kindle, I wanted a real book, so as from today Daphne du Maurier lives with me. I can vaguely remember reading it at school, but I can't recall much detail so I'll look forward to curling up with this tonight.'

'Okay, we've a choice. We can either go and ask that family if we can join in their game of rounders, or we can have half an hour of reading.'

Doris turned to Wendy and they high-fived. 'Reading it is then,' Wendy said, and she delved into her own bag to get one of the books she had bought.

Quarter of an hour later, the peace was disturbed by the tones of Doris's phone.

She looked at the name on the screen and turned to Wendy. 'It's Rosie.'

'Answer it. She wouldn't ring without good reason, would she? Maybe she simply wants you to know Shirley is home.'

Doris clicked answer. 'Hello, Rosie. Are you okay?'

'I... I don't know. We've heard on the news that a woman's body has been found in some woods about three miles away. The thing is... Shirley isn't home. I don't know what to do. Mark hasn't reported her missing, and I'm getting into a proper panic here. They've not identified the body yet, and I don't know what to do.'

'Okay, first of all take some deep breaths. The body they've found is probably unconnected. But, apart from that, if Shirley's still not home, and you've heard nothing from her, you need to notify the police, no matter what her husband says. You're her sister, and you've every right to report a missing person. If the body isn't Shirley's, they will be able to rule it out quickly, and they'll instigate a search for her anyway.'

'Thank you,' Rosie said, a sob catching in her throat. 'I knew you'd show me the sensible course. I'll ring the police now, and tell Mark when it's done and dusted.'

'And will you ring me later? Let me know what's happening?'

'I will. I can't thank you enough, I feel so much more in control. I've only known you three days, and yet you're the first person I turn to for help. You must think I'm crazy.'

Doris gave a small laugh. 'No, I think it's your subconscious telling you I

investigate missing persons cases for a living, and I'd be the obvious one to approach for information. Good luck, Rosie, and don't forget to ring me.'

'I won't, I promise.'

Doris turned to Wendy. 'You got that?'

'Most of it. Shirley still hasn't turned up?'

'No, but a dead body has. Unidentified.'

'That doesn't surprise me in the slightest, Doris Lester. You're like a magnet for them. When you said let's go and visit dead people, I didn't think you meant the newly dead.'

Doris gave her friend a slight punch in the shoulder. 'Sarcasm, Lucas, sarcasm. And I'm not involved. Rosie has recently lost her mum, so probably has nobody to ask for advice. I've come on the scene with those bloody qualifications for my job listed on my business card, so she's turned to me. It's all a bit long distance.'

'It's not that long a distance. You want to go see Rosie?'

'No, not at all.' Doris was a little too quick to answer. 'I can't help. She needs the police, although if this body is Shirley, the police will be needing her.'

The body was finally manoeuvred up the incline away from the water, and into the back of the ambulance waiting to transport the dead woman to the morgue. From his quick check by the side of the river, pathologist Owen Bridger was mulling over in his head that this was more than likely a case of strangulation; bruises were showing around her neck and he guessed he wouldn't find fluid in her lungs that would indicate death by drowning. Intuition and years of post-mortems told him this lady was dead before she went into the stream. It would be up to Grace to sort out the whys and wherefores.

He climbed wearily back up and along the path leading to where he had left his car. Once again he vowed not to stay up late because it seemed to him that whenever he did, somebody died in odd circumstances, and he was called out before even the sun had thought about getting up.

He slumped in the car for a moment, then saw the ambulance carrying his deceased client set off. He turned on the ignition and followed it. He knew it looked like being a long day, and he yawned widely. Bed by seven, he decided, Saturday or no Saturday.

The ambulance didn't rush, and he followed at the sedate pace set by the paramedic. By the time he had parked his car in his designated space at the morgue, the body had been transported inside, and delivered to the autopsy suite.

He checked his list to see his work for the day and decided the young lady from the stream had to be a priority. He'd seen a couple of reporters hoping for some information at the scene, and knew it would be in the evening papers. They needed a name.

Owen gave a small wave to Grace Stamford, standing on the viewing platform. He knew she wouldn't come into his autopsy room itself; she freely admitted to nausea and dizziness when up close and personal with his cuts and the odours emitted by the corpse, but was fairly happy to observe from a distance.

His first job was to take fingerprint copies from the deceased, and send them off for checking against identification records, as well as a DNA swab. With the basics out of the way, he did a thorough examination of the body, talking into his microphone, making sure he missed nothing. Photographs were taken of the bruises around her neck; he commented on it, and moved on to examine the rest of her.

The Y incision made down her front, and the part of the procedure that always made Grace turn away, told Owen so much more. The hyoid bone was fractured, ratifying his diagnosis of asphyxiation. She would have died quickly. To confirm his vocalised thoughts, there was no water in the lungs. The woman had been dead before she reached any sort of water.

Grace, watching the procedure now the Y incision was out of the way, held up a thumb to indicate she was getting his words and she understood. There was no doubt that this was a murder victim; she couldn't have strangled herself without a rope hanging from a hook, and the marks around her neck would have been completely different.

The DCI leaned forward and spoke into the microphone on the viewing platform. 'Owen, I'm heading off. I'll wait for the rest when you finalise your report, but I'm going to chase up those fingerprints now. We have to know who this poor woman is. We also need to find where she was killed. Thank you, Owen.'

He waved a hand in acknowledgement that he had heard her, and continued with the weighing of the liver.

Grace headed back to her office, and pulled up a map of the local area. She found the small river, the Whyburn, known locally as Town Brook, then zoomed into the map so that she could see more detail. It widened as it went higher, and there were a couple of small bridges that went across it. Nothing suggested it would be an easy place to strangle someone and shove them in the water, so she plotted out six small areas that could be of interest, then went out into the main office.

'Okay,' she said. 'Our lady from this morning was strangled, then either she fell into the water or she was put there. We still don't have a name...'

'Excuse me, boss. There's an email, came through seconds ago, confirming the fingerprints are on record, and the person is a lady called Melanie Brookes.'

11

Rosie could feel anger emanating from Mark.

'Why the hell did you bother notifying the police? She's left, there's nothing more to say.'

Ten minutes earlier she had sent Mark a text to say she had reported Shirley's disappearance, and now, to her horror, he was standing in her kitchen, his face apoplectic with rage.

She felt an overwhelming sense of relief that Dan had taken Megan to the cinema; if Dan saw Mark in this mood it would lead to a brawl, and that she could definitely do without. If anybody was going to batter Mark Ledger senseless, she wanted it to be her.

'Mark, it's Saturday afternoon. Nobody has seen or heard from Shirley since Wednesday evening, and you saw her last. I shall be saying that to the police, so prepare yourself for a visit. There's a body, Mark, haven't you heard the news?'

For a second he looked shaken, then reverted to his belligerence. 'A body? Where?'

'Town Brook woods, the other side of the park. A woman's body. You've clearly not heard, because even you might have started to connect your missing wife with a woman's body having been found.'

'Don't be bloody sarcastic, Rosie,' he snarled. 'Are they coming here?'

'In about half an hour. I suggest you stay; it won't look too good if I have to tell them you were here, but you decided not to wait for them. They might start to think you had some involvement in Shirley's disappearance. And I swear to you here and now, Mark, if that poor woman is Shirley, and I find out you had anything to do with it, you'll be looking over your shoulder for the rest of your life.'

'Shirley was alive and well as I walked out of that house on Wednesday evening. She sent me a text after midnight, telling me not to come home because I wouldn't get in.'

'You've not told me that before!'

'It's nothing to do with you.'

'Show me the text.'

He handed over his new phone. 'Fortunately they've recovered everything from my old one. But that's all it says, what I've told you.'

Rosie read the text and handed the phone back to him. 'The police will want to see that, because whether this woman is Shirley or not, they're going to be looking for her. I've made it official by reporting her, and after nearly three days they're going to want to know where she is. As I do...'

Mark seemed to be calming a little, and he pulled out a chair from underneath the kitchen table, and sat. 'You mashing?'

Rosie switched on the kettle and brushed away a tear. This should be Shirley sitting at her table, not her obnoxious husband. He'd seemed so nice when they first met, supportive throughout the pregnancy especially when they learned it was twin boys, but once he had Shirley tied to the home and the boys, unable to go to work, he changed.

Rosie and Mark were cradling their cups when the knock sounded. Rosie stood and hurried down the hallway, keen to let in the police.

DC Sam Ellis and PC Fiona Harte, both seconded to Grace Stamford's team for the duration of the case, stood on the doorstep and showed their warrant cards.

'Down to the end of the hall and through the door, it's the kitchen. My brother-in-law is in there.'

Mark stood as the two officers entered the room, and shook their hands.

'Please, sit down,' Rosie said. 'Can I get you a drink?'

'No, we're good, thanks,' Sam said. 'We need to take details of your sister, any thoughts you might have of where she might be–'

Rosie held up a hand to interrupt. 'You've found a body in the woods, a suspicious death it said. A woman.' Rosie picked up her phone and opened her pictures file. She handed it to Sam. 'This is my sister. This is Shirley. Have you seen the... the body?'

Sam looked at the screen. 'When was this taken?'

'About a week ago.'

'Is she still blonde?'

'She is.' Rosie held her breath.

'Then we can tentatively say that your sister isn't the lady we have found in the stream. She is fairly petite and has short dark hair. So, we need to take some details. Her name is Shirley Ledger? Address?'

Mark said the address and confirmed he was her husband.

Fiona was busy taking notes, and Sam asked the questions. He sat a little straighter when Mark mentioned that the boys went to Springbrook Boarding School for Boys.

'And how long have they been there?'

'They went in September, so it's coming up to the end of their first year in July. I went there, and it did me no harm.' Mark sounded defensive to Sam's ears, and even Fiona looked up from her notetaking.

'Shirley didn't like the boys being there,' Rosie said. 'I've rung round the hotels that are within five miles of the school, thinking she maybe was going to see them this morning anyway, despite Mark saying their plans had changed. She was desperate to see them. I also rang the school this morning to ask if the boys had been taken out by their mum, but they said no, both parents were due to visit next Saturday instead, following a change in circumstances.'

'Do the boys like it there?' Fiona asked, pausing from taking notes for a moment.

'Of course,' Mark said.

'No,' Rosie said.

Both police officers turned to look at Rosie. 'No?' Sam raised his eyebrows in query.

'They don't like it at all. They'd had a perfectly normal education at the local primary school up to reaching their eleventh birthday, then they didn't follow their friends to the comprehensive, they were shipped off to Springbrook. Their education is currently male-orientated, they only see their mum when Dad allows it, and I thank God every day that they're twins because at least they have each other. I've watched my sister become more and more depressed, more and more withdrawn over the past nine months than I would have thought possible. And now she's missing. And he,' Rosie pointed to Mark, 'didn't want me to report her as missing.' Rosie slammed her cup down on the table with a thud and there was a moment of silence.

'Mr Ledger, do you have anything to say?' Fiona's hand hovered over her notebook waiting for his answer.

'Look.' It was almost a bluster. 'My sister-in-law has never liked me; she's said that to make me look bad. The boys love it at Springbrook and of course I don't stop my wife from visiting them. She has her own car; she can go when she wants.'

'But that's the thing, she can't go when she wants. They only allow visiting at the weekends unless there are exceptional circumstances for a start, and you've usually got some function or conference to attend where you have to have your wife with you.' Rosie looked at the police officers. 'Since the boys went to the school, Shirley has been allowed to visit them twice. She has them home for Christmas and Easter of course, but ordinary visiting times at weekends seem to go by the wayside.'

'Where do you think your wife is, Mr Ledger?' Sam asked.

'I have no idea. I thought she'd be home with her tail between her legs long before now. I suppose she could be somewhere near the school, but I don't know where.' For the first time, Mark Ledger was starting to show some emotion. He ran his hand through his hair, and turned to face Rosie. 'Has she got somebody else?'

'I wish,' was the terse response. 'But no, not as far as I'm aware, and I think she would tell me something like that.'

'But why would she leave me, if it's not for somebody else?'

Rosie couldn't believe he was asking the question. If this was how Springbrook turned out its pupils, then Adam and Seth had to be removed as soon as possible. 'Mark, do you really want me to give you a list of reasons?'

'Please,' Fiona said. 'We're here to find Mrs Ledger, and arguing between the two of you really isn't going to help. Mrs Steer, did you keep a list of the hotels you rang?'

'I did.' Rosie stood and walked to the kitchen drawer. She pulled out a small piece of folded paper and handed it to Fiona.

Fiona glanced at it and tucked it into her notepad. 'Thank you. We'll set somebody to work on this tomorrow, see if we can track down B and Bs, smaller hotels, places like that. You haven't tried any pubs?'

Rosie shook her head. 'No, it was a bit overwhelming, to be honest. She could be anywhere; it doesn't even have to be near the school. And if it was near the school, she would have gone to see her boys this morning. That's what I was counting on, but the school said she hadn't been, or rung them.'

'Okay. Mrs Steer, can you send that picture of Shirley to my phone, please? Here's my number.' Sam passed her his card. 'And if there's anything that comes to mind, or you have any sort of contact with Shirley, can you use that number and call me?'

Rosie tucked the card inside the flap on her mobile phone cover after sending the requested photograph.

Sam checked it had arrived and the two police officers stood up. 'I'm going back to pass this information on to the team, and we'll be in touch as soon as possible to let you know what's happening. Unfortunately it's the weekend and we have a murder to investigate alongside Mrs Ledger to track down, but be assured it will be started tomorrow.'

Sam's phone rang, and he went out into the hall to answer it. Fiona stayed in the kitchen, to prevent either of the two warring adults from following him and hearing any part of the conversation Sam was having.

The front door banged open and Megan, followed by her father, came bounding through. 'Mum, why is... oh.' She stopped speaking when she saw the figure of DC Sam Ellis standing in the hallway, speaking on his phone. Her father touched his finger to his lips to tell Megan to be quiet, and they edged past Sam to get into the kitchen.

'Everything okay?' Dan asked, looking at his wife's face for confirmation that she wasn't about to murder Mark.

'It's not Shirley,' she said. 'The body from the woods has short dark hair. It's not Shirley,' and Rosie burst out crying.

Dan pulled her into his arms, and they were quickly joined by Megan. All three stood there, only pulling apart when Sam returned to join his colleague in the kitchen.

'Can we sit down, please,' he said. 'I have some further questions to ask of you.'

'You've found her,' Mark said, his voice cracking. 'She's dead, isn't she?'

'No we haven't found your wife, Mr Ledger. I understand Mr Patrick Ledger is related to you.'

'He's my younger brother. Why?'

'And he lives with his partner, a Miss Melanie Brookes?'

'He does. What's he done? It can't be much; he never does anything wrong. Does he need me?'

'Probably. Our colleagues are with him now, telling him that the lady we found in the stream has been identified through fingerprints, and it's Melanie Brookes. He has asked that we take you over to his home, so can you follow me there, please?'

Rosie stifled a sob. 'Mark? Will you be okay? Do you want me to go with you?'

'I'll be okay, thank you, Rosie. You stay here in case Shirley turns up. I'll get over to Patrick.'

Mark spoke and acted like an automaton, and knew his control had temporarily deserted him. For heaven's sake, he'd been nice to bloody Rosie. Melanie, dead. How? His mind whirred with thoughts of her and their Monday nights. He hoped there was a reasonable explanation for her death, because if not the police would start to dig, and they might come up with little things that pointed directly to him as being someone Mel knew well. He shivered, and pulled his coat around him.

'Will you take me?' he asked Sam. 'I think maybe I shouldn't drive. Rosie, I'll leave my car here until I know what's happening, if that's okay.'

'That's fine, Mark,' Dan said. 'Give our condolences to Patrick, and tell him we're here if he needs anything.'

Mark left with Sam, and once again Dan pulled Megan and Rosie into his arms.

'I liked Melanie,' Megan whispered. 'I liked her a lot.'

12

Patrick's face was ashen. 'I last saw her Thursday lunchtime. We were at a function on the Wednesday night to see my brother speak, and we both booked the morning off work knowing there would be a fair amount of drink. I took her to my home after the do, and we both went off to work about twelve on Thursday. She was going to York with her job on Friday and staying overnight, so we said we wouldn't meet up until tonight. I've been ringing her since about lunchtime, but assumed she was shopping or something.' His voice faltered at the end as reality was starting to hit home.

'You didn't live together?'

'Mostly. My place is bigger, and we spent a lot of our time here, but her home office was perfectly set up in her second bedroom, and sometimes she needed to be at home. It was easier to run both places, and it was also good to have time out. We had a really good relationship. We loved each other...'

'Who would want to hurt your partner, Patrick?' DCI Stamford tried to speak gently.

'I have absolutely no idea. What killed her? Did she fall into the stream? She liked to run, maybe she tripped...'

'I'm sorry, Patrick, it wasn't accidental.'

His eyes widened in horror as thoughts invaded his brain. 'Murdered? She was murdered?'

'She was.'

'We have officers with your brother at the moment on an unrelated matter, and he has been informed of Melanie's death. He's on his way over here with my DC.'

'How did you know Melanie and I...?'

'We went to Melanie's house. Her neighbour came out and told us about you, luckily they knew where you lived.'

It was obvious to Grace and DS Harriet Jameson that Patrick's mind wasn't able to function properly, and Harriet leaned across the table. 'Mr Ledger, would you like me to make you a cup of tea?'

Patrick nodded; it hadn't reached the extremities of his brain that these two women knew of Mark's existence.

Harriet stood and switched on the kettle. She ran a hand through her short blonde curls, trying to decide which cupboard was likely to hold mugs, then busied herself making the drinks. She brushed away the beginning of a tear in her grey eyes; she hated this part of her job, the notification of death.

Sam drove Mark to his brother's home, leaving Fiona at the Steer home. He felt it was the best call, hoping Fiona would be able to get the family talking, maybe get some information as to possible places Shirley Ledger could be.

. . .

Patrick was slumped over the kitchen table, his head in his hands. Grace was trying to question him, but getting little in the way of answers.

'Can you think of anyone who would want to hurt Melanie?'

'No.'

'Had she fallen out with anyone recently?'

'No.'

'Do you have a key to her place? We had no way of getting in the first time we went.'

'Yes.' He made no move to produce it.

'Can I have it, please? We'll return to her home as soon as we leave here.'

'Yes.' Patrick stood and walked carefully to a kitchen drawer, removing a bundle of keys. He carefully selected one, prised it off the ring and handed it to Grace.

'Thank you.'

He looked up momentarily as he heard the front door open.

Mark strode through to the kitchen. He stopped in the doorway and looked at the abject sorrow on his brother's face, then moved across to him. He hugged him, not even registering that it was probably the first time he'd hugged his brother for quite a few years.

'God, Patrick, I'm so sorry, mate. Couldn't believe it at first.'

Patrick didn't speak, as if unsure what to say, unsure how to feel. Mark knew it wouldn't seem real, Mel not being around anymore.

'Mark,' Grace said, 'for the record, when was the last time you saw Melanie?'

Mark turned to her. 'At the do on Wednesday night. I think Patrick and Mel went home around eleven but I can't be sure about that. I was a little worse for wear by the time they left, and

I ended up walking home. Didn't get home till six the next morning.'

'Six?'

'Look, I'm not proud of it. I threw my phone at a tree in temper, then ended up sleeping propped up against another tree. As I said, I was wasted. A postman on his way to work woke me up and I carried on to my house, where I found out my wife had disappeared. It's been a shitty couple of days, as you can imagine.'

'I certainly can,' Grace said, having formed her own opinion of the man in front of her. 'So, while you're both here, I want to check timelines with you. You two plus Melanie attended the same seminar or whatever it was on Wednesday evening. Melanie went home with you, Patrick, and not back to her own place. In the meantime, you staggered home eventually, Mark, getting home after six. Am I right so far?'

Both men nodded, and Mark added that he actually had a taxi for the final part of his journey, after using the postman's phone to call one.

'Okay. Patrick, you and Melanie went to work at lunchtime on Thursday. You didn't see her Thursday night because she had work to do at home to prepare for a trip to York on Friday, where she planned to stay overnight, returning home on Saturday. Mark – have you been to work?'

Mark shook his head. 'No, Shirley leaving has thrown me a bit. I rang in and booked a couple of days off, didn't explain why because I thought Shirley would be home by now.'

'Can I ask... how long Mel had been in that stream?' Patrick winced as he said it.

'I can't answer that yet, we're waiting for the forensic reports. We don't believe she went in where she was found, we think she went in higher up where it's much deeper and faster flowing, and the current took her down until she was snagged on tree branches that were in the water.'

'And she was... murdered? You're positive about that?'

'Yes, we do know some things, it's the finer details we're still waiting for. She was strangled, we believe manually and not by ligature, and we do know she was dead before entering the water because there was no water in her lungs.'

Grace allowed that to settle in their minds before continuing. 'We're now at Thursday night. Patrick, you definitely didn't see Melanie?'

'No, I rang her to wish her goodnight about elevenish. I went to bed with a book, read about two pages and then went to sleep. I didn't speak to her when I rang her, it went to voicemail, but that's not unusual, before you jump to conclusions. If she has something that really needs her concentration, she switches off her phone. I assumed she was busy, so didn't bother her again. I wished her good luck for her presentation the following day, and then said I loved her and goodnight. If you get hold of her phone, you can hear it for yourself.'

'You didn't hear from her on Friday?'

'Not at all, but I wouldn't expect to. It wasn't only about presentations with Mel, she had to network, to chat to people. Her enthusiasm for her job absolutely shone out of her, and although she wasn't in sales, she sold the idea of a new system to a lot of people merely by talking to them. When she was away, I never rang her. I waited for her to ring me, then I knew I wasn't interrupting anything important. We did have a system for emergencies. If I needed her for anything urgent, I would ring twice in quick succession, then she would call me as soon as she could. We've only once used that, when her Mum was rushed into hospital with pneumonia. Mel was in Germany for the week, but she cut it short and came home.'

'And today? You tried to ring her?'

'I did but not until after lunch to give her time to get sorted from her journey home. She didn't answer, so I left a message to say ring me when she could.'

'And you, Mark.' Grace turned to the older brother. 'Have you spoken to Mel since Wednesday night?'

'Me? No, I'd have no reason to speak to her. To be honest, since I collected my car on Thursday morning, I've done nothing. I haven't been out, I've constantly rung my wife who doesn't respond at all, and I've watched bloody daytime television.'

'Where does Melanie work, Patrick?'

'It's a company in Newark called Global Systems.' Patrick took out his wallet. 'This is Mel's business card, with the office number on it. God, I'd better ring them...'

'I'll notify them,' Grace said. 'We'll be speaking to them tomorrow, so I'll tell them what's happened. They'll probably ring you.'

'But they're not open Sundays.'

'They are for us.'

He gave a brief nod. This woman could open doors to hell, he reckoned, if she was so inclined.

'Okay.' Grace handed both Patrick and Mark business cards. 'If there's anything, and I mean anything at all even if it seems minor to you, I would like you to ring me. Patrick, we will need you to identify Melanie fairly soon. I'll confirm that later. In the meantime, can you provide a list of all Melanie's friends, addresses if you have them but phone numbers if not, and we'll start interviewing them tomorrow. My email is on the card, so send it as soon as it's complete. I'll leave you two for now, but obviously I'll have to speak to you again. We'll need a statement from both of you, but it can wait a couple of days.'

PC Fiona Harte was in the lounge with Dan and Rosie sitting opposite her, on the sofa. They were holding hands and Rosie kept wiping away a tear.

'All of us really liked Patrick and Melanie, which I know sounds odd considering how much we dislike Mark. Shirley once told me Mark was seriously bullied at school because he stammered and wore glasses, and that's why he is how he is, but he's compounded the issue by sending Adam and Seth there. Surely, if you'd had such a miserable time at a school, you wouldn't want your kids anywhere near it!'

'And didn't Shirley see any of this when she first met Mark?' Fiona was carefully probing, trying to understand the dynamics of the family.

Rosie gave a short laugh. 'No, he was Mr Charm until they got married, then the dictatorial side of him really shone through. He didn't want her going to work and meeting other men, so she quickly became pregnant. She's been on the pill since the twins were born, but he doesn't know. I wish she'd ring me, we'll help her, and she knows that.'

'There wasn't another man?'

'She's never even hinted at anything like that. She comes round here most days because we have an Etsy shop. We make stuff. It gives her an income without him knowing about it. Before Mum died, Shirley had nothing, but Mum left us a large insurance policy. Shirley has money that Mr Big knows nothing about, plus the regular small income from our shop. She uses our address for her mail concerning her account and so far we've kept it from him. She hasn't withdrawn anything since she went missing...'

'Do you see anything of your father?'

'No, he apparently died fifteen years ago. We only found out on Wednesday when our father's wife came here to tell us. She knew nothing of us until a couple of weeks ago. It's been a strange sort of time all round.'

'You hadn't seen this person before?' Fiona went on full alert. 'This woman married to your father, she was a newcomer in your life?'

'She was, but I've had contact since. She's nice.'

'Name and address, please.' Fiona bent over her notebook.

Rosie picked up her phone and removed Doris's card from the front cover. 'I don't have her home address, but that is her business card, I'm sure you can track her down from that.'

'Connection? Doris Lester of Connection?'

'You know her?'

'Not personally, but believe me, their excellent reputation goes before them. She met Shirley?'

'She did. We've spoken since, Doris and me, but only by phone.'

'Ring her. Tell her what's happened now. You'll not regret it.'

13

Doris and Wendy decided not to go to church, partly because Doris didn't want to get out of bed; a late Saturday night, a surfeit of wine and a good film on television had made her realise that Sunday was indeed a day of rest.

Wendy was reading the newspaper when Doris finally made it downstairs. 'I'll get you a coffee,' she said, and Doris smiled at her.

'You don't have to wait on me, you know.'

'Hey, this is a free holiday for me, I'm happy to help. You want breakfast?'

Doris shook her head. 'No, I don't think so. Shall we go out for lunch instead?'

'Sounds like a plan, my treat.' Wendy stood. 'I'll get us a coffee.'

She heard Doris's phone ring as she was switching on the kettle. She made the drinks and could still hear Doris talking. She hesitated, not wanting to disturb the phone call, but heard Doris say goodbye, so pushed open the door into the lounge.

'I waited,' Wendy said.

Doris seemed deep in thought.

'You okay?' Wendy put the cup down in front of her friend, and Doris shook her head, clearing her thoughts.

'I've got an apology to make,' she said.

'You need me to go home?' Wendy said, a catch in her voice.

'Not at all. The apology is because I said the only dead bodies on this holiday would be long-time dead corpses. That's not proving to be strictly the case.'

'You haven't been anywhere to find a dead body. And if you have, how come I missed out on it?' There was indignation in Wendy's tone, and Doris laughed.

'No, I haven't found one, but there is one, nevertheless.'

Wendy sat down. 'Who was the phone call from? No – let me guess. Rosie. Is Shirley…?'

'It was Rosie, but Shirley is still missing. That's what the call was about. She asked if I would take the case on an official footing, find some trace of Shirley. I kind of said we'd go out and see them. The body found in the woods wasn't Shirley, thank God, but it was somebody who was part of the family, somebody called Melanie Brookes. She was the partner of Mark's brother Patrick. I think I've got that right.'

'And Mark is?'

'Oh, sorry. Mark is Shirley's husband, so the dead woman is sort of his sister-in-law. Rosie sounded a little lost, and she's worrying herself silly that there is some connection between Shirley disappearing and Melanie Brookes' death, which, by the way, was murder.' Doris pulled a notepad towards her, and quickly sketched out a family tree showing who was who, then pushed it across to Wendy. 'Commit that to memory, then you'll know who we're dealing with.'

Wendy stared at the piece of paper. 'We?'

'You want me to make you a deputy's badge? Look, we'll go out to Hucknall and talk to Rosie, but this is nothing to do with Connection. I won't be sending Rosie an invoice; we'll be there simply as friends trying to find her lost sister. If we're killed in action, it won't come under the Connection insurance cover,' she finished with a smile. 'If I start involving Connection, the whole rigmarole of Harry and his ever-ready penis will come out, and I want to choose the right time to tell Mouse about it, not have it all come tumbling out because we have to issue an invoice. You up for it?'

'Do I get a gun?'

'No, only Sheriffs carry guns. I'll have a quick bacon sandwich in view of the fact we're not looking like getting lunch, and we can go to the Bowling Green tonight for a meal, if that's okay with you.'

An hour later saw the two women in the car and heading towards Hucknall. Wendy was really enjoying being driven about, her own car still hidden inside her garage back in Sheffield. She took every opportunity to stare around her at the scenery, mentally wondering how anybody would ever choose to live down south when there was all this beauty north of the Watford Gap.

They pulled up outside Rosie's house and the front door opened. Megan was standing there, a huge smile on her face.

'Mum said you're here to help us find Aunty Shirley.'

Doris smiled at the young girl. 'We'll try, Megan, we'll try. Is Mum in?'

Megan held open the door. 'Go straight through. She's drinking lots of tea.'

'Good. Best thing to do.'

'That's what Mum says. Dad says whiskey is best.'

They walked through into the kitchen to find Rosie and Dan sitting at the table. Rosie jumped up. 'I'm so sorry, I didn't know you'd arrived.'

Doris laughed. 'It's okay, Megan's been looking after us.'

'I've been watching out for the car,' Megan said. 'I went to meet them.'

Dan was on his feet, and he stretched out his hand. 'Dan Steer.'

'I'm Doris Lester, and this is my friend Wendy Lucas.'

'Can I offer you a drink?' Rosie asked.

'Water for me, thanks,' Doris responded. 'Wendy?'

'Me too.'

They sat around the table while Megan got water from the fridge, and Doris took out her notebook.

'I need to know exactly what's been happening since we were here last Wednesday afternoon.'

Once the timeline was completed, Doris sat back with a sigh. '*Cherchez l'homme*,' she said. '*Cherchez l'homme*.'

'What?'

'Find the man, Mum,' Megan helpfully explained.

'I know what it means, Megs, I'm not sure of its relevance to everything we've told Mrs Lester.'

'Okay, let's stop with this Mrs Lester and Mrs Lucas malarkey,' Doris said. 'It's Doris and Wendy from here on. For a start, this will be nothing to do with Connection, the company in which I'm a partner. There will be no bill at the end of it.'

'The PC, Fiona, the one with us yesterday, was full of admiration for your agency. You have an excellent reputation. But we can pay...'

'No, you don't understand. I'm officially on holiday, so I won't bring Connection into it unless I need to use a bit of clout with my business card. It opens doors,' she said with a smile. 'And if anyone mentions the fact that we're in our seventies, I will respond.'

Megan moved to stand at Doris's side. 'Can I do my work experience with you?'

'It's a long way from here to Eyam every morning,' Doris said. 'But I'm more than happy to talk to you about how you can prepare for a future in investigations.'

'What qualifications do you have?'

'Megan!' her mother interrupted. 'Leave Doris alone.'

'It's fine,' Doris laughed. 'I have a wall full of qualifications to the highest level now, all relevant to the job I do, plus a degree in IT, and I am a black belt, fifth Dan in karate.'

'And I can knit and crochet,' Wendy added.

The tension eased around the table with the mention of Wendy's skills, and everyone laughed.

'Okay, I want honest answers to any questions I may ask, and I'm going to record from now on. It makes it easier.' She took out the small recorder that lived in her bag and placed it on the table after switching it on.

'Rosie, has Shirley ever mentioned being friends with another man? Either as friends or something a little stronger.'

'No, definitely not. She never goes anywhere; Mark sees to that. She comes here most days, we sort out any orders we have for our Etsy customers, and she calls at the post office on her way home to post them out. Everything is done through this address. We have a room upstairs that we use like a mini-factory, and it's kept locked as a precautionary measure in case Mark goes walkabout in here at any time. She's paranoid about him finding out she has any money at all. I seriously don't know where she would find the time to meet another man. She's not the same Shirley I grew up with, the one who was there until she married Mark. Then he shackled her, and now she is so timid it's awful to see. Mark must not find out about the Etsy shop. He would find some way of stopping her, and to be perfectly frank, she's so much more creative than I am and is the leading partner in our business. It would fold without her.'

'So tell me about the children.'

'Seth and Adam. They're quiet kids. When you consider they're almost the same age as our little minx, and they're cousins, you wouldn't even think they lived on the same planet, never mind in the same family. I don't think they like their dad, especially as he's sent them to Springbrook. I haven't seen them since Easter when they came home for the holidays, and I know Shirley misses them dreadfully. She's lost weight, she looks miserable all the time – do you think they're the reason she's disappeared? Is she setting something up maybe, so she can take them out of school and have them living with her? Somewhere Mark can't find her...'

'Have you got a picture of the boys?'

Rosie picked up her phone, selected a photo and sent it to Doris. 'They look more like Shirley than they do their dad.'

'They look like their granddad,' Doris said quietly.

Wendy took the phone from Doris and looked at the picture. 'Hmph,' she said.

Rosie looked concerned. 'I'm sorry, this must be painful for you.'

Doris smiled. 'Don't worry about it. I certainly won't. Can you give me a list of the hotels in the school locale that you checked to see if Shirley was there, please?'

Once again, Rosie delved into her phone and swiftly despatched a document to Doris. 'The police have that information. The policewoman who was here said they would look all around the area for other smaller places, in case you get anybody saying the police have already been asking for her.'

'The boys – they're due to see their parents next Saturday, aren't they?'

'They are. I can't see Mark going without Shirley, he's not

particularly paternal. I'm keeping everything crossed that Shirley will be home by then. It's been strange without her for the last few days. And on top of that, of course, we've lost Melanie.'

'You think the two things are connected?'

'The police do. No, that's not strictly true. They've not actually said that, it's more a feeling I had. Their questions were about Shirley knowing Melanie, and were they friends. That sort of thing.'

'Were they? Friends, I mean?'

'Not close friends. In fact...'

'Go on.'

Rosie looked uncomfortable. 'I always thought Melanie was a bit more friendly with Mark than she was with Shirley. I'm not saying there's anything in that – Mel was Patrick's partner, after all – but...'

Doris waited.

'I did a meal for everybody at Easter because the boys were home, and Mel sat between Patrick and Mark. She hardly even looked at Patrick, who talked most of the night to Megs, but she certainly chatted a lot with Mark. What's even more telling is that Mark was happy all the time he was in her company. But honestly, that's as much as I know. I can't imagine he would cheat on Shirley with his own brother's partner.'

14

It briefly occurred to Doris that she was becoming rather bitter – her thoughts were rapidly turning towards the theory that all men were born with the cheating gene already present. She could imagine Mark cheating with his brother's wife.

But cheating is a two-way thing. Melanie Brookes could have said no to Mark, she could have said *I'm with your brother, get away from me.* Perhaps she hadn't, maybe she had opted for the excitement of being with the brothers, rather than a brother. If this was the case, it was probably going to put a whole new slant on who had put an end to Melanie.

'Where's Mark?' Wendy asked.

'He's with Patrick at the moment. He says Patrick's falling apart, can't understand why anyone would want to hurt Mel, let alone kill her. I'm going to tell him we've asked you for help, and it's mainly because he doesn't seem to be bothered. I wanted him to report Shirley's disappearance right at the start, because it's so unlike her.'

'Okay,' Doris said. 'Tell me about Shirley. I know she's a

devoted mother, doesn't like her children being at Springbrook and doesn't seem to be particularly happily married. Would she agree with those statements?'

Rosie nodded. 'She would. She has something to say about Mark every day, and it's rarely complimentary. Her dislike of him grew when the boys left. She's a quiet person now, it's as if he squeezes the life out of her. He doesn't hit her, or at least she doesn't say he does, but he... controls her. He talked her into giving up work when the boys were born, and has found reasons ever since for her not taking on any part-time work. He needs her to be at the other end of a phone all the time, to have meals ready when he gets home, to make sure he always has an ironed shirt.' She gave a short laugh. 'It's a good job he doesn't live here. Ironing isn't my favourite chore.'

'Nor mine,' Doris agreed with a smile. 'You're absolutely certain she doesn't have a friend on the periphery somewhere? Male or female.'

There was quiet for a moment while Rosie dug deep into her mind. 'I don't think so. I can't even remember anyone in the past. I suppose her closest friend was Melanie, purely because she was Patrick's partner, but they didn't socialise, they merely chatted whenever their paths crossed as a result of a Mark and Patrick get-together. I was her sister, her friend, and after Mum died, her mother. I've helped her get some self-respect back with our Etsy shop, and she loves the crafting we do together. She deals with the technical side, she's so much better than me at all that, and she has really good ideas for things we can do. But that's her life. I can't think of anywhere she would go to escape that life.'

Doris drew a line under her notes, knowing if there was anything she'd missed it would be on the recorder. 'Leave it with me. I'm going home to do some digging. Did Shirley keep a diary?'

'She did, but everything she put in it was mundane stuff – things like shopping reminders, days she came here to work on crafting – all simply written in case Mark saw it.'

'She's so secretive, isn't she?' Wendy observed. 'It must be hard work, having to live that kind of life.'

'It wasn't like that for her at first. Before they got married, I mean. We all thought Mark was lovely, her friends were somewhat envious because to look at him he's definitely a catch. But I think he thought marrying her meant she became his mother figure. She was expected to do everything. It came as a bit of a shock, but she loved him so she became what he wanted, instead of what she wanted to be.'

'She had friends?' Doris looked at Rosie.

'Years ago, she did. She worked in an office with lots of other girls around her age, and she loved it. She'd been promoted to section supervisor when she found out she was pregnant. He'd been a bit of a control freak prior to that, but as soon as that first scan told them it was twins, he shut her down. It was the excuse he needed to have a little slave to follow him around and make sure he never had to lift a finger for the rest of his life. It's why he's so gutted she's taken off and left him.'

'What did she take with her?'

Rosie frowned. 'Take with her?'

'Clothes? Did she take everything, or a small amount, to indicate she's going to return.'

'Oh my God, I've no idea. Mark doesn't encourage me to pop around, and I can't remember the last time I was there. I do know she took her car, because he said he was pissed off at having to take a taxi to go and get his car back on Thursday morning, after that environmental talk he did. If Shirley's car had been there he would have used that, and left her with the problem of having to get her car back from the venue. She has a little Ka. It's her freedom, the only bit she has really. She calls her Katherine. It's dark blue. I can't remember the registration number, but I've got a picture of her in front of it, from the day she bought it.'

Rosie dug into her picture file and exclaimed in triumph when she found the required one. She sent it to Doris, who checked she could see the registration clearly, then copied it into her notes, speaking it aloud for the recorder at the same time.

'Have the police searched the house?'

'I believe that was the next move when the news came through about Melanie. They took Mark straight over to be with Patrick.'

'Do you have a key to Mark's place?'

'I do. Another secret. Shirley gave me one – just in case, she said.'

'I can only give you this as a suggestion, not an instruction, but if it was my sister who had gone missing, I'd be texting my brother-in-law to find out exactly where he was, and if he wasn't at home and not looking like returning home in the next couple of hours, I might have a look around the bedroom he shares with his wife.' Doris gave an exaggerated wink.

'Mrs Doris Lester! You're a wicked woman! I'll text him now,' Rosie said, returning the wink.

'I thought you might. And if I was giving further advice out, I'd do it with these gloves on.' She delved into her handbag and produced some bright blue latex gloves. 'If you haven't been there for a while, the police might wonder how your fingerprints have been lifted.'

'Do you always carry these around with you?' Rosie was clearly intrigued.

'It's not normal when I'm on holiday, but the holiday has been moved to July or August, so I carry them now.'

'Wow.' Megan had been quiet for some time, but picked up the gloves. 'These are brilliant. Mum, when you've finished casing the joint at Uncle Mark's house, can I have the gloves, please?'

Doris took out a second pair. 'Have your own, but don't go with your mum. Stay here with your dad. Casing the joint?'

Rosie laughed and ruffled her daughter's hair. 'She loves black and white movies. She's picked up all sorts of odd phrases as a result.'

'Okay, I'm going home to start to find Shirley.' Doris slipped her notepad and the recorder back into her bag, and stood. 'There may be other questions, but I will ring unless we really have to come back out here. It depends what I can find. I think that little car is a priority, because where that is, so is Shirley. She can disguise herself, but she can't disguise the car. I'll ring you soon, Rosie, to give you an update, but it may be tomorrow. When we get home today it'll be time to go to the pub.'

Dan's head lifted. 'That sounds like the best idea I've heard in years.'

'We've booked a table for our evening meal.' Doris laughed. 'Mind you, we might manage a glass of wine or two, we are on holiday after all.'

Megan stood and walked with Doris and Wendy to the front door. 'I'll go to the car with you.'

'We're fine.' Doris smiled. 'Honestly.'

'You're seventy, you said so. I have to help you.'

'God bless you, child,' Wendy said. 'Do we look ancient? But come to the car with us if it'll make you feel better.'

The twelve-year-old nodded solemnly. 'It will. And Mum always goes to the car with guests so it's obviously what should happen.'

'Come on then.' The trio headed down the path, and Rosie reached the doorway, waving a key at them. 'Found it!' she called, 'and he's staying at Patrick's for the night.'

Doris held up a thumb, and the pair settled into their seats. She wound down the window to say goodbye to Megan.

'Here's looking at yer, kid,' Megan said, and blew a kiss through the open window.

Doris drove away, the older women giggling hysterically.

Rosie let herself into the house quietly, keyed in the code for the alarm, saying a little prayer that Mark hadn't changed it, and exhaled heavily when the beeping stopped.

She ran quickly up the stairs and into the master bedroom. The bed was unmade, the sheets half on the bed and half on the floor. It was clearly beneath him to do something as mundane as tidying the room.

Rosie crossed to Shirley's side, and smiled to herself as she recognised the old copy of *Jane Eyre* on the little table. It had been their mother's book, and they had taken it in turns one memorable afternoon to divide up the books between them. Alternate choices had been the order of the day, and somehow they had both ended up with a copy of *Jane Eyre*.

'Where are you, Shirl?' Rosie whispered, and she glanced around the room. Nothing seemed out of place; blood splatter on the wall simply wasn't there. She opened the drawer in the small table, and it contained some paracetamol, a packet of Tampax and Shirley's everyday diary. Seeing it sent a shiver through Rosie. Shirley would have taken it. It contained phone numbers, addresses, contacts, things she might need. She wouldn't have gone anywhere without dropping it into her bag.

Rosie put the diary in her own bag, and moved across to the wardrobe. It was a large double wardrobe, and Rosie opened both doors at the same time. It was full.

'My God, Shirley, where are you? You've taken nothing with

you,' Rosie groaned. She closed the wardrobe doors, had a further rapid look around, then went in the other rooms. Nothing. Downstairs it was the same. It was untidy, pots hadn't been washed, and it was definitely lacking a woman's touch. Shirley's touch.

15

Adam and Seth Ledger looked quickly across at each other, then stood in unison. They didn't think they were in trouble, but it was never good to be collected by Eva Peters and escorted to the headmaster's office.

'Don't worry, boys,' she whispered as they walked, one on each side of her, down the herringbone-floored corridor that gleamed in the bright sunshine. 'You're not in any trouble.'

Neither of the boys spoke; it had been their mantra from day one that if they weren't speaking to each other, they wouldn't speak at all.

They were surprised to see their father sitting with two women as they entered Norman Rodgers' office.

Still they didn't speak, and Mrs Peters pointed to two chairs that had been set out for them. 'Sit down, boys,' she said, and they looked at each other before doing as requested.

Seth was next to his father, but there was no contact, not even a hello from Mark to his sons.

Norman Rodgers spoke first. 'Seth, Adam, these two ladies are police officers. DCI Grace Stamford and DS Harriet

Jameson. They would like to have a few words after your father
has spoken with you.'

Mark Ledger visibly took a deep breath. 'I have two things to tell
you, boys, and the first thing is that Aunty Melanie has died.'

The twins turned to each other, Seth almost reached for
Adam's hand and thought better of it. Dad wouldn't like it, he
decided.

'Does Uncle Patrick know?' Seth asked.

'Yes, of course he does. He's upset, and he sends his love.'

'Why?' Adam asked, wanting to cry but knowing Dad wouldn't
like it. 'Why has she died? She's not old like our nan was.'

Mark glanced at the two policewomen. 'She was found in a
stream, a deep stream.'

They thought this fact through for a few seconds, then Adam
spoke again. 'She drowned? But she was a good swimmer. She
taught us to swim.'

DCI Stamford looked across at Mark, her eyebrows raised in
query, and he nodded.

'Adam, Seth, my name is Grace. I'm in charge of the case
involving Melanie, and it isn't as simple as you're thinking.
Aunty Melanie didn't drown, she was strangled, and someone
put her in the water.'

'Strangled?' Adam turned to his father. 'Strangled? But why?'

'We don't know yet,' Grace continued. 'But we will find out.
Our best people are out working on it right now, and as soon as
we know anything we will come back here and let you know. We
know she was an important person in your lives. But we have
something else we'd like to talk to you about.'

Grace gave a brief glance towards Mark, and he coughed to
clear his throat. 'It's your mum, boys.'

'She's dead as well?' There was a wail from Seth, and Adam did clutch at his hand this time, not caring what his father thought.

'Is she?' Adam demanded.

'No, but we don't know where she is. She's been missing since last Wednesday night.'

'But it's Monday now.' Seth spoke slowly, his face white. 'Why have you waited all this time to tell us? We could have helped to look for her.'

'Seth, we don't know where to look. She hasn't contacted you in any way, has she?' Grace spoke gently to the worried child.

'No, Dad won't let us have mobile phones until our next birthday.'

'But I understand you have iPads,' Grace was quick to point out.

The boys shrugged, not daring to admit that the iPads had been taken off them by boys two years older than them.

'Seth, Adam,' Grace said slowly. 'It is important that you're honest with me. Has your mother been in touch since last Wednesday night?'

'No, we said she hadn't, didn't we?' The stress was evident in Adam's voice.

Mrs Peters stood. 'I'll go and get the two iPads and you can see for yourself because there's maybe something the boys have missed.'

'No!' they said in unison.

'What's wrong? Adam? Seth?' DS Harriet Jameson spoke for the first time, but she was damned if she was going to let this crowd of vultures descend on two terrified eleven-year-olds.

They both turned towards the friendly voice. 'We haven't got them now,' Seth whispered.

'They took them.' His brother qualified his statement.

'Who took them?'

Seth dropped his head, so Adam spoke. 'Carl Dewhurst, and I think the other one is called George Ireland. They're in year nine. But you can't take them off them, they'll hammer us he said.'

'Who said?'

'Carl Dewhurst.'

For the second time, Norman Rodgers spoke. 'Mrs Peters, please go and collect these iPads, then place Messrs Ireland and Dewhurst in separate isolation rooms until I can deal with them.' He then turned to Adam and Seth as Mrs Peters disappeared out of the door. 'Adam, Seth, you will have nothing to fear from these two. This isn't their first disciplinary hearing, but it will be their last. You should have come to me when it first happened, and if ever anything else happens I expect you to knock on Mrs Peters' door, and she'll sort everything out. Did these boys hurt you?'

The twins nodded, and Mark half stood.

'Sit down, Mr Ledger. I'm not the headmaster you had here; if I say something will be done, it will be. How did they hurt you?' he asked, turning back to the boys.

'Twisted our arms up our back until we handed the tablets over,' Seth said. 'It really hurt.'

'We'll get our tech team to check the iPads,' Grace said, 'and then they'll be returned to you. If your mother has tried to contact you via the tablet, they will have deleted it, but we can always find it again. Thank you for being so brave, and now Mr Rodgers knows what's going on, I'm sure he will put things right. We don't really want to have to give these two year-nine boys a criminal record, but if things aren't handled properly, that's what will happen.'

Rodgers recognised her words as the threat that they were, and he inclined his head in acknowledgement.

. . .

With Carl Dewhurst and George Ireland deposited in separate rooms, feeling slightly worried that they couldn't talk their way out of it this time, Mrs Peters hurried back to the headmaster's office, clutching the two iPads.

She handed them to Rodgers, who photographed them and passed them over to Grace.

'I'm sure you can do more with these than I could ever hope to do,' he said with a smile.

Adam watched what was happening with some indifference. His mother was missing, his aunty Melanie was dead, and these idiots were wittering on about missing iPads. And he knew without a shadow of doubt that they would pay for snitching on George and Carl; there were a lot of other kids in year nine, friends of the two boys.

He became aware Grace was speaking to them only when Seth gave him a nudge.

'Sorry?'

'I said can you remember the names of any of your mum's friends? Anybody she would be likely to visit?' Grace gave him a gentle smile of encouragement.

'She doesn't have friends, only Aunty Rosie and Aunty Melanie. She has to stay in the house.'

'Why?' Grace saw Mark shuffle uncomfortably as she asked the question.

Seth and Adam looked at each other, then Seth spoke. 'Dad doesn't like her to go out. She only ever goes to Aunty Rosie's house.'

Grace turned to face Mark. 'Mr Ledger?'

'That's a load of rubbish. I don't stop your mother going anywhere, as you know, boys. Stop telling lies.'

'Rosie Steer has confirmed this situation, I believe. Is there some reason you don't allow your wife to have friends?' Grace's lips were firmly set, and she stared at him.

'She's not well,' he mumbled. 'I protect her.'

'Why is she not well? Would her doctor say the same thing, or don't you allow her to go to the doctor either?'

'Of course she can go to the doctor.' Mark's face was suffused with blood, and he looked extremely angry. 'I don't stop her doing anything.'

Grace saw the look that passed between the twins, and she decided to drop the questioning of their father for now. She would have him down at the police station for the next round. The boys were suffering enough without having to watch their father dragged over the coals.

'Boys, I can release you from school a little early if you would like that. We're only a week away from the end of term.' Norman Rodgers watched the twins' faces carefully. What he saw told him what he would hear.

'No, we're okay at school, thank you, Mr Rodgers.'

He nodded. 'That's fine also, but if you need to talk, or simply want to know if there's any information on your mum, please do come and find me. You can go back to your classes now.'

The two boys stood and Grace and Harriet said goodbye to them. Mark didn't attempt to give them a hug or a kiss, merely said, 'Be good, lads.'

The twins didn't go back to class. Mrs Peters took them to the dining hall, got them a drink and a cake, and sat and talked to them for a while. Eventually they smiled, and she asked them what they wanted to do.

'Can we read?' Seth asked.

'Good idea,' Adam agreed. 'We'd like to go to our dorm and read, if that's okay?'

'I think we can let you do that,' she said with a smile. 'I want to stress to both of you that if you get any comeback at all from what you've told us this afternoon, you're to go straight to any teacher, or myself and Mr Rodgers. The other teachers will be told what's happening and what's happened to you two, and they'll know immediately what to do if this bullying continues. Do you both understand?'

They nodded, not sure what to say.

'And let's pray they find your mum before much longer. I'm sure you could both use a hug from her right now.'

'What will happen if nobody finds Mum?' There was a hint of fear in Adam's question.

'Oh, I'm sure they will,' Mrs Peters said, trying desperately to inject a note of jocularity into her answer.

'Nobody has so far,' Seth joined in. 'Will we have to go home to Dad? On his own?'

It was achingly obvious to her that these children most definitely did not want to go back to a motherless house. 'Look, boys, there's still a week before school closes for the break, I'm sure your mum will turn up before then, because she knows school holiday dates.'

Seth actually stamped his foot, and Adam looked at him a little shocked. 'I'm not going home to him. If Mum's not there, I'm going to Aunty Rosie's, she'll look after us. And she'll help us find our mum.'

Eva Peters felt helpless. 'Come on, let's take a drink up to your dorm, and you can have a free afternoon. I'm so sorry this is happening to you, but I'm sure those lovely police ladies are working hard to find your mum, and to find who killed your aunty.'

16

Both iPads had a story to tell but it was a short one. Neither Carl nor George had deleted the information that a Messenger call had been missed from Shirley Ledger; in fact, they had deleted nothing, not even the pornographic pictures downloaded by both of them.

The tech department took the tablets apart trying to find some clue as to the whereabouts of the missing woman, but nothing was evident. Shirley Ledger had tried to contact her sons on the evening she had disappeared, but to no avail.

Seth and Adam returned to classes and it was clear that something had been said to their classmates. They were invited to join in any activities the others were doing, and suddenly their peers were speaking to them. One of the boys, Freddie Holland, explained to his form master that they hadn't left out anyone from their games, they all thought that the twins only wanted to hang around with each other.

Carl Dewhurst and George Ireland were permanently excluded and sent home to explain to irate parents how they had acquired brand new iPads without actually paying for them, and other year nine pupils breathed a sigh of relief that they no longer needed to pay protection money to the two ex-pupils of Springbrook School for Boys.

Doris pulled the laptop towards her, and typed swiftly. She had sent the vehicle registration number of the Ka to a colleague and asked if ANPR cameras could help with any information. His response had been swift. The car had been tracked leaving Hucknall on the night Shirley had disappeared. It had headed towards Nottingham but had then vanished. There was no confirmation of who was driving it.

She gave a deep sigh.

'No luck?' Wendy placed a cup of coffee down on the table by the side of her friend.

'No, but it was a bit of a long shot. I'm going to start on hotels and bed and breakfast places today, but I'm really starting to feel uneasy about this. It's obvious those two lads were her entire life, but according to Rosie she hasn't tried to contact either them or the school.'

'What if she's told the place where she's staying that she doesn't want anybody to know she's there? And she doesn't even need to have used her own name.'

Again Doris sighed. 'I know, but I have to do this. What if she *has* used her own name? We could miss her by not checking.'

'Is there anything I can do to help?'

'You can take half the list, if you want. There's no other way to do this but getting on the phone and asking if she's there. Give me half an hour to find as many as I can, and then we'll make a start.'

'Okay. I'll go and put a stew in the slow cooker, because after this lot neither of us will feel like cooking tonight. I'll leave you to it.' She walked across the room to where her bag was by the side of the armchair, and delved around inside it to find her phone.

She placed it on the table, and handed Doris a box of Ferrero Rocher. 'Will these help?' she said with a grin.

'Might do,' Doris said, and picked up the box. 'Twenty-four,' she mused. 'That's a hefty size box.'

'Certainly is,' Wendy agreed. 'Might last us an hour.'

Wendy stood at the island in the kitchen and chopped the carrots before tipping them on top of the meat in the slow cooker. Onions, celery, potatoes and other bits of leftovers from the fridge followed, and eventually she was happy that she had made enough to feed the entire village of Bradwell. She switched it on and went out into the garden. It was cool, but the sun was starting to burn off the early morning mist.

The bench at the end of the garden looked welcoming, so she made her way towards it, careful to let none of her coffee spill down her. Belle jumped up beside her and they sat patiently waiting for the growing warmth of the sun to reach them. The headache she had woken with had worsened, so she swallowed two tablets, and stroked the cat's smooth fur.

She had come to love the cottage, and could understand why Doris had immediately offered the full asking price for it when it came on the market, even if the previous owner had been a killer! The money she had spent on it since buying it had been money well spent, and it was truly a comfortable haven now. Wendy knew this would stay in her memory as one of her best holidays ever, despite it taking a sudden turn in a different direction after she'd just met Lord Byron.

In fact, she decided, to honour the great man, she would learn one of his poems. One of his smaller poems.

And then the sun broke through and she closed her eyes, feeling the warmth on her face. Belle pawed at her skirt, then climbed on to her lap, and the two of them sat contentedly, and relaxed.

Doris leaned back, then picked up the list and counted the number of places where Shirley could possibly have taken refuge. Thirty-five. She carefully tore the page, leaving twenty on one sheet and fifteen on the other, then went in search of Wendy. The two of them, cat and friend, looked extremely comfortable. Belle didn't move, ignoring the fact that Wendy was giving Doris a small wave.

'Shall we make a start on these now?' Doris asked, and handed the smaller list to Wendy.

'Is this it?'

'It's almost half of it. If you finish before me, check where I am on my list, and carry on. Be prepared for them to say data protection says they can't tell you. There's no real argument against that.'

'Look, Doris Lester, I spend most of my life on the telephone lying to people, telling them their taxi is seconds away when in reality their driver has just dropped off a customer on the other side of Sheffield, so don't think I need advice on how to con people, because I don't.' She laughed loudly. 'I'm looking forward to doing this. No snippy little receptionist is going to get the better of me.'

'I'll make us a drink, and we'll get cracking. I'm not convinced we're going to have much success but it's worth a shot. If this fails I've got other things I can try, but...'

'But they might fall a bit short on the legality side? God, I'm so in awe of you, Doris Lester. Can you teach me how to spy on Downing Street?'

'Downing Street? Why on earth would you want to hack that set-up?'

'I don't like her. Theresa May. Maybe I can hack into their system and get her out. I would do a better job. I'd get rid of this Brexit rigmarole for starters.'

Doris laughed. 'How long have you been a member of the Conservative party, because it's sort of a requisite for becoming prime minister. And I rather think that if you get rid of Mrs May, her replacement will be a lot less palatable.'

'Okay, I'm not, and never likely to be a member. Wouldn't it be fun to hack into it though, and send the country into turmoil.'

'It already is. It doesn't need our hacking skills to help that. But before you can hack into anything, I'd have to teach you how to do a bit more than simply turning on a computer. So shall we go inside and make these calls, or do you want to stay out here?'

'We'll go inside. You go into the lounge where you've got the laptop set up, and I'll use the kitchen table. We don't want whoever we're calling to think it's a con because they can hear another conversation. I'll need some paper and a pencil.' Wendy looked down her list. 'None of the bigger places?'

'No, Rosie had already done them. Shirley's not going to go to one of those anyway, because Mark would be able to track her down. The big ones are easy to locate. He'll not take the trouble to do what we're doing.'

Wendy placed Belle on the seat at the side of her. There was a loud miaow to show her displeasure, but after a quick head stroke from Wendy she ignored the disappearance of her slaves and settled back down to snooze.

Wendy pulled a sheet of paper towards her, picked up her phone and rang the first number. 'Oh, hello. I wonder if you can help me. I've been trying to contact my daughter but her phone keeps going to voicemail. She's either in a bad reception area, or her phone is broken, which is perfectly normal for her. Last time this happened she'd dropped it into a pint of lager. She's having a few days' break from work, and she's walking in your area, but she didn't tell me where she was staying because she didn't pre-book, she booked when she got there and I need to speak to her urgently. Her name is Shirley Ledger.'

'I'm so sorry, but we can't give out information about our guests.'

'I know, but she's left her dog with me and yesterday I had to take him to the vets. He was poorly, and the vet says he needs to be put to sleep. He has a huge tumour. I can't take that decision without her knowing first...'

There was a moment's pause. 'One moment, Mrs...?'

'Lucas, Wendy Lucas. My daughter, as I said, is Shirley Ledger.'

'I'm not supposed to do this, but I'll look for you. If she is here, I can leave her a message to contact you.'

'Thank you so much.'

There was a couple of minutes' silence and the receptionist came back on. 'No, Mrs Lucas, I'm sorry. She isn't here. There are a couple of small bed and breakfast places I know of, if you'd like their numbers.'

'Thank you. I would. I really don't know what to do about poor Cujo.'

'Cujo?'

'My daughter has a warped sense of humour. He's a black curly-haired poodle. Those numbers?'

Wendy wrote down the names of the other bed and breakfast locations, along with their numbers, and said goodbye. She also wrote down details of Cujo. After crossing out the hotel, she started a new list for any other suggestions that might crop up once she'd got every receptionist in the area concerned for poor Cujo.

'Brilliant. Absolutely brilliant, Wendy Lucas. Who knew you could lie with such conviction?' Doris clapped her hands. 'I had no luck with my first one, data protection flying around in spades, and I could hear you rattling on as though you were best friends. So we've got a dog called Cujo?'

'We have. He's a black curly-haired poodle with a tumour. Vet's going to put him to sleep tomorrow but I need to tell my daughter about it.'

'Oh, bless. Poor dog. I take it Shirley wasn't there.'

'Not under her own name. The receptionist gave me a couple of B and Bs to try, so I've written them on a separate sheet in case we haven't already got them. Didn't they teach you at your fancy MI5 or MI6 or MI whatever that if you bring an animal into it you're on a winner straight away?'

Doris laughed. 'It's the talking I don't like. I can send off an email with thousands of words on it, invent a million Cujos on paper, but talking to people I usually keep short and sweet. After listening to an expert, I now know I was wrong. Dropping a phone in a pint of lager indeed. I think that's what swung it for you.'

'I did.'

'You did what?'

'Dropped my last phone in a pint of lager. A full pint. I tell you, Doris, no amount of bloody rice could dry that one out. That's why I've got this one that I don't know how to work.'

'What did you do with the lager?'

'Drank it.' Wendy's tone suggested it was a stupid question.

'Right,' Doris said, keeping her face straight. 'I'll go back into the other room. It's not good to be around anyone who's probably highly radioactive.'

She held the smile in until she reached the lounge, and then she heard a strangled 'What...?' from the kitchen. She gave in to laughter.

17

Identifying Melanie had drained him. Patrick acknowledged it, grabbed a beer from the fridge and went to lie down. His sleep the previous night had been sporadic and light because he knew what was to face him the next day. *Take what time you need*, work had said. If he took them at their word he would still be at home in six months' time.

He puffed up the pillow and stood it against the headboard, then sat with his back against it. He popped the ring pull on the can and took a long slow drink. His fingers reached across to the other side of the bed, and he stroked her pillow. Her silk nightie was underneath it, and he lifted it up to his face, rubbing it against the two days of stubble on his chin. The smell of her calmed him in one way, but brought tears.

'Why, Mel, why?' he whispered. 'So many plans...'

He placed the can of beer on the bedside table, yanked at his pillow to lower it onto the bed, and hugged the nightie in his arms. Sleep came quickly, but his daytime dreams were as strong as his night ones and his nap was as light as it could possibly be.

He heard the key in the door, and for a moment he thought it was Melanie coming home: for a moment. Reality hit and he called out, 'Hello?'

'It's me, bro. You okay?'

'I'm upstairs, Mark. Put the kettle on, will you? I'll be down in a minute.'

Patrick heard Mark turn on the tap to fill the kettle, so he swung his legs off the bed, tucked the nightie under his own pillow and took a sip of the beer. It tasted disgustingly flat, so he took it and poured it down the bathroom sink before splashing his face with water.

His legs felt stiff, and he went downstairs carefully, carrying the empty beer can.

Mark lifted his head as Patrick walked into the kitchen. He raised his eyebrows. 'You want tea or beer?'

'Tea. I've poured this away, it went flat.'

'How did it go?'

'This morning? How do you expect? I hope I never have to do anything like it ever again. It was Mel, but it wasn't. I'm glad you didn't go with me, at least one of us can still see Mel as she was and not the white-faced body on that table. I'd asked her to marry me, you know.'

'And she said yes?'

'She did. We decided to go out on the Sunday and choose her ring together, then announce it to everyone. She didn't live long enough to get to the Sunday.'

Mark handed him a cup of tea, and they moved into the lounge. His backpack was standing by the side of the sofa. 'I've brought some stuff in case you want me to stay tonight, and I've told Rosie where I am.'

'How did the boys take it?'

'Devastated to lose Aunty Melanie, and talking about coming home so they can help search for Shirley. In the end they decided to stay at school. They had their iPads stolen by two louts from year nine, but that's been sorted.'

'For God's sake, Mark, get them out of that school. Shirley doesn't want them there, and they've hated it from the first day. It did you no good, and it will certainly be bad for Adam and Seth.'

'It's not the same headmaster, this one seems okay.'

'You're not listening, Mark. Get those lads out, and send them somewhere normal, somewhere where they can see their mum every day. If you don't, you'll lose them like Mum and Dad lost you. By the time it was my turn to go there, they'd realised their mistake, thank God. And if you don't let Shirley have her boys back, she'll take them. Then you'll have lost everything.'

Mark shrugged. 'Maybe that might be for the best. She can take the kids and go, as long as I get the house.'

'You'd trade your kids and marriage for a house? For fuck's sake, Mark, open your eyes.'

The look of disgust that passed from younger brother to older brother stopped Mark from saying anything else, but on the way over to Patrick's it had occurred to him how much easier life was without the encumbrance of wife and children.

Maybe he shouldn't have voiced those thoughts out loud.

Shirley's diary lay on the kitchen table, unopened. Rosie stared into the far distance, trying to gather her thoughts. She knew without any doubt that when Shirley came back, she would do everything within her power to get her out of the poisonous atmosphere in that house. In the meantime, while they waited for Shirley's reappearance, she would ask Mark if the boys could come to her for the upcoming school holiday; they would be company for Megan, who she knew would value bossing-around time.

She picked up her coffee and took a long drink before opening the first page.

Shirley Ledger. It was as simple as that. No address, no mobile number, no name on the 'next of kin' line. Rosie ran her finger over her sister's name, and sighed. Loneliness oozed out of the little book.

She carefully picked her way through each page, wanting to cry at the annotations that said *helped Rosie to make some notebooks*. The reality of the matter was that she didn't, Shirley was the clever one, the talented side of the partnership who experimented and created, advertised, corrected Rosie's work when she struggled on the days when the pain from fibromyalgia didn't let her do all she wanted to do. It was obvious that this was Shirley's way of making a note of her work days; she didn't want Mark reading through this and finding out she had a life away from him.

There were appointments; doctor in February, dentist in April – she had a face the size of a melon after that visit – hairdressers also in April, and one that simply said ME, 2.30. That was dated the third of April, but it gave no indication of what it meant. Rosie smiled. Was it a tiny rebellion on Shirley's part? Was she kicking back at her time being constantly needed for others? Did it simply mean that at 2.30 on that day Shirley had kicked off her shoes, switched off her phone, locked the door and laid down on the bed or the sofa with a book? Rosie hoped so.

So what had she really done with this ME time? Rosie

flicked through the rest of the diary, but nothing else showed up. All the visits to the boys had been inserted, written in red with a little heart drawn by the side of each boy's name. School holidays were in green. Rosie laughed at the thought of her organised sister with one of those pens where you pushed the colour up from the bottom, depending on which of the six colours available you needed at that moment in time.

She trawled through the little book twice but apart from the strange ME annotation there was nothing out of the ordinary. There was a section for notes at the end of the main part of the diary, and Rosie ran her finger down the inner seam to hold the two sections flatter on the table.

The notes said little. The measurements for their Pearl Journal had been written down because they had decided that it had to be uniform – it was their top seller. She had made notes of the ribbon used as standard, then underneath she had written *SAL wants a fuchsia ribbon*. They were used to special requests for personalisation, and Shirley must have taken this one when away from a computer.

Rosie flipped over to the addresses, read each one carefully, although it didn't take long. Shirley had minimal friends that she kept in touch with. Rosie sighed. Where was the Shirley who left school full of life, had far more friends than she had, and buzzing to get on with her future? She wasn't in the pages of this book, that was for sure.

She read down all the names and addresses, reaching the I/J page quickly. She hesitated and flipped back a page. Enid Hill.

Enid was an ex-teacher of theirs and had ordered a Victorian journal for her granddaughter for her twenty-first birthday. Rosie had packaged it up and left it for Shirley to drop it in at the post office on her way home, but Shirley had said she would hand deliver it as it was only the next village.

She had been insistent.

The Rothery address in Shirley's book didn't match Enid's Woodbridge address in the computer files, and Rosie knew the details on the package were correct because they had visited Enid to show her samples so that she could choose which one she wanted. She definitely lived in Woodbridge.

Strange. She stuck a Post-it note on the page, a flash of bright yellow lighting up the navy-blue diary. She looked through the rest of the addresses and found nothing unusual.

She picked up her phone as soon as the first peal of the ringtone began.

'Doris? Any news?'

'Maybe... I'm not sure. Did you manage to find Shirley's diary?'

'I did. I used the gloves to read through it, because I'm going to put it back. I don't think there's anything in it...'

'There is something?'

'A little niggle.'

'Okay, we'll come over and see if it niggles us. Then you can put it back because the police will want to check the house soon if Shirley doesn't turn up. That diary needs to be back there by then. We'll be there in about an hour.'

Wendy lifted her head. 'Thirty-nine phone calls and we only got one who was unhelpful. Did that one niggle you? It seems both you and Rosie have niggles.'

'It did. She was too abrupt. Didn't want to listen about the poorly dog, she wanted me off that phone. And it's half a mile away from the school where Shirley's boys are. Rosie has the diary, so I said we'd get out there and have a powwow.'

'Powwow. Do I need a feathered headdress? Always fancied being a Red Indian.'

'You're a nut job, Wendy Lucas. Can you top up the cat food, please, in case we're late home? I'll take my laptop with me, along with these indecipherable notes you've made.'

'Oy,' Wendy said. 'I understand them.'

'It's why I'm taking you. Only you could make any sense of them. Come on, let's go see this diary and talk through where we go next.'

18

R osie poured coffees for the four of them – Megan insisted she needed to be there – and the diary was opened.

'There is little in it that would make alarm bells ring, except for where I've marked it.' There were three yellow Post-it notes standing up from the top edge of the book. Rosie pushed it across to Doris. 'I've photocopied all of it.'

Doris frowned as she read the cryptic *ME 2.30*. 'An appointment with someone with the initials ME?'

Rosie laughed. 'And that's why I'm not an investigator. I read it as Shirley booking some me-time for herself. Possibly shutting the world out and reading a book or something. You saw it as something mysterious, a meeting with... oh, I don't know, Michael Elphick!'

'Michael Elphick? Does she know him?' Doris tried to keep her face straight.

Wendy didn't even bother. She spluttered. 'Michael Elphick died about twenty years ago, don't think she's meeting him.'

Rosie grinned. 'First celebrity I could think of with those initials. So we simply have to work out who has those initials, and we've cracked it?'

'Hardly. ME hasn't necessarily spirited her away. In fact, it may mean nothing at all. How's her health? Could it be some sort of specialist appointment?'

'As far as I know she's healthy. I've never seen any sign of illness, and she's certainly never mentioned anything,' Rosie said. 'She's a lot quieter than she used to be, but that's Markitis. Divorce would cure that.'

'So, the next one. *SAL wants a fuchsia ribbon.*' Doris waited for comments.

Rosie stood and went into the lounge, returning a minute later with a thick journal, covered in lace, vintage pictures, and filled with tags, pockets and all sorts of other ephemera. 'This is our best seller,' she explained. 'The measurements on that page are the ones we use for every one we send out, and our standard ribbon fastening is sari silk in a pale green. However, we will always personalise, and if someone wants a fuchsia ribbon, it's not a problem. It would be noted on the computer. It seemed odd that she'd made a note in her diary, when nothing else to do with the business is in there.'

Wendy took the journal from Rosie and stroked the front. 'How beautiful. You couldn't buy this in a shop.'

'That one we've never put up for sale. It's our prototype, it's the one we show to clients who want a personalised one, and we make their journal to their instructions. I don't know who Sal is, or if she got her fuchsia ribbon.'

'Mark knows she helps you, but he believes it's your venture. Am I right?'

Rosie nodded. 'We have to do it like that. He doesn't know it's a business, we have a fifty per cent share each. And it's a good growing concern. We'll never be Richard Bransons, but we do okay. Shirley is our super-talented designer.'

'Then I suspect this is nothing whatsoever to do with fuchsia ribbons. It's a reminder of something to her that will mean nothing to Mark. He'd take it at face value as you have. Sal wants a fuchsia ribbon on her journal. Tell me, does Shirley have a middle name?'

'Anne.'

SAL. Shirley Anne Ledger. We need to work out what the significance is of the fuchsia bit. Thoughts?'

Megan had sat quietly, listening to the adults talking about her Aunty Shirley, not wanting to interrupt. She put up her hand, and the three ladies laughed.

'Megs, you're not in school,' her mother said. 'Just speak.'

'We, it's... could it be a road?'

'Fuchsia Ribbon Road?'

'No, silly. Roads have flower names, don't they? Acacia Avenue, my friend Sarah lives on that one, Daffodil Crescent where my other friend Colette lives – there's lots of roads with flower names. It's called the flower estate.'

'And it's that newly built estate outside Woodbridge.' Suddenly Rosie came to life. 'Look at the third Post-it note, Doris. I'm starting to think I'm not daft.'

The blue gloves made Doris's hands clumsy, but she eventually got to the correct page. There were only two addresses. 'Which one has raised your hackles?'

'The Enid Hill one. Enid Hill taught both of us at our secondary school. She's retired now, of course, and not far off her ninetieth birthday. We see her around the place, always have a chat with her, and she knows what we do with the journals. She asked to see one, and so we went to her home in Woodbridge. She ordered one for her granddaughter, and that was the one Shirley insisted on delivering to her. This address,' Rosie pointed to the entry in the diary, 'isn't her address.'

'Would Mark know it wasn't her address?'

Rosie shook her head. 'No, I can't imagine for a minute he

would know her at all. Mark went to Springbrook, the one the boys are at now.'

'So this address is an aide-memoire meant for Shirley only. Woodbridge is a connection, and I think we have to seriously consider that fuchsia may be a road. Rosie, it's good you've made copies of the diary and you need to get it back to Shirley's home as soon as possible.' Doris pushed the diary across the table and removed her gloves before lifting her laptop onto the table.

Once more with full coffee cups, the laptop gave them information not discoverable from the diary. The address attributed to Enid Hill was in a small hamlet called Rothery. It proved to be about ten miles away from Hucknall, and after using Google Earth, it was shown as an end-of-terrace property. It had been painted cream, and whoever owned it had made it cottagey in appearance. Roses had been trained to climb the walls, and it had a small garden that went around three sides of the small house. Doris expertly zoomed around the screen, then pulled away. That was when she spotted the for sale sign in the garden.

'Bingo!' she said, sitting back. 'That's solved another mystery. Look.' The others moved around her back and Megan saw it.

'ME,' she squealed. 'It's a house-selling thing.'

'Estate agents,' Doris said with a smile. 'Do we think Shirley could be buying this little house for her and her boys? Maybe she's already bought it and is hiding out there until the boys finish on Friday for the school holiday.'

Megan peered closely at the screen. 'What's that sign say by the front door?'

Again, Doris zoomed in, then laughed. 'Well spotted, Megan. It says Fuchsia Cottage. Rosie, what do you want to do?'

'I want to go and check it out. Will you come with me?'

'Of course we will. I'll drive if you want. Where's Mark?'

'He's with Patrick. Staying overnight.'

'Then maybe you should take the diary back, minus its Post-it notes, while you have the chance. We can do that before we go to Rothery.'

Quarter of an hour later Doris's car pulled up outside Mark and Shirley's home. Doris watched Rosie walk up the garden path and knock on the front door twice. She then inserted the key, and slipped inside.

Two minutes later, Rosie was fastening her seat belt. 'Mission accomplished. I thought I'd better knock to be on the safe side, but it's empty. I put it back in the bedside drawer, then legged it out again.'

Doris had already entered the postcode into the satnav and they set off.

It was a twenty-minute drive through pretty countryside; Wendy's head swivelled back and forth as she tried to stamp the views into her memory. Sheffield City Centre had never looked like this.

Rothery was tiny. Doris guessed that it held maybe thirty houses at the most, and wondered if, in a past life, it had been a mining village. If it had been, the houses had certainly been upgraded since then. She parked the car around the corner from Fuchsia Cottage, then swung round in her seat.

'What do you want to do, Rosie?'

'What I want to do is go in and batter her for scaring me like this, but I won't do that, I promise. Do you think I should go in on my own?'

'No,' Megan protested. 'That's not fair. We've all done our bit in tracking Aunty Shirley down; we should all go.'

Rosie thought about it for a moment, then nodded. 'Megan's right. Come on, let's go and have a cup of tea with my runaway sister.'

The garden gate squeaked, and Megan giggled. 'I'm scared,' she whispered. 'What if it's a mad axeman who lives here, and not Aunty Shirley?'

'We'll find out who's the fastest runner, won't we,' Doris said. 'You stay behind me, and I'll deliver a targeted kick.'

'At his balls?' Megan's eyes were wide.

Rosie glanced back at her daughter. 'Megan! Don't say that!'

'Sorry, Mum. Testicles.'

They followed one another, Indian style, around the cottage. There had been no response to their first tentative knock on the front door, so a back door was being sought. Another knock and again there was no response.

Peering through the windows didn't help either. Not only was the cottage seemingly devoid of humans, it also held precious little furniture: a stool and three wheelie bins that clearly belonged outside.

'She's not here,' Megan said, disappointment evident in her voice. 'Did we get it wrong?'

'Let's go back to the car,' Doris said. 'I have a plan B.'

Doris handed out the sheets she and Wendy had used for contacting the hotels, guest houses and bed and breakfast places within a five-mile radius of Springbrook School.

'We contacted all of these, and there are thirty-nine in total. Thanks to Wendy's lying skills everybody was really helpful, except one. We told them some cock and bull story about a dog that had to be put to sleep and we needed to contact Shirley, its owner, before we could agree. We'd got it down to a fine art, almost had some receptionists in tears, but until we got to the next to last, nothing worked. Nobody knew her or had seen her. And then we got a negative response. It was a bed and breakfast place, about half a mile from the school. She couldn't get me off the phone quick enough, didn't buy the dying dog act at all, despite me turning on the waterworks to try to convince her I was serious. She put the phone down on me. That woman was the only one who didn't fall apart at this sad dog being put to death. I wonder why. Is Shirley there, and has she told the woman she doesn't want to be found? Perhaps told her some story about domestic violence?'

There was a moment of silence in the car as they digested those few words. Doris started the car. 'Let's go visit this Oleander House, see what the lie of the land is. It's all about flowers today, isn't it?'

Quarter of an hour later they pulled up a short distance before Oleander House, and Doris glanced up and down the street for signs of Shirley's car. There was nothing visible, but it was obvious Oleander House had a gravel drive, with large iron gates, currently open.

'We need to go through those gates, and possibly round the back of the house. Keep your eyes peeled for any sign of that Ka. If there's a garage we need to look in it. If we're spotted, we tell the truth. And don't forget the dying dog.' Doris put the car into drive, and edged forward. She indicated to turn into the driveway.

The Ka was on its way out, and the two cars faced each other off, as if lead characters in *High Noon*.

Rosie jumped out and strode towards her sister. 'What the hell do you think you're playing at, Shirley?'

19

Trudy Dawson, owner of the bed and breakfast business, carried a tray of drinks through to the five people sitting in her guests' lounge, and turned to go out of the door.

'No, Trudy, please stay, unless you have something you need to be doing.' Shirley sounded panicked at the thought of Trudy leaving the room. This woman had protected her and kept her safe since her arrival.

'Only preparing you a meal,' Trudy said, smiling at her guest.

'Then go and get another cup, and join us.'

'Shirley, tell us what's going on. You've heard about Melanie?'

'I have. It was on the news. How's Patrick?'

'We don't really know. Believe it or not, we've had other things on our minds, like finding you. That's been my priority, anyway.' Rosie's tone hadn't softened at all. The anger towards her sister had been evident in her face when she had jumped out of the car, and it was still there.

'Stop shouting at me, Rosie. You would have known I was

okay come next Friday or Saturday anyway, because I'm going to collect my boys from that awful school and they're never going back. I'm moving into a little house in Rothery...'

'Fuchsia Cottage,' Megan said.

Shirley's eyes turned towards her niece. 'How the hell did you know that?'

A smile flashed across Rosie's face for the first time. 'Because we're Team Doris. Nobody is safe from her. But leaving that side alone for a minute, can you start from the beginning? Why did you take off without letting me know? When they said they'd found a body in the woods, I thought...' And finally her anger morphed into grief, and tears rolled down her cheeks.

Wendy pulled a pack of tissues from her bag and handed them to the distraught woman. Finally, Rosie calmed down. 'You took nothing with you, Shirley.'

'That's because I didn't know I wasn't going back. My head was all over the place. I missed the boys so much, and Mark – I felt sure he was having an affair. Little things started to point to it – you know how it is when a man is playing away. Then I found something in his suit pocket that convinced me. He'd been gone about an hour last Wednesday, and I was sick of thinking things through, feeling shut off from the world I had known before I married Mark. I decided to take myself out, put some petrol in Katherine and drive around, give myself some thinking time. I came up with a sort of battle plan. I would go home, lock the doors and windows so he couldn't get back in, and we could fight it out in court over who kept the house. I felt pretty sure I would win because the boys would be with me. Trust me, I was sure of that, the boys don't really like him much. My plans changed ten minutes later when I drove past Enid Hill's place and she was standing by the garden gate, no coat on and it was after eight, dark and cold. I stopped and went to her.'

Shirley paused for a moment. 'She'd gone over on her ankle

putting out the wheelie bin. That woman is a marvel, you'd think she was twenty years younger than she is. She was trying to work out how to get back inside without crawling on her hands and knees. I helped her in, got her ankle raised and made her a drink. The conversation turned to what I was doing. That's when she offered me Fuchsia Cottage for the third time. It's been on my mind for weeks to simply move out, and I'd told Enid about my problems. She immediately offered me the cottage, but it was still only a thought in my head.

'It's where she used to live before her husband died, but then she inherited the bungalow she's in now, so they moved into it and put a tenant in Fuchsia Cottage. She decided to sell it when the tenant moved on, but last Wednesday night, when Enid saw the state I was in, she offered me the cottage again, and I said yes. It's perfect. I'm renting it until I get some money from the sale of our present house, or until Mark buys me out, then I will buy Fuchsia Cottage. I actually went to an estate agent a couple of months ago to go on their books for a house to rent. Even then I knew I had to leave, but they didn't have anything in my budget at that time.'

'You think Mark will sit back and let this happen?'

'He's no choice.'

Rosie recognised a little of the old Shirley starting to come through. 'But you didn't go back home?'

Shirley gave a small laugh. 'No, when I was talking to Enid it suddenly seemed very... liberating. There was a way forward, I have some money as you know, Rosie, and it's enough to get me and the boys away from a poisonous family life. They deserve so much more than they've had. To go back to Enid, I rang her daughter who came around to see to her mum, then I left. Enid is a friend of Trudy, and told me if I ever needed a bed temporarily, Trudy would give me one. They spoke while I was there, and she made sure Trudy knew my name.'

Shirley smiled at Trudy. 'Instead of driving home, I drove here. I sent Mark a nasty text designed to put him on edge, saying he wouldn't ever get back in the house, and that wasn't for any reason other than to be horrible to him, and Trudy and I talked long into the night. Luckily she had no other guests here, and she's been really good about me not paying, but when you arrived I was on my way to Nottingham to get some money. I was happy to resurface if I was caught on CCTV, but I didn't want anybody knowing where I was staying. So that's really it. I didn't intend leaving Mark that night; I only took my bag with my purse and phone in. Trudy lent me a nightie, and went shopping for knickerless me. I owe her a fair amount by now. I simply intended driving around and thinking.'

'You could have rung.' Rosie was clearly still hurting.

'You're right, I could, but I think Trudy will confirm this when I say I was in a bit of a state when I arrived here late last Wednesday night, and since then has been a healing time, and a planning time. There have been three or four guests and I've helped with that stuff, making beds and suchlike, and it has been a good time. I tried calling the boys on their iPads on that first night, but it didn't connect so I haven't tried since. I want to be able to go and get them Friday or Saturday, take them to Fuchsia Cottage and spend the school holiday setting up our new home.'

Doris finally spoke. 'And you think the school will let you take the boys without notifying their father? They do know you're missing.'

'Yes, I'll tell them, and Seth and Adam, that I've moved back home, that we've talked everything through and we're back on track. I don't imagine the boys will be over the moon, but I'll explain the truth when we're out of school.'

Doris couldn't help but feel that Shirley had inherited far more of her father's genes than Rosie had. Being away from the unhealthy atmosphere at home had given her a somewhat cavalier attitude and she knew that Shirley hadn't really thought this through properly.

Everything depended on whether Mark had had the foresight to say to the school that they weren't to release the boys to anyone but himself.

'Shirley,' Doris began, 'I think you should contact the police and let them know you're safe, merely taking time out. This will free up the people investigating your disappearance, take the pressure off you, and they will notify Mark that you've been found. Rosie can tell him, but you need to contact the police. They may want to speak to you in person, because I imagine you're on the suspect list for the murder of Melanie Brookes, but if you've been here since last Wednesday night, and haven't been out since, I'm sure Trudy will confirm that.'

Shock flashed across Shirley's face. 'Suspect? Of course I haven't killed anybody.'

Rosie shook her head in disbelief. 'You can't be this naïve, Shirley. Mel's dead, and you've gone missing. To the police, that probably means you're either another victim, or the killer. And why didn't you come to me last Wednesday? You know we have a spare bedroom.'

'I couldn't. I knew Mark would arrive the next day looking for me. I've reached the end, Rosie, can't you see? I won't be bullied any longer, any decisions concerning my life will be made by me. I want a divorce, I want out.'

The briefing room fell silent. Grace moved across to the whiteboard and pointed to the photograph of Melanie Brookes.

'I believe the murder of Melanie Brookes and the disappearance of Shirley Ledger are connected in some way. Although we have been running them as two separate enquiries, it's time to merge them. Hence this afternoon's briefing. We have results from the post-mortem I need to share with you.'

Grace flipped through the sheaf of papers in her hand. 'Melanie Brookes died between nine and eleven last Thursday night. She was manually strangled, and we cannot say whether it was a man or a woman who did it, because Melanie was petite and extremely slim. It could easily have been either sex. The marks on her neck indicate she was attacked from behind, and pressure held until she was dead. We need teams out at every bridge crossing of this river, every ford, I want the bank combed upstream for any signs of a struggle because we're sure she came downstream from where she entered the water. She only stopped on her journey at that point because of a low-hanging tree with branches in the water.'

Grace lifted her head to look around the room. 'The pathologist has established the time of death because of her stomach contents. She had a meal shortly before being killed, and she had eaten Chinese food. Prawn balls to be precise. And chips. We believe she went out that Thursday night, despite her having told Patrick Ledger that she was staying in because she had an early start the next day. We don't know if she went alone or if she had a partner. Patrick Ledger denies having seen her after Thursday lunchtime when they both went to work; says he came home and also had an early night after trying to contact Melanie to wish her good luck for her Friday in York. He confirms her phone was turned off, so he left a voicemail. We don't have Melanie's bag, or her phone. These are things to look out for, people, when you get out there to that riverbank.'

Grace pointed to Shirley Ledger's picture. 'I want a team to go to Mark Ledger's home and turn it upside down. Make sure it looks fairly tidy when you leave it,' she added with a laugh. 'I need anything; a diary, clothing, photos, laptops and iPads, anything that will need investigating. I want to know how close a friendship she had with Melanie Brookes, and if Mark Ledger had any sort of a relationship with our victim. Find me anything you can. Try not to find a body. Thank you everyone, spend the next half hour organising tomorrow, then get off home. I want you in early, especially the teams doing the riverbank work. If there's no one at Mark Ledger's place, he'll be with his brother. I know he's been staying there a couple of nights. Get his key, the search warrant will be ready to pick up as you go. Good luck, bring me some results.'

20

It was agreed that Shirley would stay with Trudy until she could move into Fuchsia Cottage at the end of the week, but it was also agreed that Shirley would ring DCI Stamford the following day.

'Don't avoid doing it, Shirley. They're out there looking for your dead body.' Rosie frowned. 'In fact, don't tell her, I'll ring first thing in the morning and let her know where you are. They'll be here to see you by lunchtime, or even earlier, I'm sure. I don't trust you to do it. You've morphed into somebody I don't know at all.'

Shirley sighed. 'I'll ring her at eight. If she's not there I'll leave a message with somebody, I promise. I haven't changed towards you, Rosie, I've changed towards the thing that I married and who thinks he has control over me. He doesn't.'

'I'll make sure she rings the police,' Trudy said. 'She'll not be on her own, either, when they do come to see her.'

'Okay, thank you, Trudy. Let's go and sort this bill out. I'll pay it, Shirley shouldn't use her credit card until she's told the police she's not dead, not even missing. They're monitoring her account.'

ANITA WALLER

A look of fear flashed across Shirley's face. 'Mark doesn't know I have a separate account, does he?'

'No, I haven't told him. Of course I haven't, numpty.'

Doris smiled. 'Will you two kiss and make up? You shouldn't be fighting battles in opposite camps; you should be on the same side. Rosie, I know you're worried for Shirley but she isn't involved in the death of Melanie Brookes. All she did was leave her husband and not tell anybody. Not tell you. Be good girls and stop fighting.'

Rosie erupted into laughter. 'You're a star, Doris. Come here, Shirley.'

The two sisters hugged and Shirley wiped away a tear. 'It's been a bad few days, but I will get my boys. I've left Mark and I'm not going back.'

'What about his ironing?' Rosie tried to keep a straight face.

'Balls to his damned ironing,' was Shirley's immediate response.

'It's testicles, Aunty Shirley,' said Megan. 'Mum says so.'

Doris delivered Megan and Rosie back home, and set off for the long drive back to Bradwell. She was tired; it had been emotional, but it would have been so much worse if the alarm bells hadn't rung when she contacted the guest house owner, now proven to be Trudy, and recognised the response as being a little off kilter.

The journey was fortunately uneventful, and Doris and Wendy were glad to see the outside lights of Little Mouse Cottage.

'This cottage looks so pretty at night,' Wendy mused. 'No amount of fancy lighting could make my semi look like this.' She

144

opened the passenger door. 'I'll unlock while you put the car away. Cuppa?'

'I'll go with Horlicks, please. I'm tired but suspect I'm too wound up to sleep. We need to talk about whether we carry on with this relationship with the Hucknall people, or not.'

Wendy looked as though she was about to say something, but merely nodded, and walked up the small front garden path.

Satiated after a Horlicks and a slice of chocolate cake, Wendy said, 'Well?'

'They asked us to find Shirley, and we've done that.'

'So we abandon them?'

'We can't help them solve Melanie's murder, that would be stepping on police toes.'

'You've done that in the past.'

'Yes, but we are good friends with the police officers who are tied to our area. We don't know this force at all.'

'Apparently they know you.'

'That young PC at Rosie's house knew me, but that doesn't mean everybody else does. No, I really think we have to walk away now.'

'You don't feel a tiny little bit that they're family?'

'No, I bloody don't.' Doris was a shade too quick with her response. 'So let's leave it at that. They're the family of my ex-husband.'

'Late husband. Not ex.'

'I was right when I said ex. If you could do posthumous divorces, I would.' Doris finished her Horlicks and stood. 'I'm off to bed now, it's been a long day. We'll do something tomorrow, something different. No computer work, no chasing off to Hucknall, and tomorrow night there's every chance I might go to the dojo for an hour. It's over two weeks since I've been, they'll think I'm dead.'

Wendy grinned. 'Sounds like a plan. And while you're dojoing with your karate killers – strange word, did I make it up? – I'll do some work on the journal. I've some bits to stick in, some notes to make, bit of research to do.'

Doris smiled. She knew Wendy had given in too easy; the discussion would arise again. 'Night and God bless, Wendy. Everything's locked up, so nothing to do.'

She climbed the stairs, listening to the gentle sound of Wendy having a conversation with Belle. Doris's bedroom was her haven and she sank down onto the chaise longue, deep in thought. Had she really meant it when she said she didn't see Rosie and Shirley as family? Was she being honest with herself?

Rosie, Dan and Megan – especially Megan – had touched a chord in her heart, and much as she tried to squash it, it wouldn't stay down. She knew she would ring to check that Shirley was okay, that she had contacted the police, but then it was over. She'd never met Melanie Brookes, had no interest in trying to find her killer.

What had Rosie said? That Melanie had spent all evening chatting to Mark, leaving her partner Patrick to talk to Megan. Why? Was there some sort of relationship building between the attractive Melanie and her partner's older brother? Would the pair of them do that to Patrick? If the answer was yes, then it put the brothers firmly in the frame for the murder. One of them anyway.

Doris stood and moved across the room. Then she moved back again, deep in thought. She crossed the room again; seconds later she sat on the bed. It was going to be a long night.

.   .   .

Rosie rang at eight. 'Shirley's spoken to DCI Stamford. They're going out to see her, but Trudy has promised she will be with her. Should I go as well?'

'Calm down, Rosie,' Doris said, trying to get her voice to work properly, considering she had only been awake for twenty seconds. 'She's done nothing wrong. She left her home, but she doesn't have to explain to anybody why she did it, as long as there was nothing illegal going on. Now if she had bumped off Mark first, that would be a different matter, but she didn't. They're only checking that she is who she says she is, that she's gone of her own free will, that sort of thing. They'll also want an alibi for the night Melanie was murdered, but she was with Trudy anyway, so no, you don't need to rush off to her. She'll need you to be there for her when she moves into the cottage, and when she fetches the boys, but she's okay for the moment.'

'Thank you, Doris. I knew you would make me feel better. We wouldn't have found her without your help. I have the job of telling Mark; that should be fun.'

'You didn't tell him last night?'

'No, I couldn't bring myself to do it. He's going to want chapter and verse of what she's doing, who she's with, and Shirley's made it clear her life with him is over. I was too tired last night to cope with Mark Ledger's temper tantrums. He was at Patrick's anyway, which probably means they were working their way through a fair amount of alcohol.'

Doris's brain was starting to surface. She swung her legs out of bed to get a little more comfort. 'I'm sorry all this has happened to you, Rosie, especially after finding out you're not going to meet your genetic father. You've had a tough time. If I can ever do anything else for you, please get in touch.'

'Whoa! What are you saying? Are you abandoning us? What about Shirley? What if she needs help? It's a big thing she's doing.'

'Rosie, I've done what you asked. I tracked Shirley down. What else can I do?'

'Be our friend?'

Doris had stood, but hearing those three words made her sit once again, with a thud. Be our friend? She didn't know what to say. 'Rosie, can I ring you back in a bit? I need a coffee or something to bring me round, I didn't sleep too good last night. Did you?'

'Hardly at all, Shirley is causing me so much worry at the moment, I can't sleep. I'm sorry I've disturbed you, I'll go now. Ring when you're awake properly. Bye, Doris.'

Doris stared at her phone. Be our friend.

Wendy hadn't surfaced to face the day when Doris went downstairs. She put on a pot of coffee, fed Belle and opened the back door. She stepped out into the early morning sunshine, and took a deep breath.

She had decisions to make. She hadn't counted on Harry's illegitimate daughter turning out to be two illegitimate daughters, and certainly hadn't counted on liking them. And Megan; there was another issue. She was a delight; bright, chatty and funny. Should she continue the relationship, build on what she had tentatively started, or should she walk away, sending them a Christmas card every year?

Belle wove around her ankles, happy to be in her company, and both of them wandered down to the bench. Doris sat and Belle leapt up to snuggle into her lap. Her purring filled the air, and Doris smiled. She realised there was always room in her life, her heart, for others, and knew she couldn't walk away from Harry's daughters. It was too late. She had met them, had accepted their request for help, had got to know them. Much too late.

'Belle, I need to move you. If I don't get my coffee soon, there will be murderous thoughts in my head and that's not good for anybody.'

Belle looked up, then settled back down again.

'I meant you need to move.' Doris smiled. She gently lifted the cat and placed her on the ground. Belle shook her head and stalked off, an unhappy cat for the moment.

Doris poured her coffee, and within seconds Wendy was in the doorway.

'I timed that well.' She laughed. 'You decided where we're going?'

'Not yet. Have a coffee, I need to talk to you.'

'Do we need the Ferrero Rochers cracking open?'

'Could do.'

Wendy stared at her friend, nodded and picked up the coffee pot. It was serious talk time if the little round chocolates were required.

'You are funny, Doris. Did it take this much thought and worry when we first met?'

'No, of course not. But Harry hadn't fathered you. He hadn't, had he? This potential friendship isn't as straightforward as sharing a game of bingo, or a night out at the cinema. I don't make friends easily; my job stopped me doing that.'

'So, out of curiosity, why me? Why did we have such a strong bond?'

'You made me laugh. Sometimes you made me cry with laughter. That's a proper friendship. Rosie said this morning *be our friend*. Dare I?'

'What's stopping you? Mouse? Knowing your granddaughter

as much as I do, she'll welcome them with open arms. There isn't a nasty bone in that girl's body. So that's ruled that objection out. Take it slowly. Learn about them by seeing them, I think eventually they'll become proper friends. Friends who will buy you Ferrero Rochers whenever you're a bit down. Don't turn your back on them because you married a dickhead.'

21

DS Harriet Jameson was standing in front of the twelve officers on temporary allocation to the team by seven o'clock. She spoke loudly over the general hubbub that always accompanied a large group of people, and silence descended.

'Okay, various courses of action today. This,' and she tapped a list of names pinned to the whiteboard, 'is to tell you where you're heading as soon as we've finished in here. There's been considerable activity overnight. Shirley Ledger is no longer missing. She simply walked away from her husband. The boss and I are going to interview her this morning and we'll feed back to you later, but as it stands at the moment, she has done nothing wrong. So... on to the riverbank. It is imperative we find where Melanie Brookes was killed, and where she went into that river. Remember, she was dead before she went in, she didn't slip, she was lifted or pushed into the water, and we need to find out where that happened.'

Harriet moved across to the glass screen and pressed it. A map appeared, and she used a pointer as she talked. 'We've taken the fact that she had eaten a Chinese meal shortly before she was killed. However, that particular meal of prawn balls and chips could easily have come from a takeaway, and eaten as she walked. It doesn't mean she went to a Chinese restaurant. We've taken a three-mile radius from her home, and there are, believe it or not, four restaurants and eight takeaway shops. Within a four-mile radius you can add two to each of those categories. On the table by the door there are packs for everybody. It includes this map, and two pictures of Melanie Brookes. By the end of today we want to know where she got that meal, and if she was accompanied by anybody, even if it's a bloody leprechaun.'

There was some laughter in the room and Grace turned back to the map. 'Now we move on to the riverbank. There are four bridges upstream of where she was found, which takes us to a five-mile cut-off for our search. If we find nothing by concentrating on this area, then we'll extend until we do find something. No skimping on this. It will be a lot of hands and knees work, use knee protectors where it's necessary, because it's going to be a full day.'

Harriet heard one or two comments about going over old ground, and spun round. 'We may be going over old ground, but if we are it's because you damn well missed something the first time. Don't miss it this time, and particularly keep a look-out for Melanie's bag. It's out there somewhere, hopefully with her phone in it.'

One or two cast their eyes downwards, and everybody moved towards the whiteboard to check their job for the day, before heading to pick up their pack. Within ten minutes the room was clear, and Harriet slumped at her desk, her head in her hands.

'You okay, Harriet?'

She looked up at Grace. 'Yes, boss. Tired. Addie has chicken pox, and one or other of us has been up most of the night. I'll be fine, it's hard work telling an eighteenth-month-old Adeline Jameson that she mustn't do something, and when it's a "don't scratch" directive, it's nigh on impossible.'

'Who's she with now?' Grace looked concerned.

'Daddy's stayed home from work. She's chuffed to bits. He's booked all week off to try to take the worry away from me, but I'm not worried, I'm tired.' She smiled. 'Don't ever have kids, boss.'

Grace laughed. 'Not an earthly chance. I'd need a feller first, and this job doesn't encourage having a private life, does it?'

'Nope. We always laugh about it, because we know that if I hadn't met my feller in primary school and stuck with him, I wouldn't have had time to find another one. And then there would have been no chicken pox in my life. We going to see our runaway now?'

'We are. I'll drive, you close your eyes until we get there. And if you're spark out when we arrive, I'll leave you and lock the car doors so nobody can abduct you.'

'Thanks, boss. You're all heart.' Harriet stood, and joined Grace as they walked the length of the briefing room.

The gates of the guest house were open. Grace pulled in, and followed the driveway around the back. She spotted the little Ka straight away, alongside two others. Visitors' cars, she assumed.

The back door opened and a woman, Shirley Ledger, came out to meet them.

Shirley held out her hand. 'Hi, I'm Shirley Ledger.'

'Hello, Mrs Ledger.' Grace shook her hand, but decided to keep it formal for the moment. This woman hadn't done anything illegal, but she'd certainly taken up police time spent looking for her, when a simple phone call would have told them she was okay, but didn't want to be found.

Grace and Harriet followed Shirley through to the residents' lounge, and within a minute Trudy had provided a tray of tea and biscuits. She sat down beside Shirley, then leaned forward to pour out the drinks.

'Do you mind if Trudy stays,' Shirley asked. 'She's been good to me since I arrived last Wednesday night, and at the moment I need a bit of support.'

'That's fine, Mrs Ledger,' Grace said. 'I'm pleased we haven't found your body in a river somewhere, we have enough with finding your sister-in-law like that.' She was deliberately harsh with her words, hoping to provoke a reaction.

'Melanie wasn't my sister-in-law, in law,' Shirley said, then smiled. 'That sounds stupid, doesn't it? What I meant was that she was Patrick's girlfriend, not his wife.'

'You didn't leave any sort of message for your husband?' Harriet asked.

'No, I only went out for a drive around the area, to get some thinking time. I enjoy driving. I grabbed my purse because I knew I might need petrol, my phone and my coat, and went. I drove around then saw a friend in some difficulty. Her name is Enid Hill. She'd gone over on her ankle and was stuck at her front gate, couldn't put her weight on her foot. I pulled up, helped her get back inside and we chatted while I put frozen peas on it. It was while I was doing that, and telling her how much I miss my boys, that things escalated a bit. She had a house for sale, but was happy to rent it to me for as long as I needed it, and she rang Trudy to tell her to expect me that night.

'It was fate, I felt. Everything happened at the right time. I came here, I left my phone switched off in the car along with my purse, and until last night when Rosie turned up, I've lived here free of charge. I made sure Trudy kept a tab open for me, and she's been wonderful, but Rosie paid it all last night. I daren't use either my phone or my bank card, because I didn't want Mark to know where I was. I can pay my own way now, because I move into my house on Friday, come what may, and I'm going to collect my boys, probably also on Friday.'

Shirley gave a huge sigh as she finished speaking, and picked up her cup of tea.

'Do you have any idea how many police hours have gone into looking for you?' Inexplicably, Grace felt angry with this woman.

'I can imagine, but I also know how I felt, and continued to feel until last night when Rosie and Doris turned up here.'

'Doris?'

'Doris Lester. She's the one who found me. Part owner of Connection, in Eyam.'

'Rosie Steer employed Connection to find you?'

'No, Doris is my late father's wife, but it's a bit complicated. And Doris didn't use Connection to find me, she's actually on holiday. Believe it or not, she used her brain.'

Ouch. Grace felt it was a slight slur on her team. 'I'll need your new address, Mrs Ledger. You'll be available here until Friday?'

Shirley nodded. 'I will. I'm going to ring Springbrook today, explain everything and tell them I'll be picking my boys up Friday afternoon for the school holiday. I won't be telling them they're not going back there, I'll do that when I've found a new school for them.'

Harriet spoke to Trudy. 'For the record, Ms Dawson, can you confirm that Mrs Ledger was here Thursday night and didn't go out?'

'I can,' Trudy said. 'She went to bed early as she has done every night except last night. Her car hasn't moved, until she decided she had to go and get some money and clothes last night. She was driving out of the gates when her sister arrived.'

'Thank you. We'll prepare statements for both of you to sign, and then we won't need to trouble you again. Not about this issue anyway.' Grace hoped Shirley noticed the inherent threat. Grace too could make veiled comments.

The Rainbow boasted Chinese and Cantonese cuisine to take away, and a manager with the exotic name of Ernie. When DC Sam Ellis queried it, Ernie said his mother was English and as a result he ended up with Ernest Chan for a name.

Ernie took his time looking at the pretty face of Melanie Brookes and then confirmed that he believed she had been in his shop that night.

Sam felt a tingling in his fingers, all too aware that this was the breakthrough they had been seeking. 'Was she alone, or with someone?'

Ernie thought for a moment. 'She was alone in the shop. She spoke of going away the next day, and she couldn't be bothered cooking. Yorkshire?' He hesitated. 'No, it was York. She said she was going to York.'

The tingling increased. 'So there was definitely nobody with her. She was on her own?'

'I didn't say that. I said she was alone in here, but somebody was waiting outside for her. And her order was for two lots of prawn balls, and one lot of chips. She said they would eat it as they walked home.'

Sam was scribbling furiously in his notebook. 'So they definitely didn't come in a car. Thank you so much for this, Mr Chan... you've been really helpful.'

'Ernie.'

Sam grinned. 'Ernie. Could you see if it was a man or a woman waiting for her?'

'No, I'm sorry, I didn't take any notice. They had their back to me. And apart from that, at night-time you can't see much outside because the lights are on in here. I was only vaguely aware there was somebody standing there. Sorry I can't help on that.'

Sam nodded. 'Somebody will be out to talk to you again, and get your statement, but I have to get this logged, get somebody out here.'

'I'll be here,' Ernie said with a smile. 'I'm always here. You want some chips?'

Sam rang Grace as she was driving back from her visit to Shirley Ledger. He tried to contain his excitement as he passed on the information, then waited for a moment when Grace said she wanted to stop the car so she could consult her map.

Harriet had heard the conversation and as soon as Grace pulled into the side of the road, she was handed the map.

Grace ran her finger along the B road on which the takeaway was sited, following it in the general direction of the river. A small bridge carried the road over the river, a small bridge half a mile from Ernie's shop.

The DCI stared through the windscreen; she knew. She knew this was the most significant thing to surface, and would eventually give them their answers. And it had been done with brain work, no matter what bloody Shirley Ledger thought of their skills.

'Boss,' Harriet said. 'If you follow that road beyond the bridge, it comes to one of those mini roundabouts. Turn right there and it's only a couple of hundred yards to where Melanie lived.'

22

'Sam? Did you hear that? That road leads directly to Melanie's home, but before you get there it crosses the river. A small bridge. We're coming straight to you. Get as many as you can to that bridge, and we'll be with you in fifteen minutes. Is anybody at the bridge now?'

Sam pulled out his list. 'No, boss. Ian and Trevor are working their way towards it from the next bridge downstream, I'll be the first one there.'

'Then don't let anybody do anything until we arrive. I'm getting a diver. The river is pretty deep there and we don't want anybody going in who doesn't know what they're doing. Thanks, Sam, I'll be there in a bit.'

Grace and Harriet arrived at the same time as Ian Garwood and Trevor Mitchell, two young PCs newly attached to the murder team for the duration of the searches. Sam was already there, ready for instructions.

Grace greeted them as she clambered down the bank and looked around. 'I guess we're too late for footprints, but looking at that bridge, its sides are quite low and Melanie Brookes could easily have been toppled over. There would have been no need to come down to the water. It's a quiet road, perfect for committing the odd murder without being spotted.' Grace glanced at her watch. 'The divers will be here shortly, so can we make a start with the search? This has to be where she went in, it fits with where she bought that Chinese meal.'

Harriet was on the road, cordoning off the bridge with crime scene tape; it was obviously going to be a long day, and somebody would have to work out some sort of diversion scheme to take locals the circuitous way home. It didn't look as though they would get chance today to go and speak to Melanie's employers – for the second day running it had been put on the back burner. Maybe...

'Boss!' Harriet leaned over the bridge, carefully trying not to touch it with any part of her. 'Do you need me here?'

Grace thought for a moment. 'You thinking of covering the Global Systems interview?'

'I am. I can't imagine it taking long, they're not exactly suspects, are they?'

Grace laughed. 'Pin it on them, it'll save a lot of time. No, that's fine, Harriet. You head off and do that, it doesn't need the two of us here supervising this ramshackle lot.' She threw the car keys up to the sergeant.

'Ey,' Sam protested. 'Who found us this spot?'

Harriet waved and headed off to the car, grinning at Sam's disgruntled face.

Global Systems (Newark) PLC was on a business park outside Newark, and from the outside it looked spectacular. Plenty of glass, outstanding signage, and pretty rose gardens surrounding the spotlessly clean car park. She pulled the squad car next to a

Jaguar, and headed towards the door. She had to wait for permission to enter, then walked into a welcoming reception area. There she met Imogen North, or so it said on the badge pinned to her left breast.

Imogen smiled gently, and in a practised smooth voice said, 'Can I help you, officer?' Her thick long brown hair framed a round face, and she removed her glasses as she spoke, revealing pale blue eyes. Her make-up was flawless, and Harriet regretted not even applying a touch of mascara.

'I hope so.' Harriet prayed her Yorkshire accent was having a good day. 'I need to speak to whoever is at the top.' This young girl intimidated her as a woman.

'You'll need our HR section, I expect.'

'The very top. The peak of the mountain. Not the HR section.'

The smile wavered. 'I'll see who's in.'

She tapped away on her computer, and then sparkly Imogen resurfaced. 'Mr Vickers asks that you give him five minutes and he'll come down and get you. He's on a conference call at the moment.' She passed a visitor's pass to Harriet.

Harriet gave a brief nod, hung the pass around her neck and turned away to walk across to an armchair area. She helped herself to a glass of ice-cold water from the on tap machine, and sat. Mr Vickers must be Kevin Vickers, the man who had started the company ten years earlier, and who had orchestrated its amazing growth; the man she had investigated during the early hours while trying to comfort her itchy daughter.

Harriet flicked through a magazine showing wonderfully designed homes with immaculate interiors, and thought of her own home, lived in, full of toys and wanting a bit of a dust and a quick hoover.

. . .

Kevin Vickers, immaculately dressed in a smart grey suit and sporting a royal blue tie, appeared in front of her. Harriet stood, placing the magazine on the small table.

'Is your home like that?' he asked with a smile. His brown eyes locked on to her face and she knew this man was a first-class flirt. He certainly had the looks to match the personality.

'I wish.' Harriet held out her warrant card. 'DS Harriet Jameson. I'd like a quick word please, sir.'

'No problem. I'll get us some coffee when we reach my office.'

He led her towards a lift, and they went up to the third floor.

Vickers' secretary produced the coffee, and Harriet moved away from the window with the not-so-spectacular views of the car park to take her place opposite Kevin Vickers.

'Melanie Brookes,' he said. 'One of our brightest stars. I can't begin to tell you how much we're going to miss her.'

Harriet waited for a few seconds, then inclined her head in acknowledgement of his words. 'I need to ask you where you were on Thursday evening, Mr Vickers.'

'You suspect me?'

'I suspect everybody.'

'Oh.' He looked a little nonplussed, as if unable to believe what he was hearing. 'Hang on...' He stopped. 'Give me a minute while I get my brain into gear. I deal with computer systems, not real brains. I was...' Again the pause. 'I wasn't anywhere. I left here around seven and went home. I was there until coming into work on Friday. I was alone, my wife and children stayed at her mother's.'

'So you have no alibi.' Harriet made a note in her notebook, then lifted her head to look at him. 'Tell me about Melanie. Did nobody contact you on Friday to say she hadn't turned up in York?'

'No, they didn't. Alarm bells would have rung immediately, because she's never missed a conference or a promotion of any sort during the time she's worked for me. She booked Thursday morning off because her and that boyfriend of hers had been out to some function or other the night before, but worked Thursday afternoon from home on her slide show presentation. I spoke to her about five on Thursday to make sure she had everything she needed, and she was fine. Said she was leaving early for York, train about seven I think she said, and I wished her good luck. That was it. Until DCI Stamford rang on Sunday to give me the news, I had no idea anything wasn't as it should be.'

'What was she like?'

'Mel? Beautiful. Inside and out.' He closed his eyes for a moment. 'An amazing woman, she deserved somebody better than Patrick Ledger. She was earning so much more than him, and we believed he was with her for her money.'

'But you said she was beautiful. Why would he be with her for any other reason?'

'He used to gamble, big. He had debts. Now he doesn't have debts. Logic says he got the money to clear what he owed from Melanie.'

'In my book that's fine, if she loved him.'

'If.'

'You don't think she did? Or was it that you didn't want her to love him?'

'What are you inferring, DS Jameson?'

'I'm inferring nothing. I'm asking. Did you have feelings for Melanie Brookes?' Harriet felt a shiver run down her spine. Suddenly this whole case was widening, and she knew she had to handle it carefully. His words were sending mixed messages.

'She was a much-valued employee, and we've lost her.' His tone had become icy. He picked up his coffee cup and drank deeply. Harriet left hers where it was, on his desk. She wasn't going to lose the momentum for the sake of a drink of coffee.

'You know that's not what I meant.'

'I'm a happily married man, DS Jameson. I have feelings only for my wife and children, and as I said, I resent the inference.'

'That's okay, then,' Harriet said, deliberately making her tone flippant. 'Will your wife corroborate that?'

'Of course she will. Have we finished, DS Jameson?'

'For the moment. We will probably need you to come into the station to make a statement, but I'll be in touch to let you know more about that.'

Harriet stood, and walked towards the door. Kevin Vickers remained seated at his desk, and she hid the smile as she left him. One rattled boss. Why?

The secretary escorted Harriet to the lift, and she exited into the immaculate reception area, still guarded by Imogen. Harriet handed over her visitor pass, and turned to walk away.

'You've left something, DS Jameson,' Imogen said, her voice pitched low. Harriet turned and looked back. There was a small piece of paper on the reception desk.

'Sorry, I must have dropped it,' she said with a smile at Imogen, whose unease was reflected in her eyes and the set of her lips.

Harriet tucked the piece of paper into her pocket, and walked away from Global Systems wondering what the hell was going on.

. . .

Harriet didn't look at the note until she had driven some distance away from the car park. She pulled into a layby and sat still for a moment. That hadn't been a pleasant hour or so, and she felt as uneasy as Imogen had looked.

Harriet recovered the note from her pocket and smoothed it open.

DS Jameson, Melanie had an affair with Kevin Vickers. She finished with him about two months ago but he wouldn't leave her alone. If you need more information please ring me after six tonight when I will be home. My number is 05880 321405. Imogen

Harriet reread the words, tucked the piece of paper inside her notebook, and put the car into gear. She needed to tell the boss about all of this, about her own feelings that Kevin Vickers was holding something back, and about a girl called Imogen who was too scared to speak out.

The bridge and the riverbank seemed alive with uniformed and non-uniform police. Two divers were in the water, but so far had found nothing. The men and women scouring the riverbank had come up with a hoard of goodies that would need testing. In a small area they had found four empty soft drink cans, and more telling was a tray containing the remains of a Chinese meal. This had been carefully bagged for forensic analysis, but it was becoming increasingly obvious that this was the spot where Melanie Brookes had met her death before being tipped over the bridge wall into the fast-flowing river.

Grace and Harriet were huddled in close conversation, filling each other in on their activities while they had been apart.

'There's only one meal container?' Harriet asked.

'Unfortunately yes. It seems we have a tech-savvy killer to

contend with. I'll place every bet in the book that this was Melanie's meal. So what's this Kevin Vickers like?'

'I thought he was okay for the first five minutes, a genuine employer devastated he had lost an employee in such horrible circumstances. By the time I left I felt he was acting, and he said last Thursday his wife and kids were at her mother's. Why? It wasn't a school holiday last Friday. It seems strange. He didn't offer any explanation, and it was starting to appear to me that we needed to get him in an interview room, and get his answers down on tape.'

'Couldn't agree more. We'll organise it for tomorrow, send a squad car to collect him from work, I think. That'll give his staff something to think about. Okay, the divers are moving further downstream now, it seems, so let's hope the bag drifted along with the body. We've found nothing yet that says it belonged to her. You get off home, Harriet, and I'll ring this Imogen tonight.'

Harriet shook her head. 'I think she'll open up to me, boss. She might clam up when she realises it's not me. I'll go home, give the husband a break,' she said with a smile, 'and I'll ring Imogen from home tonight.'

23

Harriet rang the number on the slip of paper, and Imogen answered within a couple of seconds.

'Hi, Imogen, it's DS Jameson. I'm at home, not at work, so you may hear some disturbance. I have a little one.' She gave a slight laugh, hoping Imogen would feel at ease.

'Thank you for ringing. I wanted to make sure you knew the facts about Melanie. I'm not going to slag her off, I liked Mel a lot, and she taught me quite a bit. She had a strange lifestyle, but that was her, and I'm sure he won't have told you anything.'

'He?'

'The big boss, Kevin Vickers. He... he... pursued her. I think that's the best way of explaining it. He wanted her and he was going to have her. So he did. She was ambivalent about it. It's only sex, she said. But it wasn't only sex for him, he proper fell for her. They were a secret item for about four months, then she got fed up and moved on. She found Mark Ledger.'

Harriet was carefully writing down Imogen's words, but she suddenly stopped. 'Mark? Don't you mean Patrick?'

'No, Patrick was her steady, the man she would probably have ended up marrying, maybe even having his children. But then along came Mark. She really fell for him, said the sex was the best she'd ever had, and I think she was changing. She was starting to realise that you don't need to sleep around, you can get everything with one man. It didn't bother her that Mark was married, she planned on him getting a divorce. Everything was easy to Mel.'

'You spent a lot of time with Mel?' Harriet's head was reeling. Melanie Brookes had been seen as a career woman at her peak, loved by all who knew her, and who would be sorely missed. It seemed that there was so much more to the dead woman than they had been led to believe.

'He didn't tell you, did he? Mr High and Mighty Vickers. I don't know whether his wife has discovered what he's really like, but she left about three weeks ago. He spends a lot of his time on the phone, trying to persuade her to come back home.'

'Really?' This was turning into a gossipy conversation.

'I'm the receptionist, DS Jameson. I deal with telephone calls. As I said, Mel taught me a lot. Anyway, at one time Mel had all three men on the go, Mr Vickers, Patrick and Mark, but it was Mark who'd finally stolen her heart. She was worried; she thought he was cooling off.'

'You didn't know who she was planning to meet on Thursday night?'

'No, as far as I knew she was having an early night because she had to get up at half five the next morning. I spoke to her Thursday afternoon, checking she didn't need anything for her presentation, and that's what she said. If she met somebody, it was arranged that evening.'

Harriet thanked Imogen for being so open, and Harriet disconnected. She sat deep in thought. Melanie Brookes was a definite Jekyll and Hyde; on the surface a bright, talented woman, but underneath a woman who craved attention and got it by any means.

They urgently needed the data from the mobile phone company. They might not have the phone, but that didn't stop a list of numbers landing on the desk. Tomorrow, she decided, that document would be available for her perusal come what may.

Doris buckled on her seat belt, and started the car. She was beginning to feel that she could make the journey to Hucknall with her eyes closed; no satnav needed.

'Let's call and pick up some flowers for Rosie, shall we?' Wendy said, wriggling about to get more comfortable. 'I think she needs to know it's not all doom and gloom.'

Doris nodded. 'We will. I've been thinking. Melanie Brookes, this body in the river, why was she even out that night? Listening to what everybody has said, it seems she had an early start Friday morning for her visit to York, so what persuaded her to go out Thursday night for a Chinese takeaway?'

'What? How do you know she did that?' Wendy's eyes widened. 'I've not heard anything about that.'

A small smile hovered around Doris's lips. 'If I told you how I knew that, I'd have to kill you.'

'You've gone Connectiony on me. What time did you go to bed last night?'

'About three.'

'You're up to date with the investigation then?'

'Kind of. I did find out one or two things I hadn't known before. Like this Chinese meal. It's with forensics at the moment because they found the polystyrene box with some left in it. But it doesn't make sense that she was out buying the damn stuff in the first place. She told Patrick Ledger she wouldn't be seeing him until Saturday afternoon. She needed an early night on the Thursday, and she would be staying overnight in York on the Friday. Rosie said that, that's nothing to do with me and whatever I was doing that kept me up until three. So what made Melanie decide to go out that night for food? Or maybe the food was an addition? Maybe she didn't go out to get something to eat, maybe she went out to meet somebody who said let's have a Chinese.'

Doris touched her brakes lightly, then swung into a layby. The roadside stall had mainly fruit and vegetables for sale, but a large galvanised bucket held bunches of brightly coloured flowers. She bought one and put it into the boot before resuming her place in the driving seat.

'Do me a favour, Wendy, when we get there. If I say something that I can't possibly know, don't question it. And let's hope Rosie doesn't. Megan, on the other hand, is a dead cert to query everything, so we might not get away with it.'

'Doris, I rarely check anything with you, I assume you know things anyway. You give off an air of confidence that fools everybody. Let's go see your extended family, and you can offer your help. Let's talk these questions through with them and see what we come up with.'

Doris and Wendy pulled up outside Rosie's house, to see Mark on the front path holding Rosie and pushing the back of her head against the stone wall; he was screaming into her face. Megan was hovering inside the doorway crying, and Rosie was attempting, unsuccessfully, to push Mark away from her.

'Stay in the car and film this,' Doris said to Wendy, then ran up the path towards the irate man and the clearly frightened woman and child.

· · ·

Mark didn't see, or hear, Doris's arrival behind his back. 'Where the fuck is my wife, bitch?' were the words that Doris heard, and she went into action.

Doris hooked her right ankle around his leg and tugged. He fell away from Rosie and turned around. 'What the...' he roared and lifted his hand to grab at her.

Doris brought up her foot, and the pain that must have reverberated through his groin was the trigger that brought him to his knees, the roar changing to a scream. The right-handed chop to his shoulder saw him tumble to the floor, in too much pain to move. Doris pushed her foot towards his face. He didn't move; he couldn't move.

'You can sue me if you want, Mr Ledger,' she said quietly and sweetly, 'but I do have to tell you that every part of this has been videoed and I am sure that when your friends find out you were... demolished... by a seventy-year-old granny, your street cred will be shot to smithereens. Facebook is a powerful tool. Now, we're going to leave you here on the path until you feel you can walk again, then I want you to go home, Mr Ledger, forget you have a wife and children because they've certainly wiped you from their memories and don't ever come near this house again unless it's by invitation. Should I ever find out you've touched any inhabitant of this house, or even threatened them, I will be back and next time I won't hold back, I will mash your balls.'

Wendy had climbed out of the car to do the filming, and now walked up the path, still aiming the camera at the man lying prostrate on the path. She zoomed into his face and grinned.

'Hello, Mr Ledger. Smile for the camera please.'

His answer was a groan, and they walked around him and through the front door. Rosie was holding tightly on to Megan, who was still sobbing.

'Shush, sweetheart, it's over. When Uncle Mark's able to walk again, I think he'll go straight home. Let's go and make a nice cup of tea, and maybe we can have the scones you made this morning?'

Megan stifled a sob and nodded.

All four of them headed for the kitchen and sat around the table. 'Thank you, Doris,' Rosie said quietly. She touched the back of her head. 'Ouch. He was bashing my head into the wall before you arrived.' Megan stood and moved behind her mother. She inspected her head and pronounced it free of blood, just a couple of scrapes.

'I'll give him a couple of minutes, then go and make sure he's still alive,' Doris said. 'He deserved that, but I do think there was an element of if you're a male you've got it coming, at the moment. It's been a strange couple of weeks for me,' she finished with a laugh.

Megan stood to go and butter some scones, while Rosie made a large pot of tea. Rosie's hands shook slightly, and Doris knew she had been afraid.

Doris stood and walked down the hallway. She opened the front door but there was no sign of Mark. He'd clearly decided retreat was his best option.

'He wanted to know where Shirley is?'

Rosie nodded. 'He did. And he says he's going to go to the school on Saturday and get his boys, then she'll come home to be with them. Arrogant bastard.'

'She needs to get the boys for definite on Friday.'

'I know. I'll speak to her later. Megan and I are going over for the day on Friday anyway to help her move in. She's apparently having new beds delivered really early. She's managed to get a suite from a charity shop and that's coming Friday, so they'll be comfortable enough until it can be made into a proper home for them.'

'You're off school, Megan?'

Megan nodded. She pulled up her top and showed Doris and Wendy her back.

'Shingles,' Rosie explained. 'She's been a bit off for a few days and two days ago that rash appeared. I took her to the doctors yesterday and it's shingles. She's on a pretty intense course of treatment, five tablets a day, but the pain is easing. She'll be okay by the end of next week's holiday, hopefully. As a result, she's free to help on Friday. Good news all round,' Rosie said with a grin.

'And,' Megan interrupted, 'it's given me time to look up where there are some karate classes. Mrs Lester, that was the most amazing thing. I've seen it on TV, but that's the first time I've ever witnessed it used in a real situation. I want to be able to do that when I'm a PI.'

24

The briefing on that Thursday morning saw everyone issued with different jobs, unlike the day before when the work had been concentrated on the riverbank area and the bridges.

They had some answers. Melanie Brookes had been thrown in from the bridge closest to the Chinese takeaway where she had last been seen alive. The Styrofoam packaging had been confirmed as being of the same type used by Ernie Chan. Ernie's statement also confirmed he had provided two boxes with prawn balls in, and one portion of chips. He could not confirm it was a man who accompanied Melanie on her last walk, but there had definitely been a second person waiting outside his shop for her to buy the meals. Ernie also confirmed she had worn a backpack, but could give no further details other than it was either black or navy blue.

Harriet gave the account of her visit to Global Systems (Newark) PLC, and of her impressions of the owner. She described her visit in detail, and how that visit had ended with a surreptitious action on the part of the receptionist, the proverbial note-passing so that the boss doesn't know what's going on.

Harriet read from her notebook, telling them of the conversation she had with Imogen the previous night, a conversation that upped the suspect count to three definites: Mark Ledger, Patrick Ledger and Kevin Vickers.

'She was sleeping with all three of them?' The query came from the back of the room.

'Not currently. She had broken off with Kevin Vickers, but he wasn't happy about it. He was even more unhappy when his wife left him. The boss and I will take this interview as soon as possible, we'll have to speak to Vickers to get the address. He's not going to want us talking to her, he wants her back in the marital home and we might kill off any chance of that by talking to her, but we need to know why she decided to go. It may be that she was fed up, and it was nothing to do with Melanie, but we must hear her reason so we can rule him out or in. If it turns out to be him who killed Melanie, he certainly killed his golden-egg-laying goose. She was a real star at the company, earned massive bonuses for arranging contracts for new work, which is why I'm hesitant to think it's him. He's definitely not ruled out though. She was currently living most of the time with Patrick Ledger, he was her acknowledged boyfriend, but she was having an affair with Mark Ledger, Patrick's older brother. You know, the brother who's devastated his wife has gone walkabout, and who desperately wants her home to do his ironing.'

There was laughter around the room at her words. 'You get the idea, then. So, I'm leaving...' she glanced around the room, 'Fiona to organise what everybody is doing today. DCI Stamford is working from her office and is available if needed. She's checking everything that's come in, chasing up some details we're still waiting for, and is generally in charge. The divers are moving further downstream and Sam will be with them. Sam, take two more bodies with you, continue with that bankside search. The phone and bag still haven't been found. I have the phone records now, for Melanie's number. I shall be working on them at my desk. Any queries, see either the boss or me. Okay?'

There was a general shuffling of feet, a drift over to Fiona Harte, and an exit by Sam Ellis who took Ian and Andrew with him. They'd been up to their knees in mud the previous day, and yet hadn't complained once – they'd do for him.

When everyone had left for their various visits and tasks, Harriet went through to Grace's office.

'Okay, everybody's out doing things, and I'm about to be glued to my desk. You need anything, boss?'

Grace sat back with a sigh. She opened her purse and took out a ten-pound note. 'I want a large cappuccino with loads of chocolate on it. You fancy going and getting us one each before you start? I can't, I'm waiting for a phone call, but you've not started yet.'

'It'll be a pleasure. Look at the sunshine,' Harriet said with a smile. She picked up the money, and closed the door quietly behind her.

The queue in Costa was long and Harriet had changed her mind about which drink to have by the time she reached the front. In the end, she decided to go with the cappuccino also, and gave her order to the girl behind the counter. She paid and moved to the end section where she would collect her order.

'You found who murdered Mel yet, then?' a voice said quietly. She spun round, suddenly scared.

'Pardon?'

'Saw you cross the road after you'd come out of the police

station. Mel was a friend, so thought I'd ask.' The man, around twenty-five if Harriet had to guess, smiled.

'I'm sorry, I don't discuss work outside of work,' she retorted. 'You want to know anything, join the police.'

'Okay, okay!' He held up a hand in surrender. 'I didn't mean to upset you. I liked Mel, we got on, so I thought I'd ask.'

'You haven't come forward as being a friend of Mel's. If you are, we need to interview you.' Harriet felt uncomfortable. The situation was out of her control. 'What's your name?'

'Ray Taylor. Raymond really, but I don't like that. Everybody calls me Ray.'

'Ray, I need to talk to you. An hour? Don't be late. She handed him her card and picked up her two coffees which had arrived. 'Don't make me have to come looking for you.'

'As if I'd dare,' Ray said with a laugh. He picked up his own cup, and carried it to a table.

Harriet headed back across the road, and delivered both drinks to Grace's office, where she told the story of her coffee shop trip.

'Think he'll turn up?'

'Oh yes. I might have threatened him. Only a little bit. I reckon he'll come, and I reckon he'll be early. I don't suppose for a minute he'll have anything to add, I wanted to pay him back for making me jump.'

Ray Taylor was ten minutes early for his appointment, fully believing that the officer he'd tried to get a bit cocky with would indeed go out and search for him, possibly with a view to keeping him locked up overnight.

He confirmed that for a period of about three weeks he had slept with Melanie Brookes, about five times in all. But more if you counted the number of times per night, he hastened to add.

Much to his dismay, she then ditched him. Ray thought her boyfriend was starting to click on, so it was bye bye, Ray. Yes, he had said, he did still think about her a lot, and was sad to hear of her death. She didn't deserve that.

He did come up with one interesting comment – when she went out walking or running, she always took a backpack. It had a side strap for holding a water bottle, and it was lightweight.

'How do you know this?'

'It was how I met her. The running, I mean. I run as much as she does... did, and I spotted her by the side of the road having a drink. I stopped because she was proper tasty, but she'd stopped because her drink holder strap had snapped. We ended up in bed that night, and the next night I took her a new bag.'

'Can you remember what the bag looks like?' Harriet felt a small frisson of anticipation.

'Yes, it was black, Nike on it, lightweight, made of nylon I think.' He took out his phone and scrolled through his pictures. He passed the phone over to Harriet. 'That's it. Scroll to the next one as well.'

Melanie was in the pictures, totally naked, her back to the camera and wearing the backpack, her thumb held up indicating she was happy with it. The second picture was a full-frontal shot with Melanie leaning forward to blow the photographer a kiss.

Harriet sent the pictures to her own phone, then thanked Ray for his co-operation.

'I miss her, you know,' he said. 'I really liked her, but she's like a free spirit, not tied down to anybody. I hope you find whoever did this, he deserves to hang.'

Harriet walked him to the car park, and waved as he went. *Nice bloke*, she thought, *I misjudged him.*

.   .   .

Unable to use Ray's pictures of the bag, they found one on the Internet and showed it on the evening news, asking everyone to keep an eye out for it as it was still missing despite carefully searching the crime scene. Grace was the spokesperson, and she also asked for any sightings of Melanie on that journey between the Rainbow Chinese shop and the bridge where they believed she had been killed.

They didn't have a single call in response, and frustration was starting to set in.

Finally Harriet managed to get around to checking the data for Melanie's phone. She couldn't help but wish they had the actual instrument, with its photos and a list of contacts, but they didn't so the file sent by O2 was vital to the investigation.

Melanie had had five incoming calls between four and seven on the evening she died. One was from Patrick, one from Mark, one from Shirley, one from Rosie and one from Global Systems. Patrick's had gone unanswered, but she had spoken to all of the others. There had been no incoming calls between Melanie leaving Patrick's home at midday, and speaking to Mark at four seventeen. The call was slightly over four minutes in length.

Forty-five minutes later there had been a call from Shirley, lasting two minutes exactly, then one from Rosie that lasted thirty seconds.

Harriet realised the call from Global Systems was probably the one from Imogen – she had said that she had spoken to Melanie to check she had everything she needed for the York conference. No point seeing problems like imagining it was Kevin Vickers calling Melanie when she knew for a fact that Imogen had rung her.

Strangely, Melanie had made no outgoing calls that afternoon. Maybe she had slept – it seemed from Patrick's statement that they had had a lot to drink the previous evening, it had meant they were late in bed, and she was probably still feeling the effects the following afternoon.

With a sigh, Harriet tidied her desk and entered her report on to the computer. She would give a verbal report at the briefing of her activities, but they could check details by logging on to the file.

Harriet waved at Grace as she passed her office, and Grace flicked her wrist to tell her to go in.

'You want something, boss?'

'Only to say well done today. We're chipping away at it, and we'll get there. Is it tomorrow that Shirley Ledger gets her new house and her boys?'

'It is.'

'We might go and wish them good luck, have a little chat. You think Doris Lester will be there?'

'Boss, we can pick her up any time we want. You want me to do that?'

'God, no. Don't do that. According to Tessa Marsden and Hannah Granger, she'd run rings round us. I want to meet this paragon of virtue. Maybe we'll nip out to Rothery tomorrow and see what's what. Yes?'

'Definitely. You've got me intrigued as well. I'll give Rosie Steer a ring tonight, casually check if Ms Lester will be there. No point in trailing out there if she isn't.'

'Good girl. Now get off home to that sweet child of yours. Adeline any better?'

'Addie's fine,' Harriet said with a laugh. 'We're knackered.'

25

Megan had no idea what she was doing with the funny little hooks that apparently went into curtains when a curtain pole wasn't in place. Space evenly had been the instruction. Divide the pile into two, one half for one curtain, one half for the other. Easy.

Except it wasn't. And she'd had to iron the curtains first, to add to the chore. Could she pretend the shingles pain had returned? She moved two of the little hooks up, and slotted another one on the white tape stuff, then wondered if it would have been easier to use a measuring rule and do some proper calculations. She heaved a huge sigh, then jumped up to see who had just arrived.

She squealed in delight – it was Mrs Lester and Mrs Lucas, bearing the promised bacon sandwiches picked up from the bakery in the village. She carefully laid the curtain on the bed, knowing if she didn't she might have to do a re-iron, and ran downstairs.

There were six chairs in the kitchen brought in from the Steer garden as a temporary measure, and an old table rescued from the cottage's own garden that had required a bit of a scrub down before it came through the door.

A chorus of 'morning's was heard as the two ladies arrived bearing food, and tea and coffee was quickly made.

'Exciting times, Shirley,' Doris said with a smile. 'What time are you getting the boys?'

'They finish at three, so I shall be there for half past two. I'll say we're going on holiday so I need them out a little early. I don't want Mark turning up for them and causing problems.'

'Okay. You have beds?'

'Yes. They arrived yesterday, and a delivery of bedding is coming in the next hour. I know the carpets aren't brilliant, but they'll do for now. At least it's not bare floorboards. Megan is putting curtains up in Adam's room, and I want to make sure Seth's room is done next. Mine can wait, if necessary. I need my boys to be comfortable.' She looked around them all, daring them to disagree. 'I can make this work, you know. There's no way on this earth I'm going back to Mark.'

'Hey!' Rosie stood. 'We're right behind you. Yes, I was mad at you for not contacting me, but I do understand.' She pulled her sister towards her and hugged her. 'I am curious, though. Was there a final straw?'

Shirley gave a small laugh. 'Kind of. It was Enid Hill. She's been on her own for a long time now, and she was actually considering getting on her hands and knees and crawling back inside the house. But the point is, why the hell is she taking her own bin out? She's ninety. I thought councils had a duty of care towards their elderly residents? That's not the issue though. She does manage, and without any real problems. I don't doubt she would have crawled back inside if I hadn't driven past and sensed something was wrong. She would have managed. We talked at some length while I was putting frozen peas on her ankle, and she saw the struggle in me, I suppose. When she offered me this house once more, I knew it was right. I didn't even look at the cottage, I said yes please.'

The bacon sandwiches were handed around, and everyone chatted, steering clear of the elephant galloping around the room in the form of the murder of Melanie Brookes. It was only as DCI Stamford and DS Jameson walked past the kitchen window that everything went silent.

'Oh my God,' Rosie said. 'I forgot they were calling round. That DS rang me last night to say they'd pop in, make sure everything was okay with you, Shirley, and that you weren't expecting trouble from Mark. That's not all though...' She didn't get the chance to explain Harriet had specifically asked if Doris would be there; they knocked on the back door, and opened it slightly, peering around and smiling.

'Come in,' Shirley said. 'Tea or coffee? I can't offer you a bacon sandwich though, we've scoffed the lot.'

'Coffee please,' was the answer given by both officers, and Megan stood, offering her seat to Grace. Harriet sat on the spare chair, and looked around the kitchen.

'This is nice. Any problems, Shirley?'

'No, and there won't be as long as Mark doesn't find out where I am. I'm picking up the boys this afternoon. They can ring him tonight to tell him, so he doesn't make a trip out to the school tomorrow, but I don't really think he'll be bothered anyway. The boys have always been an encumbrance, he'll not even be bothered about getting any sort of visiting set up, I'm guessing. But we'll see. The boys are almost twelve and can make their own decisions about whether they want to see him or not.'

The room darkened slightly as a man walked past the kitchen window, and Shirley took in the delivery. She breathed a sigh of relief. The beds could be made, and the boys would welcome a takeaway meal tonight. The next day was looking like being a shopping day.

Slowly, Grace brought the subject round to Melanie Brookes, keen to hear if Doris Lester had any contribution to make. 'Did you see our spot on local TV last night? We haven't found either her bag or her phone, but thanks to a real coincidence, we know what it looked like. I showed an exact copy of it, but we've had no response so far. We're pretty sure she must have had it with her when she went out that night, because it's not in her home or her car. It's black, has Nike written across it, and it's a fabric one.'

'I saw it, the appeal,' Doris said, 'thought you handled it excellently. Don't give up, somebody will find it one day, and it will tell you everything if that phone is in it.'

The sound of Doris's voice acted like a trigger for Grace. 'It's actually an honour to meet you, Mrs Lester. Tessa Marsden and Hannah Granger speak highly of you, they tell me you've helped them several times when things needed sorting, or talking through. Have you any thoughts on this murder?'

Doris laughed. 'Several, but nothing yet where there's any proof of anything. Mark Ledger, obviously, has to be the lead suspect, but I'm not convinced he has the required skills to strangle someone then hide things as well as they're hidden in this case. He's a bit poorly at the moment, by the way, so if you feel the need to question him again, now might be a good time.'

'Poorly?'

'Sore testicles,' Doris said, and Megan burst out laughing behind her.

Shirley almost held up her hand as if asking for permission

to speak, then thought better of it. 'Why is Mark the obvious suspect?'

Rosie leaned across towards Shirley. 'Look at the back of my head, Shirl.'

Shirley gave a small cry when she saw the grazing and the redness. 'What have you done?'

'Your husband slammed me into the wall outside my home. He was trying to find out where you were, and I wouldn't tell him. Luckily, Doris and Wendy turned up.'

'May I look?' Grace stood and moved across to Rosie. 'I can bring him in on assault charges. I'm assuming you witnessed this, Mrs Lester?'

Megan laughed. 'Mrs Lester and Mrs Lucas not only witnessed it, they filmed it. It was amazing.'

First rule of being a private investigator, Megan, Doris thought, *is don't open your mouth until it's necessary.*

'You have the film with you?'

Wendy looked at Doris, and Doris nodded. 'I only fathomed how to do a video a week ago,' Wendy mumbled, delving into the depths of her bag for her phone. She found it and handed it to Grace.

Harriet watched it and shrieked with laughter. Grace watched it and held in her laughter.

'Can he walk?' Harriet asked.

'He'd gone by the time I went out to check if he was dead,' Doris said. 'He'll be sore.'

Shirley held out her hand. 'May I see it, please?'

They were silent while they watched her face. Shirley saw it through to the end, then turned to Doris. 'You hurt him.'

Doris nodded again. 'I did. I pulled back, it could have been much worse for him, but I did enough to make him think twice about hurting anyone else. I had no choice, Shirley. If I hadn't barrelled up that path like some avenging angel, he could possibly have killed Rosie. Since Connection became fully operational, this is only the second time I have had to use my skills, and I won't apologise for it. I haven't been taking karate classes for twenty years simply for the company in the dojo. I can kill. I don't kill. Not yet anyway.' She smiled.

'Dear Gods,' Harriet muttered. 'I so want to be this woman.'

Wendy laughed. 'The sucker punch was when she told him we were going to post it on Facebook. Made my day, it did, I've never seen Doris in action before.'

The police officers did a quick tour of the cottage, then drove away with a copy of the video on Harriet's phone. Beds were made and curtains put up, then Shirley locked the front door. They watched as Shirley drove off to get Adam and Seth, and Rosie asked Doris and Wendy to go home with her and Megan.

'Is Rosie scared?' Wendy asked.

'I think she's worried. Maybe not scared, but she has to consider she has Megan with her. I don't really think Mark will try it again, though. He'll not be fully recovered yet.'

'Think she'll tell Dan?'

'I think Megan will.' Doris laughed. 'We'll probably need our video to show Dan that Mark has been dealt with. It will be a step too far if Dan's locked up for attacking Mark.'

Dan laughed uproariously when he saw the video. Megan, of course, had opened her mouth as soon as her dad walked through the front door.

'I'd best take my four ladies out for a meal tonight, then,' he said. He saw Doris was about to say it wasn't necessary, so he held up his hand to stop her. 'I insist. Things could have been so much worse without you. It seems you came into our lives for a reason, Doris, and I'm truly grateful you're here.'

Shirley had no problem getting her boys. She collected them at half past two, explaining to Eva Peters that they were leaving that afternoon for a week's holiday and she needed them a little early.

'They're nice lads, these boys,' Eva said. 'The sort we need in this school. I hope we see them again after the break.'

Shirley smiled and turned to hug Adam and Seth as they came through the door into Mrs Peters' office.

'Thank you, Mrs Peters. Come on, boys. Let's go holiday.'

She led them out to her car, and they put their backpacks into the boot before climbing into the rear seat.

'Seat belts on?' she called, and put the car into gear. She felt as if this was literally the first day of her life, and her future was waiting to be taken. Mark needed to be out of that future now, she wanted nothing more to do with him.

26

Kevin Vickers' wife was called Juliet. It suited her. Her long blonde hair was straight, stopped halfway down her back and framed an elfin face that belied her true age of thirty-four years. She looked like a teenager. Her blue eyes clouded over as she opened the door to face the two women.

Grace and Harriet, full up from meat and potato pie eaten in a local hostelry they had discovered shortly after leaving Fuchsia Cottage, held out their warrant cards, and Juliet stepped aside, inviting them into her parents' home. She spoke with the lilt of an Irish accent, and she later confirmed she had been born in Dublin but had moved to England when her parents had, when Juliet was fifteen.

'I met Kevin five years later, and here we are with two children, and I'm back with my parents.'

'Can I ask how long you've been separated?' Grace asked the question, Harriet wrote the answer.

'Not long. About three or four weeks. It's permanent though. One affair too many.'

'And who was the one too many?'

'Melanie Brookes. I didn't kill her, before you ask, I'm not all that bothered. He's never been the faithful type, and finding out he'd slept with Mel was the finish.'

'How did you find out?'

'He told me. He was drunk and miserable, and I mean really drunk and really miserable. I asked him what was on his mind and he said Melanie Brookes. It all spilled out of him, there were even tears, and he collapsed on the sofa. Once he was asleep I packed suitcases for the three of us, woke up the kids and we came here. I've not been back, hardly even spoken to him although he calls several times a day, and next week he'll get the divorce papers that will start off the process.'

Grace smiled. 'You haven't seen Melanie Brookes since he told you?'

'No, I've only seen her a couple of times anyway, we don't move in the same circles. She hasn't got kids. She seems to collect men instead. I don't blame her at all. She's single and can do what she wants. He is a married man though and in my book that means you don't sleep around. Kevin does, so he's out of my life now.'

'When Kevin was doing this confessing and being miserable, did he mention anything else at all about Melanie?'

'He wanted to sack her, but she brings so much business into the company he knew he couldn't. He kept saying don't think about leaving me, I'll get rid of her, but it was too late. As soon as he mentioned he'd slept with her, I was mentally deciding which clothes to take for the three of us, and trying to calculate how soon he would fall asleep.'

'So he didn't say I'll sack her, he said I'll get rid of her?'

Juliet looked horrified. 'Let me think.' She went quiet for a moment. 'No, he definitely said I'll get rid of her. You don't think...'

'We don't think, we look for proof. It could be a figure of speech he used. He was drunk, you said.' Grace tried to smooth over the tension coming from Juliet. 'Did your husband tell you we were coming to see you?'

'Yes. He texted me last night. I've told him I won't speak to him, but if I have anything to tell him about the children, I'll text him.'

Grace and Harriet stood, followed by Juliet. 'Thank you for your time, Mrs Vickers. Are the children at school?'

'They are. They finish this afternoon for a week's holiday, so I'm thinking of taking them away for a break.'

Grace handed her card over. 'If you do, please let me know where you will be.' She smiled to lessen the impact of her words.

'You suspect me?' The blue eyes flashed between the two officers.

They gave their standard response. 'Until we get to the truth, we suspect everybody.'

Harriet sat at her desk, the telephone list for Melanie's landline in front of her. There had been only one incoming call to that during the entirety of Melanie's last day of life, and it had come from Global Systems. It was a brief call, lasting only a few seconds over one minute.

That puzzled her. Two calls from Global Systems within half an hour of each other – one she knew about, the one from Imogen. So had Imogen had to call Melanie for a second time, or had the second call come from the boss-man's phone in his office?

And Harriet needed to ask the sisters why they had rung Melanie that afternoon, Shirley in particular, because this was the only contact from Shirley during the whole of the time she had been missing. Harriet felt annoyed with herself that she had shelved this part of the investigation to head off to Rothery and then on to the interview with Juliet Vickers.

If Harriet had given the phone data her full concentration she could have questioned Rosie and Shirley earlier. Her frustration bubbled over, then her brain clicked in to tell her she couldn't do everything, to calm down and count to ten. Then carry on.

Mobile data:

1. Patrick 4.12 – not answered
2. Mark 4.17 – 4 minutes
3. Shirley 4.53 – 2 minutes
4. Rosie 4.58 – 30 seconds
5. Global Systems 5.01 – 2 minutes

Landline data

1. Global Systems 5.30 – 1 minute 8 seconds

Grace stared at the handwritten list Harriet handed to her, and frowned. 'Why would Shirley break her silence to ring Melanie Brookes? She goes away and there's no contact with anybody for five days, but during that time she rings Melanie Brookes on the day of her death. And why would Rosie ring her? I don't think they were friends, were they? Acquaintances, yes, but nothing stronger than that. I'll go and talk to Shirley tomorrow.'

'I'll go with you.'

'No you won't. You're off this weekend. Go and look after Adeline, she'll be needing her mummy, I reckon, after a week of Daddy.'

Harriet flashed a grateful smile. 'Thanks, boss. You want me to ring Shirley Ledger and tell her what time you'll be there?'

'No, she's pissing me off a bit. I'll be there for eight, let's inconvenience her a bit.'

It didn't inconvenience Shirley at all. She was up and preparing breakfast for her boys when Grace appeared at her back door.

'You're out and about early,' Shirley said to her visitor.

'I want to finish early, and something's cropped up that I need answering. Can I come in?'

Shirley stepped aside, and waved the teapot at Grace. 'Want one?'

'No, I'm fine, thanks. We've been checking Melanie's phone records and at nearly five o'clock on the day she died you rang her. You spoke for slightly over two minutes. You haven't contacted anybody else between leaving your house on the Wednesday night and Rosie finding you on the following Tuesday. So, as you can imagine, we're curious why you rang Melanie Brookes.'

'Oh, that's easy. You didn't need to trail out here, I could have told you over the phone. I rang her to tell her I'd left Mark, and she could have him.'

'You knew?'

'Of course I knew,' she scoffed. 'I've been married to the two-timing rat for a number of years. She wasn't the first, but possibly the last. I think it was getting serious, and I knew I'd had enough. You want to know what she said?'

'I do.'

'She cried. Tried to say she was sorry, she didn't mean to take him away from his kids, but she loved him. I threw in the name Patrick, and the cold-hearted bitch said Patrick would get over it. She asked if we could meet to talk things through, and I laughed at her. I can't say I'm sorry she's dead, but one thing she has done is to give me my freedom. You're looking in the wrong direction, DCI Stamford, I didn't kill Melanie Brookes, I didn't care about her enough to do that.'

Adam and Seth bounded through the door and sat at the makeshift kitchen table. 'We still going shopping, Mum?'

'We certainly are, as soon as you've eaten breakfast. McDonald's for lunch?'

The boys high-fived each other, and pulled their cornflakes towards them.

'Thank you, Shirley, I'll leave you to enjoy your day with your boys. If you decide to go away during this school break, please let me know.'

Rosie was surprised to see Grace standing at her front door. 'Hello. You work Saturdays as well?'

Grace laughed. 'I work every day really. When it's a murder case you never switch off until we've locked up the killer. I've got something I need to check with you.'

Rosie held open the door. 'Come in. Coffee?'

'Thanks, I will. I said no at Shirley's because she was getting breakfast ready for the boys, but I think I need the caffeine now.'

'You've been to Shirley's already?' The welcome in Rosie's voice had died away.

'Yes, I knew she was going out shopping, and I didn't want to miss her.'

'You could have rung her.'

Grace shrugged but said nothing.

Seated at the kitchen table, she said, 'Thank you,' as Rosie handed her the coffee. 'Megan still in bed?'

'She is, but if she hears your voice she'll be straight down. I think she fancies herself as a proper Miss Marple since meeting Doris and Wendy, and she's definitely fired up for starting karate lessons. So, what did you want to know?'

'You rang Melanie in the afternoon on the day she died. Just before five o'clock, but the call only lasted thirty seconds. Why did you ring her?'

'Is that it? That's all you've trailed out here for? I rang her to ask if she'd seen Shirley. I was desperately trying to find Shirley, if you remember, despite Mark's reluctance to admit she'd gone. I disconnected pretty quickly because she was crying, really not our normal bubbly Mel. She said no, of course she hadn't seen her, but if she decided to, she would let me know, which I thought was a bit strange. And that was it. Conversation over. Not worth reporting to you, is it?'

Grace scribbled down Rosie's answers in her notebook, and sat back. 'No, and I'm sorry I have to do this, but it's my job. Don't get pissed off with me, I'm trying to find your friend's killer and we're only getting little bits in dribs and drabs. We honestly thought finding out what sort of bag we were looking for would get some response, but we haven't had one call about it. The divers working the river from where she went in to the spot where we found her have turned up nothing, so they've packed up, and we've had everybody and their grandmother out scouring the banks all the way up, but still nothing. Either this killer was lucky, or organised. Has Shirley told you Mark was having an affair with Melanie?'

'She has. I'm not surprised. He tried it on with me once. He has a hole in his foot where I stepped back with my stiletto heels. Dirty little man. I really didn't like him. He told Shirley it was accidental, I'd stepped back without realising he was there, but I knew all right. And so did he. He's never been near me since then. Does Patrick know about the affair?'

'I don't know. We took his statement at the beginning, and are set to go and reinterview now that we've progressed a bit, but that is going to mean we tell him about his brother. What do you think will happen?'

Rosie laughed. 'Let's hope he doesn't shoot the messenger for a start.'

27

As Wendy handed her an orange juice, Doris pushed the laptop away, and smiled. 'Thanks. I was thirsty. The key to all of this is that damn bag. Somebody's got it. No, I'm being an idiot. The killer has got it.'

Wendy laughed. 'An idiot you're definitely not. Would a Ferrero Rocher help?'

'Might do. We got any left?'

'No. I only asked if it might help. Didn't say it was going to.' Wendy could sense the cogs working in Doris's brain. 'Tell me what you're thinking.'

'The thing that I'm thinking is unthinkable, and I can't see how it was done. Yet. So I'm hoping I'm wrong. How can we interview somebody when we're not supposed to be interviewing people, and we'd have to do it without authorisation?'

'Is this a rhetorical question? A quiz question? A conundrum? Or are you really asking me?'

'I'm thinking out loud.'

'Oh good. So I don't need to answer then.'

'Feel free to jump in whenever you want.'

'What have you been checking on that machine?'

'It's a laptop, Wendy, not a machine. And I've been looking at any new reports that have been entered.'

'On what?' Wendy was curious.

'Doesn't matter. Let's say I've got a friend who can access whatever he pleases. Which is why I can't teach Luke this part of his job. My friend isn't his friend.'

'I'm not asking you anything else. I don't want putting in the Tower of London for treason.'

Doris sipped at her drink, deep in thought. 'It's not *cherchez l'homme*, as I said many moons ago. It's *cherchez le sac*. It seems to me there's a chatty young woman at Global Systems who might talk to two unauthorised doddery old ladies playing at being private detectives.'

Wendy rolled her eyes. 'I knew nothing of a chatty lass at this place. How are we going to do this?'

'I've no idea. I don't even know if she'll be helpful, but we won't know if we don't ask, will we? Monday morning we'll target Imogen North.'

Sunday was a day of rest. Harriet spent the day being normal with her young daughter, and Daddy was allowed to go fishing as a special treat before heading back to work the following day. Adeline would be returning to her nan now that the spots had stopped itching and were starting to clear – and yet Harriet couldn't switch off from the case. Once Addie had gone for an afternoon nap, Harriet started to think.

Okay, Melanie Brookes was small in stature, but she was incredibly fit. She used a gym regularly, and she ran tremendous distances to keep her fitness levels as high as she could, so

Harriet was unhappy with the theory that a woman could have done the deed on that Thursday night. If there had been some other injury like blunt force trauma to the head, that would have been a different scenario, but her only injuries had been manual strangulation marks around her neck. Melanie would have been able to fight off one woman, but one man would have been a different story.

So who did they have? Who were the assorted males in this difficult case? Mark Ledger, how Harriet would love it to be him, but she doubted he would have the guts to do something murderous. Despite his roguish good looks, he presented as something of a wimp. Or did she think that after seeing the video of Doris Lester annihilating him?

Patrick Ledger came across as a caring person who had loved Melanie, but what if he had found out about her and her assorted infidelities. Would it have been enough to push him into killing her in a rage? Did he know Mark was one of her conquests?

The obnoxious Kevin Vickers was high on the list. Melanie had seemingly made it clear she didn't want him, but could it have led to him murdering her? He could have been pushed to extreme limits when Juliet walked out on him, taking their children with her.

And there was Dan, Rosie's husband. Did he fit into this jigsaw in any way? They'd only spoken to him once; he seemed to work away a lot, but he was a suspect, nevertheless. He was part of this somewhat-dysfunctional family. Harriet felt she needed to check his alibi for that Thursday night. All they had was that he was away, and didn't come home till Friday. Who was he with on the evening before his return home?

Harriet took out an A5 notebook with pictures of butterflies on the front, and made notes, dredging up everything she could remember about each of the men who were involved in the investigation. Writing things down had always helped her, made her focus her thoughts instead of trying to lump together random ideas and information.

She moved on to the next page and wrote down the women involved, making a special note of their alibis. They all had one.

Harriet sat back with a degree of surprise. They all had one. Not one of the women involved in this case could have murdered Melanie Brookes. Every single one appeared to have a solid alibi, backed up without a doubt by the people giving them the alibi.

'Well,' Harriet muttered, 'who the fuck did kill her then if everybody can prove they were doing something at the time Melanie was killed?'

Could it be some random person they had yet to discover? She thought not. There had been no sexual assault, Melanie had simply been strangled. This crime didn't follow the usual pattern for murder by a chancer in the wrong place at the wrong time.

Deep in her heart, Harriet knew what had to happen next. One of these people was lying. One of them had killed Melanie and had given an alibi that wouldn't stand up to deep scrutiny. Starting Monday morning, she would double and triple check every single one. And she would do it personally, because she doubted anybody else on the team would have spent their Sunday afternoon going over and over the case – this task was hers, and tomorrow she would take the butterfly book with her thoughts and exclamation marks into the office with her, and she would work on it until it became clear who the liar was.

She made a pot of Earl Grey and fished out her china cup and saucer, then carried her tray through to the lounge. She waited a couple of minutes before pouring out her drink. She was halfway down her first cup when she heard Adeline call out for her mummy.

Thinking time over, hello Peppa Pig, Harriet thought as she climbed the stairs. She lifted Addie out of the cot and together they counted their way back downstairs. 'One, two, three, four, five...'

'Eight!' Addie said triumphantly, and Harriet knew it was definitely *Peppa Pig* time.

Rosie and Shirley sat in Shirley's kitchen, drinking wine. Dan and Megan had gone to the cinema, dropping Rosie off along the way at her sister's new house, so they decided any excuse for a bottle of wine was excuse enough.

'So the boys spoke to their father last night?'

'Yep. He was... angry, I think is the word, but it wasn't with them, it was all targeting me. I'm not worrying, he'll have somebody else soon enough.'

'He didn't argue for having the boys himself?'

Shirley laughed. 'No, but I had no worries on that score anyway. He was always proud of having twin boys, they were a bit of a status symbol to him. Look how virile I am, I can produce two at once sort of thing, but that was the extent of it with him really. He had no involvement in their upbringing, and he's never done anything mundane like change a nappy. I knew he wouldn't want them in a situation where he had to do stuff for them. As soon as the schools are back after this break, I'll be finding one for Adam and Seth, one in which they'll be happy and can come home every night, and they'll be my responsibility.'

Rosie lifted her glass of wine. 'Here's to you and the kids. Now, do you need me to help with anything while I'm here? They're picking me up around six, so we've a couple of hours.'

'You've not seen the lounge?' Shirley smiled. 'It's a disaster. They delivered my suite first thing this morning, so that's dumped in there. I've a coffee table to erect, that's still in a box, and I've a television to sort out.'

Rosie moved towards the lounge to see for herself.

'Oh, and there's a...'

'Kitchen table and four chairs.' Rosie finished the sentence for her sister. 'Right, let's get these garden chairs folded and put outside and we'll load them into the car when Dan comes back for me, then we can move that old table back out into your garden. This room actually resembles a furniture store.'

'I know. The neighbours will think I'm having an affair with the Argos driver, he's been that often since Friday.'

By the time Dan and Megan arrived, order had been restored and Shirley had requested a vacuum cleaner from Argos, for delivery the following day. The lounge was comfortable, although lacking in softer lighting, pictures and other things that would turn it into a home, but overall, it was clear Shirley was pleased with the result.

Dan connected up the television and DVD player and switched it on. He tuned it in and handed his sister-in-law the two remote controls. 'There you go, set up for *Midsomer Murders* tonight.'

Shirley looked around her lounge, tidy, everything where it should be, and sighed. 'I'm going to be happy here, I know I am. Thank you so much for your help today. My boys haven't been exactly helpful, but to be honest I get more done if they're up in their rooms. They're in Adam's room playing on their iPads. They sleep in their own rooms, but gravitate towards one or the other during the day. They've always done that. That's why it must have been so awful for them going to that ridiculous school. It's stopped now, they'll become normal little lads and not the manufactured mini-adults Mark saw them becoming.'

Dan gave his sister-in-law a hug. 'You'll be fine, the three of you. And we're only a phone call and ten minutes away. Faster, if Megan gets on her broomstick.'

Megan punched her dad and grinned. 'I'm going up to have a few minutes with the boys before we go home. Go and make a cup of tea for these two, Dad. I would have done it, but in view of sarky comments...' She disappeared upstairs, and Dan shook his head, wondering exactly where they had found this feisty daughter, and could they swap her for a kitten?

Rosie and Shirley sat in the lounge waiting for their designated slave to appear with cups of tea, and Dan went outside to load the car with the garden chairs. He put them in, then came back inside to make the tea.

The two women were talking business strategy when he carried the tray through to them. Rosie had briefly touched on the order she had taken, but she was explaining it to Shirley. 'I'll make a start on the basic journal, but you're so much better than me at putting the whole thing into a cohesive collection of the ephemera, and this is a special one. We've six weeks to do it, and it's a bridal theme. She's given us a budget of two hundred pounds, so we'll get a special box for it. The customer is buying it for her daughter as a wedding gift. I know we said we wouldn't work through school holidays, but we're a bit behind with other orders after your disappearing act. I'll do some during this week. Megan is getting pretty good at the tiny notebooks and the journaling tags, so I can trust her with those. As soon as you've got the twins in a school, we need to get back to work.'

'That's fine. I'm so sorry I seem to have cocked everything up with my actions, but I think you saw it coming. You knew how unhappy I was, but I couldn't tell you I was leaving because I didn't know. I honestly only went out for a drive. But I'm back now, stronger and better.'

28

The sun was flexing its muscles by eight on Monday morning, and Grace took off her jacket and put it on the back seat. It would be hot in the car, and wearing something extra wouldn't help.

Her first stop of the day was her workplace, where the briefing, the first of the week, was to begin at nine. The main office was already busy, and the hubbub made her smile. She always enjoyed the early morning noise when her team were deciding who was scheduled to do what and in what order, and her face held a smile as she opened her office door.

Harriet was waiting for her, clutching a notebook covered in butterflies. 'I've been thinking.'

Grace hung up her jacket that looked like being a useless article for the rest of the day, and turned to her sergeant. 'When did you do this thinking? Would that be during the time I sent you home to look after your daughter?'

'Addie was in bed. Look...' Harriet opened the book.

'Can I sit down first?'

'Oh, sorry, boss. This is winding me up. I've written down every name of everybody who could be a potential killer amongst the people we've already interviewed, and nobody did the deed.'

'Really?' Grace grinned at the enthusiasm pouring from Harriet.

'Really. Every single person on this list has a rock-solid alibi.'

Grace pulled the book towards her and took a couple of minutes to read Harriet's copious notes. 'Mmm. Mark Ledger doesn't have an alibi.'

'I know, but he does have two phones, one a landline and one the new mobile he had to go out and buy that day because he'd lost his on the way home when he was drunk. And the data from those phones shows that he was on them constantly on Thursday night, ringing Shirley, ringing Rosie, ringing Patrick, he even rang Melanie. That man was desperate to find his wife on Thursday night, and I'm not kidding myself it's because he wanted her back, I think it was more that she had the utter gall to leave him, rather than him kicking her out. And most of the calls were made on the landline, which kind of ties him to his home.'

'You don't like him, then?'

'No I bloody don't, but I don't like him for the murder either. I don't think he's got the balls to kill somebody. He uses threats, and issues orders, but deep down he's a pathetic little man, a bully. I reckon he had Shirley properly under his thumb. Thank God she's got out.'

'I think you're right,' Grace conceded. 'About Mark, I mean. I think you've got him spot on. But he's got a brother, and that brother's alibi for that night was that he was in bed.'

'Exactly. He didn't come up with something he'd set up,

didn't involve anyone else in his alibi, he simply said he had an early night because he wasn't seeing Melanie, and they'd had a heavy night the night before. I spoke to Sam about how Patrick took the news, and he said there was no way Patrick was faking it, he was floored by it, deeply upset, couldn't even tell Mark, simply wanted him to come over. It doesn't sit right with me that he could have done it, and the lack of an alibi tells me he didn't.'

'Okay. I'll take that. I'm going to see him later, so I'll push his buttons, see what I can shake loose. You want to come? I'm going to see Imogen North also. She's the eyes and ears of that business, being on reception, so I want to tweak her memory a bit, see if we can shake anything out of her. She goes to a café down the road from where she works, The Buttered Bun it's called, so I said I'd meet her there at quarter past twelve. Her lunch break's twelve till one.'

'I will. But when I get back I'm straight on to this. One of these people killed Melanie Brookes, so somebody is lying.'

Doris and Wendy had decided it wouldn't be a clever idea to walk into Global Systems and start chatting to Imogen North, they had to attack this differently. Deducing that lunch breaks could be any time from noon onwards, they parked up outside Global Systems' fenced compound at ten to twelve, and waited. The doors opened at twelve exactly and four laughing girls walked out. Doris and Wendy reviewed the photograph Doris had found on the company website depicting a smiling Imogen, double-checking that she wasn't one of the four girls. One minute later, Imogen followed them, but stayed back.

'She doesn't want to be with them,' Wendy remarked. 'Wonder why?'

'Meeting somebody, you reckon? Boyfriend, maybe.'

'I don't know, but it could make our job impossible if she is.'

Doris started the car, and they drove slowly, watching Imogen's journey down the road. They could see the four girls who had exited prior to their quarry, but they were some distance down the road. Imogen turned to her right and went into a shop.

'It's a café,' Wendy said. 'That's a café noticeboard outside it.'

Doris pulled into the side of the road, and they both got out; within a minute they were in the café and sitting at the next table to Imogen.

The waitress took Imogen's order, then moved to their table where they ordered ham salad sandwiches and coffee.

Doris smiled at Imogen, who smiled back. 'Nice little coffee shop, isn't it,' Doris said.

'Very nice. I come here most days.'

'You live locally?'

'Work. Just up the road.'

'Really? I had a niece who worked up the road, at Global Systems. I used to meet her in here for a drink. We've come here today to raise a coffee to her, she recently passed away.'

'Oh my God,' Imogen squealed. 'You mean Melanie?'

Doris nodded. 'You knew her?'

'I did. We were good friends. That's awful... I'll really miss her.'

The waitress leaned in between the two tables, and delivered all three lunches. They thanked her and Doris, keen to keep the lines open, turned to Imogen once more.

'Was there anybody at work who would have done this to her? She was such a lovely girl... I can't imagine...'

'Everybody loved Melanie,' Imogen said, her voice serious. 'If Mr Vickers would have left her alone, she would have been much happier. But he's on his own now, because his wife's walked out on him. Oh, I'm sorry, I know you're grieving for your niece, and I didn't want it to sound as though it was Mel's fault that Mrs Vickers had left Mr Vickers. I'm sure it wasn't. It was never serious between them, at least, not on her part.'

Doris was saying a silent thank you for having been gifted with the office gossip when the door opened. She had the grace to blush. Caught in the act by the two people she would never have expected to walk in.

'Miss North, Mrs Lester, Mrs Lucas,' Grace said quietly. 'Who would ever have expected to find all three of you together in here?'

Doris and Wendy finished their sandwiches, drank their coffee and stood to leave. Grace Stamford and Harriet Jameson ordered their food, and deliberately refrained from speaking about anything important to Imogen until the two women had left. Doris and Wendy said goodbye, and went out, holding in the emotion until they were back at their car.

'Oh my Lord. Think we're in trouble?' Wendy was doubled over with laughter.

'What trouble? We know nothing. We simply called in there for a drink because our niece used to go there. Okay, she's not our niece, but that's a slip of the tongue. Can I say, Wendy Lucas, your face was a picture when they walked in.'

'And yours wasn't? Think we'll have some explaining to do?'

'I'm explaining nothing. I probably outrank her anyway. You don't though. She might arrest you.' Again Doris burst into laughter. 'Want to call and see Shirley?'

'Are we confessing to this?'

'Why not. She'll be impressed we know Imogen North, because I bet she doesn't. Let's go and buy her some flowers for a housewarming present. Let's try being nice.'

'You don't like her, do you?' Curiosity was etched on Wendy's face.

'I don't know. She doesn't seem to be anything like Rosie, but Rosie is like Harry, and so is Megan. I suspect Shirley is more like her mother.'

Doris called in to a Tesco and bought an orchid, beautiful, a deep rose pink, deciding it would last longer than a bunch of flowers, and picked up a tub of Haribo sweets for the boys to share.

Five minutes later they pulled up outside Shirley's, and spotted the boys doing some work in the garden. Shirley was giving them instructions and they seemed to be laughing at her.

Shirley waved at the two ladies as they got out of the car, and walked across to them. She kissed them both on their cheeks, and Doris handed her the orchid.

'A housewarming gift from us,' Doris said. 'We hope you have many happy years here.'

Wendy handed over the tub of sweets. 'And these are for the boys. Please don't blame us when they become uncontrollable later.'

Shirley looked at the sweets. 'Do you have any idea what these do to kids?'

They both nodded.

'Thanks. Boys, you have a gift,' she called, and Adam and Seth walked over, happy to leave the gardening.

'Oh, wow. Can we go in now, Mum?'

'Do not empty that tub,' Shirley said in warning. 'They're to last a week at least.'

They adopted solemn faces and ran.

'Cup of tea?' Shirley asked, holding the orchid and admiring it. 'This is stunning, thank you so much.'

They walked into the kitchen, surprised to see how much everything had changed since their last visit. It looked like a normal kitchen, and Shirley told them to check out the lounge.

They walked back into the kitchen as she placed drinks on the table. 'It looks wonderful,' Wendy said.

'Rosie and Dan helped. I'd kind of run out of steam, but they took over and as a result it looks like this.' She waved a hand encompassing the whole house. 'I feel so settled. I went to see Mrs Hill this morning to sort out how to pay her, and we've reached an agreement that when I have some money from my divorce, I will be buying this. It's perfect for me, and the school for the boys is a five-minute bus journey away.'

'I'm so pleased for you,' Doris said. 'And the boys like it?'

'They love it. I heard them arguing about something this morning, and I let them get on with it. That would never have been allowed with Mark in the vicinity. They weren't allowed to be children.'

Doris and Wendy sat at the table, and Shirley placed a biscuit barrel in front of them. 'Please, help yourself.'

'I don't think we could eat even a biscuit.' Wendy laughed. 'Would you like to know what we've been up to this morning? Would you really like to know how one of Doris's plans went crazily wrong, and gave us such a laugh like we haven't had in years?'

29

Grace watched the two women turn left outside the café, and she put down her cup.

'We can speak now, Imogen. Did those two ladies say why they were here?'

'Yes, they said they were aunts of Melanie Brookes. They're not press, are they?' Her eyes widened in alarm.

'No, don't worry. One of them is a family member, kind of. Did you say anything at all to them?'

She shook her head. 'No, we only said it was a nice coffee shop.'

Satisfied, Grace relaxed. It seemed that inadvertently she and Harriet had arrived at the right time. 'Okay, we have a couple of questions for you about telephone calls. During the afternoon prior to Melanie's death you told us you rang her to see if she needed anything for her York presentation. Did you ring her on her mobile?'

'I always ring her on her mobile, it's the automatic number keyed into my machine. Although I have her landline number, I would have had to look it up.'

'And you rang her before four?'

'I did. I get busy with mail between four and five so I try to get everything done by four that's routine stuff. I leave every day at five to five because I drop any mail off at the post office before I go home.'

'So what happens with the switchboard?'

'It's put on to automatic. All incoming calls go direct to the answering service, and if anyone is still working and needs to ring out, they dial nine to get a line, followed by the number. It's only admin staff who leave at five, there's always people still there when I leave.'

'This includes Mr Vickers?'

'Definitely. He's there after me every night.'

'So to confirm, you made a mobile number call to Melanie Brookes just before four o'clock, and that was the last time you spoke to her?'

'Yes, that's right.'

'So if a call was made to Melanie after five it would have to be made by someone still in the building who dialled nine first.'

'Yes. My switchboard does keep a list of which extension dialled which number though. I don't bother checking it, it's usually people ringing home to say they're on their way, but as you can imagine, working for Global Systems, everything works super efficiently, everything's monitored, and I can even print out the call log for that night if you happened to need it.' She gave a long slow wink to Grace, who burst out laughing.

'And my next question was going to be can you print the call log for us.'

Grace put the car into gear and set off for headquarters, where Harriet, she knew, was itching to get on and crack an alibi. 'She was no dumbo, was she? Her train of thought led her straight to what she knew we would want. Massive gossip though, and that's not ideal in a receptionist. Still, when Kevin Vickers realises she's telling all and sundry his business, he'll get rid of her and legitimately. She'll have learned a valuable lesson when she gets her next job.'

They had driven Imogen back to work and collected the printout. Kevin Vickers hadn't been happy to see them, but Grace had applied some charm and asked him about the phone call, made after five on the evening of Melanie's death.

He had spluttered a little, said it was only a couple of minutes, and they had discussed her presentation, and agreed on a Monday morning meeting for feedback.

Vickers said nothing about his suggestion to meet Melanie in York at her hotel, and Mel's definite no to that idea. He watched as the two women left his office, mental darts directed at their backs. Crossing to the window, he timed how long it took to get from his office to their car, and knew they had stopped to talk to bloody Imogen North. Somebody was feeding them information; they hadn't come up with the printout idea on their own, he guessed. The stupid bitch had to go when this inconvenience was all over and done with.

Grace put on her jacket to make her look more official, collected Sam Ellis for the trip to reinterview Patrick Ledger, and headed for her car. She felt enough time had lapsed since the first interview for him to have got over the initial shock, but she wasn't prepared to see how ill he looked. His weight had dropped, and he apologised for wearing joggers, saying his trousers and jeans kept slipping down. He could tie his joggers in place.

'I'm sorry we've had to turn up on your doorstep like this,

Patrick, but our initial interview was kept really brief. And obviously in the intervening time we have collected new information. We need to give this to you, and we need to hear your thoughts now that some time has passed.'

Sam Ellis was impressed. Grace had softened; she didn't come across as the most caring of DCIs, although she did appear as the most efficient. He knew what information she had to share with Patrick, and he guessed it was why she was mollifying her approach.

'Sam, can you make us all a cuppa, and then we'll chat, please?' The young DC stood to go into the kitchen.

'The milk's fresh,' Patrick said. 'Mark brought it yesterday, said he was fed up with black coffee.'

'You saw Mark yesterday? Did he make you aware that Shirley's been found, and she has the boys safely with her?'

'He did. I told him he'd lose everything by being such a dick with her, but to be truthful, I don't think he's that bothered. He's going to fight having to give her any money for her half share of the house, but he's living in cloud cuckoo land if he thinks he'll get away with that. He's not even mentioned Adam and Seth, and they're lovely kids. I hope Shirley lets me still see them, they're my nephews after all.'

'I think Shirley is taking the stance that the boys will decide. She said she's not going to make them see their father, they must choose, and that is the way it will be for all their lives. They understand. I'm sure they'll choose to see their uncle.' She smiled. 'How is Mark?'

'A mess, if I'm being honest. As big a mess as me. The difference is I'm a mess inside, he's a mess on the outside. He's wearing joggers because he's nothing else to wear, not because his trousers and jeans are falling down. He asked me how to use the washing machine yesterday. The iron will completely fox him.'

As if on cue, the washing machine kicked on to the spin cycle and Grace laughed. 'You clearly know how to use it.'

'It's an experiment,' he said ruefully. 'I've chucked four pairs of jeans and a couple of T-shirts in on a boil wash and I'm hoping between that and the tumble dryer they'll shrink. I wasn't joking when I said they're falling down.'

Sam passed around the cups of tea, and joined the other two at the table. They had gravitated automatically to the kitchen; it had been where they were when Sam had told him of the discovery of Melanie's body.

Grace sipped at her drink, preparing herself. 'We're calling in on Mark after we leave here, we have a few questions for him. When he came yesterday, what did he tell you?'

'Not much. I think he was hoping I'd heard from Shirley, that I would know where she was, but I haven't. I don't believe she'll contact me, she knows what's happened with Mel, and she probably thinks I'd tell Mark. I wouldn't. I've watched her change over the years, and I know it's down to Mark. I love my brother, DCI Stamford, but I don't like him very much.'

Grace took a deep breath. 'Okay, we have information for you that we know will come as a shock, but I need to tell you before it becomes common knowledge when we find Melanie's killer. And we will. Mark Ledger was having an affair with Melanie.'

Grace waited for a reaction, and got one. Patrick burst out

laughing. 'Don't be ridiculous. He wouldn't do that. Melanie wouldn't either.'

'Patrick, listen to me for a moment. I wouldn't be coming here saying that to you if it wasn't categorically the truth. Her affair at the moment was with Mark, but there have been others.'

The laughter stopped as Patrick recognised the truth behind her words. His face blanched. 'Others? I asked her to marry me, after we had made love on Wednesday night. She said yes.'

'I suspect it was maybe drink talking,' Grace said gently.

'But... Mark? It doesn't bear thinking about. Why hasn't he told me? He must have known it would come out, yet he's left me to hear it from you.' Patrick stood and hitched up his joggers. 'I need to see him.'

'Not this afternoon. First of all, you need to calm down. Secondly, you need to remember he is your brother, but he's not completely to blame in this. Melanie could have said no, and she didn't.'

Patrick wiped away a tear he didn't want Grace to see, then turned to her. 'You said others? What do you mean? I was marrying a hooker?'

Grace shook her head. 'Not at all, but during our investigation two other names have come to light. I'm not going to give them to you at this stage, but I may have to at some point. We felt it was important that you knew about Mark, in case any of this reaches the newspapers. And I will tell you that you will get either a visit or a phone call from DS Jameson probably today. She's checking alibis for the night Melanie was killed, and you don't have one. I suggest you write down a minute-by-minute detailed description of everything you did. She's like a ferret and she's doing this with every person connected in any way to Melanie. She's decided somebody is lying, and she's going to find out who it is. Do you have anything else to tell us at this time?' Grace placed her empty cup on the table, and saw Sam was making notes.

The spin cycle ended with a clunk, and slowly the drum stopped rotating, revealing denim in the concave window. Patrick stared at it, distracted; appearing thrown by everything he had heard.

'I can't say anything,' he said. 'I don't know what to say. I loved her, Mel. I thought we would be together for ever, and it turns out she preferred my brother. Oh my God, does Shirley know?'

'She does. I actually thought he would have had the guts to tell you himself because he's probably guessed Shirley knows, but he seems to be lacking in courage.'

'I thought he was ill when he arrived yesterday, he was limping and didn't look good. Said he'd fallen down some stairs, so I left it at that.'

Grace tried to hide her smile. 'He was in a bit of a rough and tumble. No stairs were involved, but he did end up on the floor, with seriously inflated testicles. If you want some ammunition to give you a bit of satisfaction, a woman put him there, but I haven't told you that. Have I, Sam?'

'No, ma'am, I heard nothing.'

She stood and Sam followed her lead. 'We're heading over for a chat with Mark now, please don't ring him and warn him we're coming. You owe him nothing.'

Patrick wiped his eyes and nodded. 'I feel as if she's died all over again, you know. I'm hurting as much as when Sam first said the body was hers. Does it ever end?'

'The hurting will. Just not yet, not till we can give you full closure with the name of the killer. Take care, Patrick.'

30

Grace removed her jacket for the drive to Mark Ledger's house; the sun was emitting far too much heat for her to handle. She knew she would put the navy blazer back on when she spoke to Mark; it stamped her authority and she felt she needed it with such a snake to contend with.

'Do I have to make a brew here?' Sam said.

'No you don't. Not altogether sure I believe he'll have washed any pots, so we'll pass on the drink, I think. Isn't it funny how you can take a real dislike to some people. I can't see anything nice about Mark Ledger, and yet I don't believe for a minute he had anything to do with Melanie's death, not directly anyway. Maybe indirectly...'

Sam sensed his boss was thinking out loud and he decided not to respond but to wait.

'Indirectly...' Grace repeated. 'Who knew about this affair and decided to keep quiet about it? Sam, talk to me.'

'God knows. Shirley Ledger? Rosie Steer?'

'It doesn't sit easy with me that Shirley knew about it. She left Mark the day before Melanie died and she could have easily used that as her reason, but she didn't. Nobody would have worried and I wouldn't have had half of my team out looking for her. I can't see it being her. They always say the wife is the last to know anyway.'

'Huh,' Sam said, 'my wife would know before I did.'

They reached the Ledger residence ten minutes later, and because Mark's car was on the drive, Grace shrugged on her jacket. She hoped she wouldn't be tempted to refer to the hammering he'd received from Doris Lester – and, her mind shouted at her, how the bloody hell did Doris Lester know about Imogen North, and what was she doing in that café?

'Sam,' she said slowly, 'when we get back, remind me to check out Doris Lester and Wendy Lucas.'

He grinned. 'You have Doris Lester down for a suspect?'

'No, but she's been on the periphery of this investigation from the start and I get the feeling she knows as much as we do, which is a bit disconcerting. I'd like to know more about her.'

They walked up the path and rang the bell. There was no response so they rattled on the door knocker, followed by hammering with fists. Eventually Sam bent down and yelled *Mr Ledger* through the letterbox.

'Let's look round the back. He may be in the garden.'

Grace led Sam down the paved path at the side of the house and into the rear garden, but there was no sign of life beyond a bird sitting on a branch.

'Strange that his car's here,' Grace said, and banged on the kitchen door.

Sam shielded his eyes and peered through the window. Mark Ledger was on a kitchen chair, slumped across the table, blood pooled under his feet.

. . .

The crime scene team were there within twenty minutes, and although access was available through the unlocked kitchen door, Sam and Grace knew they couldn't go in. Sam had offered to find something in the garden shed to place on the floor so he could check life was extinct, but Grace said no. 'We can't risk contaminating this, so we'll close the door, make sure nothing gets in. It's pretty obvious he's dead, nobody could be alive with that amount of blood on the floor.'

Harriet and Fiona arrived and followed Grace and Sam's lead in donning white suits. The forensic team were meticulously mapping out a splatter pattern, taking photographs, generally keeping the police officers at bay until they had something to report. They had quickly confirmed death, and that it was a slash across the throat that had caused it. The perpetrator would have blood on him or her, that much they could guarantee. There was no sign of the murder weapon.

The four team members sat around the garden table, with Harriet responsible for taking any notes. There was precious little in her book; no time of death estimate, an identification that any one of them could have given, and no weapon.

'We have to notify Shirley in the first instance, before anyone else. Then Patrick. I have no idea if the brothers have parents, but I'm assuming if they do that Patrick will notify them. What a fucking mess.' Grace was angry. They were still no closer to identifying Melanie's killer, and now they had a second murder almost certainly connected to the first one, and no further on with bringing anybody in for questioning under caution.

Owen Bridger walked over to speak with the four officers, and sat at the table with them. 'Nasty business. It took two slashes, so whoever did it didn't know what he was doing, he was hesitant. He did it from behind.' Owen stood up and moved to stand behind Sam. 'Like this.' He grabbed Sam's hair and pulled his head back, exposing his throat. He drew his hand across Sam's throat from left to right, then repeated the action. 'Twice,' Owen said. 'He did it twice. He must have been covered in blood – oh, sorry, Sam, you've gone grey.'

'Perhaps you can give me some warning next time you cut my throat?'

'I'll try, lad, I'll try. I wanted to show your boss how it was done. Whoever's done it is right-handed, and I would say fairly tall, which is why I'm saying it's a male, but a tall female could just as easily have done it. It's not a normal way of killing someone, if you're a woman. Really rare.'

'Thank you, Owen. Any idea when it happened?'

'I would say between eight and ten this morning. This hot weather is stopping me being more accurate than that, but when I do the autopsy I'll know more. I think we're about ready to move the body, and then the scene is yours. See you at two, Grace?'

She nodded, unsmiling. Maybe she could talk Harriet into going...

All four of them stood as the body was taken round the side of the house and out to the waiting coroner's van. The crime scene had been confined to the kitchen, and nobody really wanted to face it. So much blood.

Fiona and Sam had been despatched to visit neighbours' houses, asking if anything unusual had happened, had there been any visitors to the Ledger house, or even had they seen Mark that morning.

The forensic team inside the kitchen were finishing up, and with the body no longer the focal point, the blood was.

'Jesus,' Harriet said. 'Whoever did this must have had some blood on him. Surely somebody saw him. Or her.'

Grace held up a hand. 'Let me think. My brain's churning like a whirlwind. Patrick's house is in walking distance from here, yes?'

'Yes. You think he's in danger?'

'No, I think he is the danger. Supposing he went down the back garden and through the hedge. It's only privet, it's not made of iron. Is it conceivable he could go over the fields without anybody seeing him?'

Harriet stared at her boss. 'Are you serious? You think Patrick's done this? Why? You've only just told him about Melanie and Mark, haven't you?'

Grace stared down the garden, looking for damage to the hedge. She saw it. Not massive damage, not really damage at all because a couple of days would see it spring back to its normal position, but more disturbed branches. She walked down to it and looked over the top. She could see houses in the far distance, and calculated that Patrick's house was a minute further on than the ones she had in view. The whole scene as she believed it had happened flashed through her mind like a film.

Patrick had said Mark had visited on the Sunday – *the milk is fresh, Mark brought it yesterday* – and she knew with such certainty that Mark had confessed to his affair with Mel. He would have been scared of Shirley telling her version of events in an act of revenge.

'The jeans! The fucking jeans in the washer!' Grace ran her hands through her hair. 'When we were there two hours ago the machine was about to finish a wash cycle. It had jeans in it. And a T-shirt. I'd bet a year's wages they were covered in blood before he put them on a boil cycle.'

She took out her phone. Her voice was crisp as she relayed

instructions for a team to get to Patrick Ledger's home and take him in for questioning. She wanted forensics on the washer, the tumble dryer and any jeans that could possibly still be in the dryer. And she wanted a bloodstained knife finding.

They found the knife on the draining board, in the cutlery drainer, washed but with traces of what looked like blood in the crack where the blade was inserted into the handle. The jeans and top had been taken out of the dryer and folded without expertise, and an unconscious Patrick Ledger had been rushed to hospital, with a suspected overdose from a variety of tablets.

Grace didn't reach the hospital until after nine that evening. Harriet had accompanied her to Shirley's house after finishing at Mark's house, and had spent a difficult hour there telling her of her husband's death. They had waited until Rosie arrived to comfort her sister before leaving.

Rosie followed them to the door, leaving Shirley and the twins wrapped in fleecy blankets, cuddling on the sofa and all three crying.

'So it's definitely Patrick who killed him? You're sure?'

'We're sure. I'm dropping Harriet off to get her car, then I'm going to see what's happening at the hospital. I'll keep you both informed, but he will be arrested as soon as he comes round. We have enough evidence, he left it in plain sight.'

'And Melanie?' Rosie asked.

'A completely separate investigation,' Grace said with a shake of her head. 'Patrick Ledger isn't under suspicion for that murder at all. He had no reason to want Melanie dead. In fact, quite the opposite, she'd agreed to become his wife the night before.'

'Please tell me you don't think Mark killed Mel. It would finish Shirley off, I think.'

'Melanie Brookes' death is still under investigation. I can't say any more than that at the moment. Are you staying here tonight?'

'I am. The boys are shell-shocked, I think. I need to support them all, see them safely through this. Adam and Seth must be wondering what's happening, all this turmoil and upheaval in their lives, and everything in the space of a couple of weeks.'

'Go and make that cup of tea for Shirley, and I suggest a tot of brandy in it, if she has any. She needs sleep, she's going to need a lot of strength over the next few days.'

Grace drove back to headquarters and watched until Harriet drove out of the car park, heading home. Adrenaline was still racing around Grace's body, so she parked and ran up the stairs to her office.

She switched on her computer and waited patiently for it to come to life. Entering her password, Grace smiled to herself. *Right, Mrs Doris Lester, let's see what we can find out about you, and why it feels as though you're one step in front of us mere mortals.*

31

The late-night email that landed in Doris's private and password-protected inbox had thrown her completely. Mark dead, Patrick unconscious following an overdose, hospitalised and an arrest on the cards as soon as he recovered – her thoughts had flown immediately to Rosie and Shirley and their children, but she had no way of legitimately contacting them. Officially she knew nothing.

She was awake and downstairs by seven, checking to see if any more information had filtered through, but there was nothing. She knew she could tell Wendy without questions being asked, although she doubted she would get away with withholding answers.

Wendy appeared behind her, her dressing gown loosely tied around her waist, her dark grey hair a mess. 'You're ill?'

'No, I'm fine.'

'But you're up. It's only seven. That means something's wrong. And if you're not ill, it's something to do with Hucknall. You think I'm stupid?'

Doris gave a short laugh. 'No, you're spot on. If I tell you something, you have to accept that I know it, and as far as anybody else is concerned, when we hear about it we didn't know prior to just hearing it.'

'What?' Wendy sat at the kitchen table, waiting for Doris to repeat it in English instead of double Dutch.

'Something's happened, and because I know somebody who knows most things in this life, I now know it through that person. Yes?'

'Is it a man? Is it something I should know about?'

'It's a person. That person knows we have interests in the murder of Melanie Brookes and something has happened that's linked to it, so my friend has emailed me with the details as far as they go at this moment in time. Do you understand?'

'Perfectly. I might need coffee. No, strike that. I definitely do need coffee. Is it too early for a tot of whiskey in it?'

'Twelve hours too early. You want to go and get dressed while I do breakfast? I'll tell you everything when you come back down, then I think we should take a trip out to Hucknall. We might be needed and if we aren't we'll come back home.'

'Good thinking.' Wendy stood. 'Perhaps you can put your brain into gear while I'm having a shower, and tell me everything in words of one syllable only when I get back downstairs.'

Doris looked surprised. 'I thought I had.'

'Huh. I wish I'd recorded our conversation. Nobody would credit gobbledegook like it at this time in a morning. You been awake all night?'

'Most of it. Go on. You want scrambled eggs or bacon?'

'Sausage with tomato dip, on a breadcake. Don't mess me about with this, Lester, I feel as though I'm going to need maximum fuel today.'

· · ·

They were halfway through their sausage sandwiches when the door knocker rattled. Doris glanced at her watch. 'It's only eight. It'll be the postman. He'll leave it in the blue bin.'

She took another bite, and the door knocker, shaped as a little mouse, rattled again. 'Little Mouse Cottage is being invaded,' Wendy said. 'It might be Luke. Shall I go?'

'If you must. If it's a delivery man you have my permission to push him in the blue bin alongside his damn parcel.'

It proved to be DCI Grace Stamford. She sat at the table with them, and waited while Wendy cooked her a sausage and tomato sandwich. With the back door open, the sun came straight through, glancing off the top of the table and lighting up Grace's face. And her tired eyes.

'You look tired, DCI Stamford,' Doris said, sympathy in her voice. 'I wouldn't have your job for a pension.'

'And the pension's not that great,' Grace said. 'Tell me, Mrs Lester, what do you call DI Marsden and DS Granger?'

Doris looked puzzled. 'Tessa and Hannah unless other police officers are present, then we give them their titles. It's an unwritten rule at Connection.'

'My name is Grace. May I call you Doris and Wendy?'

'You can call us Jack and Jill if it helps,' Wendy said with a laugh.

'I'll be frank with you, I'm jealous,' Grace said, smiling. 'I don't have anybody who calls me by my first name. I'm usually boss, or ma'am, and I speak with Tessa a lot so I know about your friendship with her, and how well you get along. I want somebody to talk with, to discuss cases, and I know she trusts you implicitly.'

'Thank you,' Doris said quietly, wondering where this was leading. 'Another coffee?'

Grace pushed her cup across with a thank you and Wendy filled their cups from the coffee pot. 'So,' Grace continued, 'I decided to find something out about this paragon of virtue called Doris Lester, and her fellow directors. I recognised the name Katerina Rowe, of course. Being married to Leon Rowe did her no favours. And Bethan Walters, granddaughter to Doris Lester, and part of the Leon Rowe investigation. I even discovered an affiliate, Luke Taylor, a member of the elite Connection team.'

She hesitated for a moment. 'I had no difficulty finding out the basic facts about Katerina, Bethan and Luke. Then my search ground to a halt. I had to really dig deep, and everything I saw about you, Doris, was mainly redacted.'

Doris smiled. 'I'm sorry, Grace, I'm not at liberty to comment.'

'That's a relief.' Grace laughed. 'At least I don't have to arrest you for breaking the Official Secrets Act. There'll be no more questions from me about what you have done or indeed do now, but I would still like to call you Doris.'

'Of course you can, but be assured you will be given your rank if we're with your colleagues. As I said, it's our rules. I don't want you to think we're reverting back to your official name and title, it will be because it's what we do.'

'That's brilliant. Now, tell me what you know.'

Doris felt at a loss. She knew as much as the DCI, but wondered how much this spirit of bonhomie would count for, if she told her what she knew. Officially they didn't know of Mark's death, let alone Patrick's future or non-future. 'I'm not sure what you mean.'

'If I told you we had another death, possibly two, what would you say?'

'What?' Wendy said for the second time that morning. This was, presumably, the information she had been about to receive from Doris when the little mouse rattled.

Doris said nothing, deciding silence might be the best way forward at the moment.

'I'm sorry to bring you this news but Mark Ledger was murdered yesterday.'

Once again Wendy said, 'What?'

Grace noticed Doris didn't even flinch, never mind speak. 'Nobody has rung to tell you? You've not heard from either Rosie or Shirley?'

As if on cue, Doris's phone pealed out. She looked at the screen. 'Rosie.'

Grace and Wendy remained silent for the duration of the call, aware that Doris was getting details not yet divulged by DCI Stamford. Neither of them knew she'd been fully cognisant of the details since the previous night.

She promised Rosie they'd be there as soon as they could, said goodbye and disconnected. 'So you believe Patrick killed him?' Doris asked Grace.

'I do. Patrick's own words were that Mark had visited him Sunday. We think Mark told him that he had been having an affair with Melanie, trying to get his version of the relationship in before Shirley told him. It's obvious that Patrick isn't in a good place mentally, and we believe he stewed on it, went over to Mark's early Monday morning and slit his throat. We do have evidence gathered from Patrick's place, stuff that's currently with forensics for analysis. When we went to Patrick's after finding Mark's body, he was unconscious. He'd taken a load of tablets washed down with a bottle of whiskey and it's by no means certain he's going to wake up.'

'As you probably gathered, we're going over to Hucknall this morning, there may be some way we can help. They almost feel like family now, even though they're not,' Doris said.

'I understand from Rosie that your husband had an affair with the girls' mother, that you knew nothing about?'

'That's correct. I see a lot of Harry – that's my late husband – in Megan, Rosie's daughter. She makes little comments and I immediately think that's like Harry. Bit disconcerting really. I only intended making contact with them once, so they understood Harry died fifteen years ago, but we seem to be in Hucknall more than we're in Bradwell.'

'I'm loving it,' Wendy said. 'I haven't had this much fun since we won ten thousand on the bingo.'

'Did you?' Grace raised her eyebrows, as if not sure whether to believe Wendy or not.

'We shared it, but yes we won it.'

'Wow.'

Doris laughed. 'Don't think we're inveterate gamblers. That was about eight years ago, I rarely go now, and the most we've won since then is about a tenner. That ten thousand was a national game.'

'You've known each other a long time?'

'Over forty years,' Wendy said. 'I thought I would lose that friendship when Doris moved out to Eyam, but she turned to me for help with the Leon Rowe thing, because I worked at a taxi firm and she knew I had contacts. That's when I knew the friendship wouldn't fade away.'

'You lived in Eyam?'

'Yes. When Beth was first injured we went to Kat's house to recuperate. Oh my, that husband of hers might have been an evil man, a killer, but he was mighty nice to look at. Beth sold her house in Sheffield and she eventually bought our Connection shop and the large flat above it, right in the centre of Eyam. I knew about this cottage coming onto the market, so I bought it, hence why I'm living in Bradwell. No more moves for me. I've felt a bit like a gypsy for the past three years.'

Grace smiled. 'I don't think there was a police station for miles around that didn't give a loud cheer when we heard Leon Rowe was dead. I know that's awful, but he controlled the drugs, he was responsible for many deaths – a bad lot all round. I feel as if I know you two a bit better now, despite the redactions. It seemed strange that I had only known of you, and even my team were in awe of the great Connection Agency. You have any thoughts on who killed Melanie Brookes?'

The question was abrupt, and took Doris a little by surprise. 'Yes, but for now some thoughts stay with me. I don't want to send you off in completely the wrong direction, so I'll think for a bit longer. I'm certain as I can be it wasn't Patrick. Everything was so normal with him. He knew her routine with the unavailability when she was working, he loved her and believed they were going engagement ring shopping at the weekend, and at that stage he knew nothing about Mark Ledger's dalliances with Mel. And those dalliances steer me away from Mark being involved in her death. He was too up himself to sink as low as murder. Probably too idle, also. He'd expect somebody to do it for him, but again, he'd no reason to kill her. No, whoever killed Melanie Brookes found out about her somewhat chequered sexual past, and it broke their heart. Who did she sleep with, which of her male acquaintances had a wife who objected to Melanie muscling in on their territory? Or could it be a man or woman she said no to? So that's my thoughts on it. It's a crime where sex has played a massive part, but I suspect a lot of jealousy comes into it somewhere down the line.'

As she finished speaking, Grace's phone rang, and she apologised and said she had to take it. She slipped outside into the back garden, and listened carefully. Doris and Wendy heard her say okay a couple of times, then she disconnected and returned to the kitchen.

'Patrick Ledger never regained consciousness. He died ten minutes ago.'

32

Rosie and Shirley were sitting at the kitchen table when Doris and Wendy arrived. The mood was sombre. Shirley had clearly been crying, and looked lost.

All four of them sat clutching coffee mugs. 'Your boys?' Doris asked. 'Are Adam and Seth here?'

Shirley nodded. 'They are. Megan's taken them out for a walk. They're totally bewildered. Death is a new experience for them. It was hard telling them about Mark, but I had to compound it with Patrick's death.'

'I'm sure the police will come up with answers soon,' Doris said slowly. 'We saw DCI Stamford this morning, and she told us she was going back to the station to give Harriet a hand with checking alibis. They'll find a discrepancy because there has to be one. Somebody hasn't told the truth, and apparently Harriet is on a mission to unmask the liar.'

'Oh brilliant,' Rosie said. 'I don't really have one, I was simply here, Megan in bed, and I went up before the news started at ten. Shirley has a better one than me, she was with Trudy.'

'I thought you said you went to your room before eight, Shirley?'

'I did. Couldn't keep my eyes open, it had been a stressful previous night when I left Mark, and a day of decision-making, don't forget. So my alibi is good, check with the sandman.'

Wendy watched as the conversation went around the table, her brain telling her that Doris was trying to get them to open up, and if it was necessary, to slip up. The deaths of Mark and Patrick Ledger had narrowed suspects down considerably. Wendy took out her notebook and wrote down one word, taxi. Doris had told her that no known cars belonging to any members of the family or friends had shown up that night in the locality of the bridge where Melanie had died – she hadn't queried how Doris knew, she merely accepted it was accurate. But supposing a taxi had dropped someone off near to Melanie's home, and that person had gone to Melanie for their evening run. It seemed that Melanie had worn the backpack she used for running, so there was no reason to suppose she was going out for any other reason. Wendy hid a grin at the next thought. She could do more than knit and crochet, she had a fleet of taxi owners and companies in her phone, all of whom she could contact easily.

Harriet popped her head around Grace's door. 'We need to talk to Juliet Vickers again.'

Grace lifted her head. 'We do? You'd consider her a definite suspect?'

'I do. Her husband was having an affair with Melanie Brookes. Juliet's alibi is that she doesn't have one. She said she went to bed when the kids did because she was tired, and her parents would agree with that. But that only means she went to bed. It doesn't mean she stayed there, does it?'

· · ·

With Megan's return, the discussion stopped. The boys took a ball out into the garden, borrowed four cushions from the lounge for goalposts, decided who was Manchester United and who was Manchester City, then yelled their way through the rest of the morning.

'I know it's awful of me to say this,' Shirley said pensively, 'but they wouldn't have done this at our house. Mark wouldn't have let them, too noisy.'

'You're staying at Rothery?' Doris asked.

'For the moment. I haven't made any decisions yet, obviously, it's too soon, and we love our cottage.'

Doris and Wendy had lunch at Rosie's home, then left shortly after to drive back to Bradwell.

'What's wrong?' Doris could sense something was out of kilter with Wendy. 'You poorly?'

Wendy laughed. 'No, itching to try something. If I get a result I'll let you know, but I might be clutching at straws.'

Belle miaowed as she heard them go through the front door, and she ran from wherever she had been to get into the kitchen before them.

Wendy reached down to stroke her ears, and knew she would miss the dainty little cat when it came time to leave. 'Hungry, Belle?' she asked and filled up her food bowl.

'Okay, you want to tell me what's on your mind?' Doris leaned against the door jamb.

'Yes, okay. It was Grace, something she said this morning about Harriet checking alibis because somebody was lying. Now, if your information is right...'

'It is.'

'Then there are four people who have iffy alibis. Rosie Steer, Shirley Ledger, Kevin Vickers and his wife Juliet.'

'They were all alone at home?'

'Virtually. Rosie Steer was home with Megan, but Megan is only twelve, and wouldn't go to bed late because of school. She also doesn't sleep in the same bed as her mother, and Dan was working away that night.'

'Shirley was with Trudy at the bed and breakfast.' Doris's brain was racing. 'But again she went to bed early, and she said before eight. However, Trudy said her car never moved until that day we turned up.'

'Keep going. Extend that thinking.' Wendy smiled. 'Come on, I'm turning into Agatha Christie here.'

'Damn! ANPR has been checked for their cars according to the information I have, and they haven't been seen anywhere in the area, but a taxi...'

'Exactly. So I need an hour to put together the addresses, the locations in general, and I need to contact the companies I've had dealings with over the last few years. There's a lot of them, but with computerised systems that they use now, I should start to get answers pretty quickly. What do you think?'

'Genius, Wendy Lucas. You need the laptop?'

Wendy laughed. 'No, I'm good. I've got my phone and my iPad. We may get nothing from this but if we do, it will be good to tell Grace, won't it? Think they'll make me a civilian consultant?'

'Doubt it, but worth asking.' Doris smiled. 'I'll do a cuppa, shall I?'

It took Wendy over an hour to work out what she needed to put in the email, the parameters of the journeys, and the date they needed to look at. She sent it to forty-three businesses, mostly people she had dealt with in the past, and a couple of new ones who were in the right areas. She used her title from when she had been at work, Senior Traffic Controller, and signed off as Wendy Lucas. She crossed her fingers and hit send.

'Done,' she said, sitting down beside Doris on the garden bench. 'I'll keep checking, see if we get any responses.' She rubbed her forehead.

'You okay?'

'Bit of a headache. It'll go soon enough now I've finished that. I'm not the smart cookie you are, you know. Takes me ages to do anything on a computer, but I get there in the end.'

'There's some paracetamol in the kitchen drawer. Take a couple.'

'Thanks. I need to get you some, I must have used nearly a full pack since I've been here.' Wendy stood and returned to the kitchen.

Doris's eyes remained on Wendy's back, a worried frown on her face. Why? Why was she taking painkillers? She stroked Belle's fur, and the cat purred. 'Come on, Belle,' she said, 'let's go find out what's wrong with Wendy.'

Wendy was standing by the table, a glass of water in her hand. She turned as Doris came through the door. 'It's nothing, honestly. I had a couple of TIAs, those mini stroke things, about six months ago, and their legacy is I get headaches. The doctor keeps a close eye on me, so there's no need to worry.'

'No need to worry? You're having strokes and I shouldn't worry?'

'I knew I shouldn't have told you. Honestly, I'm fine. I had scans and stuff, and I'm on medication. I'm not concerned about it, so you shouldn't be.'

Doris put her arms around Wendy and hugged her. 'You

have to take care. What would I do without you? Is there anything else you haven't told me?'

Wendy gave a huge sigh. 'Only one thing. I'm marrying Idris Elba next Saturday.'

'That's nice.' Doris grinned at her friend. 'Is my invite in the post?'

'Not bloody likely. If he sees you he'll realise I'm not the catch he thought I was. No, Doris Lester, you're not invited till I've got that ring on my finger. You can come to the christenings of our children.'

'You're greedy, Lucas, greedy. He should be shared. Now, shall we have a cup of tea to celebrate this marriage?' Doris clicked on the kettle, and Wendy sat at the table.

'Seriously, Doris, I'm fine. I'm going to check my iPad, see if we've had any replies to these emails. My headache will go in a few minutes, and we hopefully will have some news to get our heads around.'

It took a mere two hours to get the first response, a lovely chatty missive from an old friend who was coming to the end of his working life, but knew everybody there was to know. He sent her a long list of twenty names to contact, four of whom were new to her. He had also contacted them himself to say Wendy was looking for information. She would be getting in touch and needed answers pretty damn quick. He confirmed that no taxis in his fleet had been in the areas she specified, and ended his email with a kiss.

'He sounds nice.'

Wendy smiled. 'He is. We used to flirt a lot in our younger days, but he's happily married so it was only workplace flirting. It brightened our day and nightshifts considerably, I can tell you. And he was funny. I can always appreciate that in anybody.

I'll get some more emails off to the four I didn't think of, and then maybe we can go for a walk or something?'

'A walk?' Doris checked her watch. 'It's nearly five. We go for walks early morning when we're fit and pretending to be youthful and full of vigour, not in the evening when we're too tired to do anything but stand up and shuffle about.'

Wendy grinned. 'My headache's clearing fast, and I thought a nice thirty second stroll round to the Bowling Green might be a good idea. Is it a bit more appealing, this walk?'

'It might be a really good idea. You're sure you're okay now?'

'I'm fine. Stop whittling, Lester.' Wendy pulled her iPad towards her and spent some time rewording the original email, as she knew nothing of the four new names suggested. She noticed they were Derbyshire and Nottinghamshire based and realised some thought had been put into the list. She clicked send, and said back with a chuckle, 'Well done, Miss Marple. You're surpassing yourself with this.'

'We'll have to set you on as civilian consultant at Connection, I can see this coming.'

Wendy laughed. 'Poor Luke, he'd never cope with two old ladies. Nope, it's the police or nothing.'

'Then I suspect it's nothing. We'll go and drown your sorrows now, shall we? You taking your iPad?'

'I will. It's much easier to read emails on that than on my phone.' She slipped it into her bag and stood, correcting the slight wobble before Doris noticed.

But Doris had noticed. And Doris was concerned.

33

Wendy woke to a long string of emails and no headache. She plumped up her pillows, wedged the iPad into her duvet, and sifted through the responses. Most of them seemed to have come from the nightshift managers, and all of them were happy to help.

Before reading them she checked the ones who had replied against her list and saw there were still nine to reply. Then she digested the responses.

Bang! Bang! Bang! Wendy hammered on Doris's bedroom door far too loudly in her eagerness to pass on news. 'You awake, Lester? Can I come in?'

There was a groan and a muffled, 'I am now,' from the other side of the door.

Wendy opened the door slightly and peered around it. 'Good morning. I have news.'

'And I have a hangover. The two are incompatible at...' Doris fumbled for her alarm clock and held it close to her face, 'nine seventeen.'

Wendy crossed the room and sat in the armchair. She looked around. 'Why is this room always tidy? Mine is a tip. I have to tidy it every morning.'

Doris's eyes were almost open. 'I have a team of fairies come in every night once I'm asleep...'

'Stop being facetious. Listen, two of the taxi companies had cabs in the right areas on that night. They've sent times when we can meet up with the drivers to ask them about it, all they ask is we let them know if we're going to see them, so they can prewarn them to hang about the office.'

Doris fought her way to a sitting up position in bed. 'Awesome, Miss Marple. Whether anything comes of it or not, that's a cracking job you've done, and definitely one I couldn't have tackled. That's the second time your taxi job has come up trumps. Two cabs in the right area, did you say?'

'Yes, and both local to Hucknall. I did a blanket send to all my contacts, a kind of fishing expedition to see if anyone had covered any part of Hucknall and district on that night, not expecting any joy from the Sheffield firms, but these two are local.'

'Okay, I'd better get up, then we'll get the map out and see what's what, and what time we're meeting these drivers.'

'You're not thinking about passing this stuff on to our new friend, Grace, then?'

'Maybe,' Doris said, swinging her legs out of bed, 'later.'

A quick cereal breakfast was eaten without enthusiasm, and they moved into the lounge where the map for the Hucknall area was laid out on the table. Doris printed off the two emails and they followed the information contained in them to locate pick-up and drop-off points for both taxis.

Several points on the map had already been highlighted in

colour; red denoted the homes of Mark and Shirley, Dan and Rosie, Patrick, and Melanie. The point where Melanie had been pulled from the river was in green, as was the bridge where police believed she had been murdered. Trudy's bed and breakfast place was in orange, as was Shirley's new home at Rothery. The purple marks represented Global Systems, Kevin Vickers' home, and Juliet Vickers' current place of residence. A small yellow dot showed Imogen North's home.

'Colourful, isn't it?' Doris said. She selected a blue marker, and placed a dot where Springbrook School stood. 'I think that's everything on it. Now, where is the pick-up point for the first one?'

'It says Hucknall Road.' She leaned over the map. 'It is a black cab, so it could have been hailed, rather than booked.'

'Hucknall Road is a long road. Damn. What's the drop-off point?'

'Layby.'

'Yep. That's all it says. The charge was slightly over six pounds, so it's not a long journey. We need to speak to these drivers, don't we?'

'We do. We'll not put these on the map until we've got the full information. Can you notify the two companies that we'll be there at the time they want us there? I'll get us some photos to take with us.'

'Photos?'

'We'll need the drivers to identify the passenger, really. I want pics of... let me see... Mark and Shirley, Rosie and Dan, Patrick, Kevin and Juliet Vickers, Imogen North, Trudy, and Ray Taylor. Can you think of anybody else in this woven tangled web?'

'Only Megan.' Wendy laughed. 'And we have these pictures? Who's Ray Taylor?'

'Somebody the police have interviewed. Another of

Melanie's dalliances, it appears. Don't ask any more questions on that one,' Doris warned, 'and definitely don't mention his name to Grace, because we don't know about him. We have some pictures already, but I can get the others either from the Global Systems website or from their Facebook profiles.'

'Okay, I'll leave you to sort that. I can send emails but anything else would baffle me,' Wendy said. 'You're okay doing this?'

'I am. Don't forget this comes naturally to me. It's my job, and okay I know I'm working a bit under the radar at the moment because I don't have the official backing of Connection or even the support of Tessa and Hannah, but I do have other help. It keeps me young and functioning, Wendy,' Doris added with a laugh. 'Let's have a cuppa while I'm printing these pictures off, and then we'll go to meet our taxi drivers.'

The A5 pictures were placed in a small plastic envelope and Doris slipped them into her bag. They had been remarkably easy to acquire from social media posts, and the Global Systems website had pictures of all employees from Kevin Vickers down to his receptionist Imogen North. Juliet Vickers had clearly not been employed by the company, and Doris used Facebook as her portal to get a shot of her.

The timings for meeting the drivers were an hour apart, so they left home at two and drove to Nottingham, to the Sherwood Taxi Company.

Arriving early, they went into the taxi office where Doris left Wendy to catch up with the owner, a man she had known for some considerable time, and who answered to Ronnie. They started chatting the second they walked through the door, remembering shared acquaintances and talking in particular about a man who had recently died unexpectedly. Doris remained in the background as she listened to their enthusiastic chatter, and she watched as her friend came alive. This was Wendy's territory, she had the knowledge in this office, and she would be the one to get the information from the driver when he walked through the door to meet them.

Doris felt her phone vibrate and she checked to see why. A message from Rosie.

Megan would like to visit you. Are you in tomorrow if we call?
You appear to be her new superhero. Sorry.

Doris smiled and replied that indeed they were in, unless things changed at short notice, and would they like to come for lunch. The response was swift.

That's put a smile on her face. 11.30 ok?

Doris returned a thumbs up, and slipped her phone back in her bag. Her attention went back to Wendy's conversation, and she was currently chatting about road closures and the amount of time it added to journeys, which in turn added to the fare structure. It seemed passengers didn't think it was their fault the roads were being repaired or dug up, and they didn't see why they had to pay increased prices.

The conversation dropped into the background, and Doris waited patiently for the driver to appear.

His name was Walt Young, and Doris estimated he was in his mid-fifties, with light grey hair, thinning, and piercingly bright blue eyes. He smiled at them as he came through the door.

'Sorry I'm late, Ronnie. Carbrook Road's got three sets of

roadworks traffic lights on it now. Ladies, you want to talk to me?'

Wendy held out her hand. 'Walt, I'm Wendy. Used to work for Paynter's in Sheffield before I retired.'

'Know them well, Wendy,' Walt said, returning the handshake. He turned to Doris, and held out his hand. 'Walt.'

Doris stood and grasped the proffered hand, replying, 'Doris. And thank you for taking time out to talk to us. We'll not keep you long.'

She went into a fairly detailed explanation of what they needed to know, and Walt walked over to a large map on the wall. 'Okay, I checked my facts last night after Ronnie told me you were popping in to see me, and this is where I picked her up.' He pointed to a place on the map. Doris took out her phone and photographed where his finger was.

'Her? It was definitely a woman?'

'Oh aye,' he said. 'Skinny bit of a thing, pretty. She flagged me down, it wasn't a telephone booking.'

'Okay, Walt, we have some photographs. Can you look at them and tell me if any look like your passenger? Don't worry if they don't, this is a bit of a shot in the dark.'

'You sound like the police,' Walt said, a puzzled expression on his face.

'I'm a private investigator,' Doris explained, and handed him her card.

He looked at it, and then lifted his head. 'I've heard of you. I've a mate lives in Eyam, Stefan Patmore.'

Doris laughed. 'Such a small world. I know Stefan too. He did our business alterations when we needed to create an extra office. Lovely man.'

'Sings your praises,' Walt said. 'Apparently you pay on time, which is a big bonus in the building trade.'

Doris took out the plastic wallet holding the pictures and

she placed photographs of Rosie, Shirley, Imogen and Juliet on the table. 'Take your time, Walt. It may be that your pick-up isn't here. Really we're on a ruling out mission, not necessarily a ruling in one.'

Walt stood by her side and looked at the pictures. There was no hesitation in his choice. 'Definitely her,' he said, tapping one, then walked back to the map on the wall. 'I picked her up at this point here, in Calverton, after the roadworks. I went straight across at the roundabout, and dropped her at the far side. She paid in cash, and I went on to my next job.'

'How do you remember?' You must have lots of jobs every day, so how do you remember this one?'

'She was crying. And I don't normally work in the Hucknall area, but I'd picked up a fare in Newark who needed taking to Calverton which was the top side of the roadworks. He'd got out, paid me and I went straight through the green traffic lights, heading back to base, when she flagged me down almost immediately. She was heading in the direction I was going anyway, so it was definitely a bonus fare, but as I say, she sniffled all the way, and hardly said a word apart from *I'll tell you where to drop me*, and *thanks* as she paid and got out. I pulled up to the roundabout and she said *here* so I told her I'd take her round the island and drop her immediately opposite. That was what I did, and she got out. Sorry I can't help any further.'

'You've been an enormous help, Walt. This will end up in police hands, so you may have to make a statement, but it's nothing to worry about. You simply did your job.'

'Who is she?' Ronnie asked.

'We can't say,' Doris said, 'but I'm truly grateful you've given up your time like this.'

Doris and Wendy moved towards the door. 'Expect a quick police response. We will be telling them within the hour.' Doris flashed a quick smile, Wendy waved and blew a kiss and they left, heading towards their car.

'Result or what?' Wendy said.

Doris shrugged. 'I don't know. Why have we got two positive responses from your mass email drop? Why two, for heaven's sake? It doesn't make sense. Let's go see this next driver, see if we feel enlightened after this visit.'

34

The second taxi office, with its neon sign telling the world that Star Taxis was in residence, proved to be much smarter than Sherwood Taxis, although equally accommodating to the two ladies.

'Linc Starr,' the owner said, 'and this is my driver, Chunk Johnson. I'll leave you to guess why he's called Chunk.'

The driver grinned at them, and patted his well-rounded stomach. 'My real name, my posh one, is Charles, but I've been Chunk for more years than I care to think about. What can I do to help you ladies?'

'Okay,' Wendy said, once more taking the initial lead. 'I'm Wendy Lucas and this is my friend Doris Lester. I worked for Paynter's for many many years which is how I knew who to contact for this big email shot. This is the result of a hunch that somebody's telling lies, and we're trying to sort it one way or another. Doris is a private investigator so is the brains. Doris?'

Doris handed over her business card to the men, who looked suitably impressed.

'You're not police then?' Chunk asked.

'No, but we will be speaking to them within the next hour

with our findings. Chunk, can you tell us where you picked your fare up on that night?'

'I can,' and mirroring Walt Young's actions, he walked across to the wall map. 'I picked up in Westville,' his finger tracked his route, 'and dropped off here, a few yards beyond this bridge.'

Careful not to lead him, Doris took out the wallet of pictures. 'Can I show you some photos, Chunk? I simply need to know if you recognise anyone in these who was your fare that night.'

He gave a slight nod, and walked back to the desk. Doris placed the printouts on the desk and stood back, allowing Chunk full access to them.

He looked through them twice then picked one up. 'This one. No doubt at all.'

Doris turned to Wendy to make sure she was aware of which picture had been chosen, and then Doris gathered them up and put them back in the wallet.

'Thank you so much, gentlemen,' she said. 'We'll leave you to get back to your work now, but the police will be around to see you, I'm sure of it. I'm assuming cash was used for the fare?'

'It was. It usually is when I've been flagged down, it's the telephone bookings that are card or account.'

The women sat in the car for several minutes, Doris making some notes and Wendy staring out of the window. Doris finished her notetaking and turned to Wendy.

'We're not cooking tonight. Let's go and eat, then I'll ring Grace.'

'Grace? It's Doris Lester. Are you still at work?'

'I am, but about to head off home. There's only Harriet here, still thrashing out these alibis.'

'Okay, about the alibis, we may have something for you. Do you want us to come to your office?'

There was a moment's hesitation. 'Doris, how have you got something for me?'

Doris laughed. 'I have a best friend called Wendy who has superpowers. Don't worry, Grace, I have done what we've done without any strange help.'

'Can I bring Harriet if we come to yours? She's been sulking all day because I've been to that little cottage without her.'

'Of course. We're not home yet, we've been for a meal but we should be home in about half an hour. Take care.'

Harriet and Grace were in animated discussion as they got out of the car, and Wendy opened the door to invite them in.

'Welcome to my temporary home,' she said with a smile. 'Doris is taking some scones out of the oven, so I recommend you say yes to a cuppa, because her scones are to die for.'

They followed Wendy through to the kitchen, where Doris greeted them with a smile. 'We should sit in here because we need the space. It's easier than me moving everything off the dining table. Thank you for coming, DCI Stamford and DS Jameson, I'll show you round the cottage later, if you'd like that.'

'It's Grace and Harriet.'

'Okay. You know my rules, though...'

'I know, but we're both signed out and off duty now.'

Harriet snapped her mouth shut. Never in a million years would she have called her boss by her first name, but it seemed it was okay.

'Harriet, I'll explain. I reached an understanding with our two super-sleuths the other day. I want to be me, basically, and they're to call me Grace and you Harriet, but Doris, in her professional life, would always call us by our official titles. Tonight it's Grace, Harriet, Doris and Wendy. Okay?'

'Yes, boss.'

Grace sighed. Sometimes it hardly seemed worth the effort...

They had scones, Harriet adding jam, Grace taking them with butter, following Doris and Wendy's lead.

Wendy eventually cleared everything away to the work surface by the fridge, then unrolled their map, coloured dots abounding.

'This is pretty,' Harriet said with a laugh. 'You want a job?'

'Got one,' Wendy and Doris said in unison.

Grace put on her reading glasses and bent over to inspect the map.

'There's nothing on there, Grace, that you don't know about,' Doris said. 'Not yet anyway. We're about to add some luminous pink dots but thought it was easier to talk you through them.' Doris slipped on her reading glasses. 'Okay, yesterday we were discussing the case, and, like Harriet, recognised that somebody was lying, whether it be somebody giving the alibi, or somebody confirming it.' She paused for a moment, keen to get everything in the right order.

'The deduction,' she said with a laugh, 'was that nobody had a strong alibi. Any one of the suspects could have been out and about that night if they'd done it under cover of darkness, and by not telling anyone they were going out. So, Wendy here, superstar Wendy, said although cars didn't appear to have been used because there was no CCTV of any sort, taxis could have been used.'

'Cars haven't shown up on CCTV because the camera

covering the roundabout near the victim's home isn't working, and there isn't one anywhere near the bridge. It's a secluded spot,' Grace said with a sigh.

It briefly occurred to Grace that in theory Doris couldn't have known about the CCTV, but Tessa Marsden had warned her not to query the stuff Doris Lester knew.

'And you checked taxi firms?' Grace's brow creased as she thought of the magnitude of such a job.

'Wendy has a vast network of taxi firms and individual drivers virtually at the touch of a button in her phone,' Doris said. 'She worked for what seemed like hundreds of years for Paynter's Taxis in Sheffield, so she narrowed her contacts down to around forty-five covering this area, and at this stage leaving Sheffield alone. We were prepared to extend if necessary. Nottingham, Newark and Hucknall itself were targeted, although we did think Hucknall was too close to home for any self-respecting murderer to consider.'

Wendy joined in the discussion. 'I do have to say at this point it was a bit of a clutching-at-straws exercise, and if I hadn't had this vast network and the knowledge to chat to these lads in their taxi offices on their level, what we did would never have happened, so if we're in trouble for what we're about to tell you, it's down to me, not Doris.'

Doris continued to look down at the map trying not to laugh at Wendy's valiant attempt to keep her out of the Tower of London. 'We're not in any trouble. I'm licensed as an investigator, and this is a pro bono case for Connection. We get our information however we have to.' She lifted her head and smiled. 'Okay?'

'Okay,' Grace said. 'Come on, carry on with this fascinating tale of how you're trying to justify your transgressions.'

'Wendy put together an email, asking for information about pickups or drop-offs in the area of the bridge where Melanie

Brookes died, although we didn't specify that obviously. We gave them the location of the bridge and the roundabout near to Melanie's home, plus a wide six-hour window. We had lots of responses, some of them remarkably chatty towards Wendy, I might tell you, but two of them gave an indication that they had picked up and dropped off in the right area at the right time. Both these firms indicated they would have their drivers drop by the office at specific times, to tell us about it.'

'So that's where we've been,' Wendy said. 'Chatting to taxi drivers who are both expecting to speak to you. They're both working tonight till midnight, so you might want to leave it till tomorrow. They need to earn their crust.'

Doris reached across to her bag and took out the photographs, then picked up the bright-pink marker. 'So... the first pick-up was here, at Calverton. A woman who cried all the time she was in the taxi and who spoke very little. He got to the roundabout near Melanie's home and "she", his passenger, asked to be dropped off. He took her straight across, heading towards the bridge, and she got out. He then went back to base. She paid cash.'

Grace and Harriet looked at each other. 'Did he describe her?'

'Better than that. I took these with me,' and Doris laid out the photographs in a line. 'I showed him the women, as he had clearly stated his passenger was female, and he had no hesitation in pointing to this one. He's prepared to give a statement to that effect.' Doris's hand remained on the photo for a few seconds. 'But that's not all.'

'Certainly isn't,' Wendy said with a grin. She stood and walked to the kitchen drawer and took out two tablets. She swallowed them down with water and apologised. 'Sorry, headache starting, so let me stop it before it worsens.'

'So we have a clear suspect now, who was out and about in

the vicinity of the murder on the night in question.' Grace looked at Doris. 'So was the second taxi company ruled out?'

'Not at all. We knew the driver had been asked to go into the office specially to meet us, so when we'd finished at Sherwood Taxis, we headed off to Star Taxis. There we met the delightful Chunk Johnson, the driver who had also picked up in the area that night. He picked up in Westville, flagged down, not a booking, then dropped his client at the bridge. *The* bridge,' Doris emphasised, 'where Melanie was murdered. Again, cash was paid for the fare, so no help there, but we asked him to look at the photos anyway. Because of the identification at the first taxi place, I had no expectation that there would be one at Star, but there was. He, exactly like Walt at Sherwood, had no hesitation in pointing to this one,' and again Doris's finger stayed on a different photo to the first one, for a few seconds.

There was silence around the table as they watched without seeing the actions of Wendy putting pink dots on the map, signifying everything to do with the taxi activity.

Eventually Doris spoke. 'The four of us round this table are the only people who know about this. Neither the taxi drivers nor their bosses know names, we simply thanked them for their time and said you would be contacting them for a statement. You'll not have a problem with that, both men were really helpful. They showed us on their map the exact pick-up and drop-off points, so I photographed them in order for us to be accurate when we put them on this.' Doris pointed to the multi-dotted map. 'Now would anybody like another cup of tea, or something stronger?'

35

Doris, Grace and Harriet settled for tea, Wendy said she would stick with water until her headache went. They moved into the lounge to more comfortable seating, and as both officers looked in appreciation, Doris invited them to look around her home. 'It really is a proper cottage now,' she explained. 'I've tried to furnish it to keep it compatible with how old it is, and I'm so pleased I bought it.'

The three women headed upstairs and Wendy remained in the lounge, checking her emails to make sure no further positive responses had arrived. Two suspects was enough for one murder, she considered.

'I absolutely love this,' Harriet said, her eyes sparkling. 'If I was given a wish list, this would be it. The whole thing. I only need to find a rich man to replace the present Mr Jameson, that's all.'

'Not worth it,' Grace said.

'Not worth it,' Doris echoed.

. . .

By nine o'clock, Grace had filled several pages with notes, had photographed Wendy's map, and was standing in the front garden taking her leave of her two hosts. She had sent Harriet off an hour earlier, ever-conscious of little Adeline at home without Mummy to put her to bed.

'Tessa Marsden is one lucky woman to have you on her side and not on the dark side of our police world. I hope she knows that.'

'We have a great deal of respect for Tessa and Hannah and their whole team, and Tessa uses us as a sounding board. She knows she can trust us with anything, and it will go no further. This that's happened today is somewhat unusual, and I'll be honest, if this had been a Connection case we would not have had the same result because we wouldn't have had Wendy's knowledge. She's the one who's made this happen, not me. I'm only the driver.'

'Is she okay? She looked a bit pale.'

'She's fine. A headache. It's been a long and exciting day, she enjoys her role as Miss Marple. It's going to seem really mundane when she goes back home after this holiday.'

'Thank you so much, Doris. I'll keep you informed as to what is happening tomorrow, although I don't doubt you'll find out from Hucknall anyway. We'll get the statements from the drivers first, then we'll be picking these two up for questioning. It'll be interesting to hear what they say.'

Grace slid into the driver seat and wound down her window. 'Take care, Doris. I'll hopefully speak to you at some time tomorrow. And thank you for feeding us, you're a star.'

Doris smiled and waved as Grace dropped down the hill and out of sight.

Now to see how Wendy was.

. . .

After the excitement of the previous day, feeding the ducks felt anticlimactic. It wasn't to the ducks; they loved every mouthful of the bread Doris and Wendy cast their way.

'I want a tartan throw,' Wendy announced. 'When we've given this lot their breakfast, shall we go and get one?'

'We'll do whatever you feel like doing. Why a tartan throw?'

'Because I love yours. It's lovely to snuggle under on a cold evening. I want one of my own.'

'Okay, it's easily arranged. I actually got mine here in Bakewell, and when I got it they had several different tartans in, so we'll go straight there if these ducks will let us go.' Doris threw the last of the bread behind them, and the crowd of ducks moved as one to get to it. 'Right, let's go while they're distracted.'

They slipped down the path that led into the town centre, called in at the bookshop simply for a browse, and bought three books each, then wandered a little further on to the shop selling high-class woollen things.

Wendy chose a red tartan, paid an extortionate amount for it, and swapped it from arm to arm for the rest of the Bakewell visit, so awkward was it to carry.

They had lunch in a pub, then headed back to the car park, primarily to get rid of the throw and the weight of the books. Doris's phone pinged as they sat back in their seats. She took it out and read the message from Grace, then turned to Wendy.

'Grace has statements from both drivers, they have confirmed everything we said and she's sent two teams out to bring the suspects in for questioning.' Doris paused for a moment. 'Why do I feel so down about this?'

'Because they've become your extended family, and this is going to be a terrible time for everybody. In that little circle of people, three have already died, and two more are going to be questioned and, in time, probably convicted. You're a caring woman, Doris, it's going to affect you. They're not even my family, I merely tagged along, but it's definitely affecting me. Let's give Chatsworth a miss and go home. We can wait for news there in comfort.'

Doris nodded, put the car into drive, and left the car park.

'DS Jameson and DC Ellis,' Harriet called through the closed door, responding to the feeble 'who's there' that had followed their knock.

'What do you want?'

'To speak with you. Can you open the door, please, Mrs Ledger?'

Shirley turned the key, but left the chain on as she slowly opened it. They both held up their warrant cards.

Shirley closed the door, removed the chain and allowed them entry. 'Sorry, I'm a bit nervous. What can I do for you?'

'We'd like you to accompany us to the station, please, Mrs Ledger. Are your children here?'

The colour drained from Shirley's face. 'No, they're not. They've gone over to my sister's to have a couple of hours with my niece. She's taking them to the park...' Shirley was aware she was babbling, and took a deep breath.

'Would you like to ring her and tell her what's happening? She can keep the children safe, I'm sure.'

Shirley appeared lost. She picked up her phone and rang Rosie, explaining the police wanted to ask her some questions, and Rosie was clearly heard to say *Don't worry. Text me when you're back home*.

Harriet dropped the mobile phone into an evidence bag, and Shirley picked up a cardigan as they left Fuchsia Cottage. Tears filled her eyes.

. . .

Grace took PC Fiona Harte with her, and they pulled up outside the property, looking at the impressiveness of it.

'Wow. This is massive!'

'Come on then, let's go and bring them back down to earth where the common people live,' Grace said, trying to stop a smile.

They walked up the path to the front door, and listened as the doorbell played a Mozart concerto. A disembodied voice said *Can I help you* and Grace held up her warrant card to the small camera above the door.

'DCI Grace Stamford and PC Fiona Harte. We'd like a word, please.'

Footsteps approached the door, and slowly it opened. It was clearly one of considerable weight.

A man stood there, elderly, grey hair that hadn't started thinning, but with a well-lined face. 'What do you want? We don't deal with people at the door.'

'That's okay,' Grace said, and stepped inside. Fiona wanted to explode with laughter at the man's shocked face, but held it back.

'You can't do that!'

'I need to speak to your daughter, please.'

'Juliet? Why?'

'Can you get Juliet for me, please, sir.'

He stared at the two officers for a moment, then turned away. 'Wait here.' He went to the end of the hallway and disappeared.

'He doesn't like you,' Fiona whispered.

'Not many people do, especially when I'm here to take their daughter away, and they're going to be left with the kids,' Grace whispered back.

. . .

They waited five minutes and Grace was about to go to the end of the hallway to track down the irascible old man, when Juliet Vickers appeared in front of them.

'Apologies,' she said. 'You should have rung to make an appointment and I wouldn't have been in the shower when you arrived.'

'Are your children here?'

'Yes. Why?'

'Are they safe with your parents?'

'Of course they are.'

'Then we'd like you to accompany us to the station, please, Mrs Vickers. PC Harte, will you go and find someone and tell them what's happening?'

Fiona moved to go around Juliet, who also moved. 'I'll tell them,' she said, snapping at the two officers.

'No. You remain with me,' Grace said.

'I beg your pardon.' The look was delivered to Grace with precision. Juliet was obviously used to getting her own way.

'Mrs Vickers, if you take one step from me I will place handcuffs on your wrists and send for a squad car to transport you. If you remain here without moving a step while PC Harte does as instructed, you will travel with us unfettered and in an unmarked car. Your choice.'

Fiona continued her journey down the hallway, aware of virtual daggers sinking into her back. She tried desperately not to smile. This Juliet Vickers bird didn't know DCI Grace Stamford at all.

Fiona's conversation with Juliet's parents told her why Juliet was so up herself; she was definitely a carbon copy of both parents. They didn't seem too happy to be lumbered with the children, but as Juliet's father said, 'It's only for the afternoon, darling.' Eventually his wife nodded her agreement, and Fiona returned to report to Grace.

. . .

Fiona sat in the back with Juliet while Grace drove them to headquarters. Grace had had text confirmation from Harriet that Shirley was in the interview room, that a solicitor hadn't been requested, and she seemed in a state of shock.

She didn't expect the same reaction from the feisty Juliet. She could almost guarantee that the first words out of her mouth would be get me a solicitor. It was only as they approached the station that the hitherto-silent Juliet showed visible and audible signs of stress.

'Why am I here?'

'We have a few questions for you, Mrs Vickers.' Fiona was polite.

'What about?'

'I would advise you not to say anything, Mrs Vickers, until you're speaking for the tape.'

Grace grinned at the audible gasp from Juliet Vickers, as the PC's words finally sank in. 'Are you arresting me?'

'Have you done something wrong?'

'No, of course I bloody haven't.'

'Then you have nothing to worry about.' Fiona turned her head to look out of the car window, effectively closing down the conversation.

Juliet Vickers was placed in interview room three, next door to interview room four, occupied by a trembling Shirley Ledger. Neither woman had asked for a legal representative, and neither woman was admitting to knowing why their presence was required.

Grace knew it was only a matter of time before one of them explained why they were both in the same place, on the same night that Melanie Brookes had been murdered, and why they felt she had to die.

Grace took out her phone and messaged Doris for the second time.

Both in custody, not interviewed yet. Shirley shocked, Juliet cocky.
Things will change.

Doris and Wendy were at home, the new tartan throw spread across Wendy's legs; she wasn't cold, she wanted the luxury of it wrapped around her.

Doris's phone pinged, and she read out the message to Wendy.

'I don't know what to say,' Doris said. 'As soon as Chunk picked out her photo, I felt sick. And I must admit, I thought he was going to pick out a man at first, but no, he hovered over Shirley then picked it up. Those poor boys. This isn't going to end well, is it, Wendy?'

36

'You do not have to say anything, but it may harm your defence if you do not mention when questioned, something which you later rely on in court. Anything you do say may be given in evidence. Mrs Ledger, do you understand the caution?'

A look of horror had settled on Shirley's face. 'You're arresting me?'

'We need to question you under caution, Shirley,' DS Harriet Jameson said. 'Please confirm you understand everything I've said to you.'

Shirley's shoulders dropped, and she nodded, before saying she understood. She looked somewhat wildly around the room as if searching for an exit marked 'escape hatch', but finally she slumped into her chair and waited.

'Thank you,' Harriet said. 'Can you please confirm where you were on the evening of Thursday, the second of May, 2019, between twenty and twenty-two hundred hours.'

'I was in bed at Oleander House. I'm sure Trudy Dawson, the owner of the Bed and Breakfast, will confirm that.'

'I'm sure she will,' Harriet agreed. 'Did you, at any time that evening, leave your room to go back downstairs.'

'No, I stayed in my room till breakfast the next morning.'

'So you didn't see the owner at any point that night?'

Shirley froze; she'd walked into her own mousetrap, and it showed on her face. 'Er... no.'

'So in actual fact, Trudy Dawson can't alibi you for that evening because she didn't actually see you. Is that right?'

'I slept. I'd had an emotional day, and as soon as I got into bed I fell asleep.'

'You see, Shirley, we have a bit of a problem. We have a witness who has identified you as being out and about that night. In fact, so much out and about that it necessitated you flagging down a black cab for your trip between Westville, where coincidentally Oleander House is situated, and the little bridge where Melanie Brookes was murdered.'

There was silence in the room, and significant blood loss from Shirley's face. Harriet waited, guessing what was coming next. She felt Sam Ellis tense by her side.

Shirley turned to the DS. 'I categorically deny I was out that night. Whoever has identified me is mistaken, and I won't be saying another word without a solicitor by my side. I have no idea why you think it's okay to set me up for this, and it's possibly because you're under pressure to deliver a result, but you've got the wrong person with me. And that's my last word.'

Harriet gathered up the papers in front of her. 'I'll organise a duty solicitor for you, Shirley. You'll be taken to a cell until that happens, and I'll see you later.'

'You said I wasn't being arrested.' Juliet Vickers was angry; the inference was that Fiona had lied. Grace said nothing, leaving Fiona to respond.

'I did not say that at all. I asked if you had done anything to merit that action, and when you said no, I advised staying quiet until you were on tape. You are now safe to speak as the tape is running, and you are about to be questioned under caution.'

Grace didn't let the internal smile show. 'Mrs Vickers, you said when we questioned you last week that you were at home on the evening of the second of May, 2019. Is that correct, or do you want to amend your statement?'

'Of course it's correct. Ask my mother and father, they will vouch for me. I went to bed early and watched television until I fell asleep.'

'What did you watch?'

'Emmerdale. I watch it every night.'

'And?'

'Nothing. I went to sleep at the end of it.'

'It seems to have been a night for going to sleep early. Your partner in crime, Shirley Ledger, says she was asleep by eight o'clock too. But, you see, I have a problem with this sleeping on this particular night. I have a witness who places you in Calverton, then a few minutes later at a small roundabout a few hundred yards from Melanie Brookes' home. Sorry, the late Melanie Brookes' home.'

'Not me,' Juliet said, her voice level increasing. 'I was at home with my parents, and my children in their room. Whoever has told you this is lying.'

'They have no reason to lie. They were out that night simply doing their jobs, taxi drivers picking up at one point and delivering the client to another. It's interesting that Shirley Ledger was picked up close to where she was residing temporarily, and dropped off at the bridge where Ms Brookes was murdered, and you were picked up where your parents live and where you are residing temporarily and delivered really close to Ms Brookes' house.'

'Not me,' Juliet repeated. 'And I need a solicitor, please. Our family solicitor, Penelope Tarbutt.'

Grace gathered together her paperwork and with dignity, walked towards the door. She paused and turned. 'You'll be taken to your cell in a few moments. We'll attempt to contact your solicitor, and if we do, I will recommence the interview later today. That will be an interesting conversation, as I believe your friend is speaking about all sorts of things.'

Grace closed the interview room door and took a deep breath. 'Cow,' she muttered.

'Yeah, but nice one, boss,' Fiona said, 'telling her Shirley is already talking. Is she?'

'Not yet, but she will.'

The note on Grace's desk asked her to contact Paul in forensics, and she smiled at the thought of the geeky young man with the round dark-framed glasses and the prominent dimple in his chin. She picked up the phone.

'Good afternoon, ma'am. I was in the middle of typing up a report to send to you with the details, but the gist of it is that Shirley Ledger has two phones, her personal one and a business one. It seems she has a business called Rosebay Willowherb. Both these phones were left at reception, along with her bag, when she was booked in. Her personal phone showed no phone calls in or out for a period from the evening of the first of May until she turned up again when you found her.'

Grace wanted to say *Doris found her*. 'She said she hadn't used it, she didn't want us tracking her down.'

'She used the other one, though. During the afternoon of the following day she made a five-minute call to the deceased, Melanie Brookes, then a two-minute thirty-second call to Global Systems, followed by a twenty-minute one, half an hour later to

Juliet Vickers, then a further two-minute call to Melanie Brookes. All were made on the business phone. She hasn't made any calls in the past to these numbers on this phone. The call to Juliet Vickers was to her landline, so presumably she didn't know her mobile number. It is an ex-directory number. It's all on the report I'll be sending in about five minutes. I'll also send you the list of everything that was inside the bag when it was left with the sarge.'

'Thank you so much, Paul, and I can definitely make an educated guess as to how she got the ex-directory number, in view of the call to Global Systems. I'll speak to DS Jameson now, she's interviewing Shirley Ledger. You've got these results really quickly. Was it easy?'

'Very easy. They'd hidden nothing. Didn't delete any calls, and the Juliet Vickers number is the last one entered in the business phone contacts. I've asked BT for phone records for the landline where Juliet Vickers is living, so we'll see if she made any calls out immediately after, or not. There's nothing out of the ordinary on her mobile phone. Lots of stuff in her bag though. She had three lipsticks!'

'Tools of the trade, Paul, tools of the trade.' Grace laughed. 'Thank you, Paul.' She replaced the receiver and stared at it for a moment. The phone calls, she guessed, were murder arrangements being made, but what had triggered the initial one? Grace tapped on her office window and Harriet looked up, then stood up.

'You want me, boss?'

'I do. I've some new information. When you booked Shirley in, she handed her bag in.'

Harriet nodded. 'Standard practice.'

'She had two phones.'

'No! I take it we didn't know this at the time she was insisting she didn't use her phone because she didn't want to be tracked by us.'

'It's a business phone. Remember Rosie telling us about the beautiful journals and books they make for their Etsy shop? Shirley has a phone dedicated to the business with the rather sweet name of Rosebay Willowherb. You might want to start off your next interview session with that little nugget of a name. I'll have a report on that phone in a few minutes, but basically she made a short call to Melanie, followed by a short call to Global Systems, followed by a twenty-minute call to Juliet Vickers, and that was followed by a two-minute one to Melanie Brookes.'

'Global Systems? Did Shirley know Kevin Vickers?'

'No, I think she probably came up with something along the lines of she'd lost her phone and she wanted to contact Juliet. But guess which gobby little mouthpiece she would speak to first, who would swallow the story and give her a number she could get Juliet on.'

Harriet swung Grace's notes around so she was no longer reading them upside down. She studied the phone call list for a moment, and then sighed. 'It tells a story, doesn't it. I've never really bought into this thing that Shirley simply went for a drive that Wednesday night and decided not to go back. What did she discover after Mark Ledger left for his function that night, that tipped Shirley over the edge? Whatever it was, it sealed Melanie's fate.' Harriet glanced at her watch. 'Where the bloody hell is that duty solicitor?'

Grace laughed. 'Calm down. You need the report from the lovely Paul before you go into that room. You can't take my scribbled notes, not with that pornographic doodle on anyway.'

'I wasn't going to say anything, but you're no Picasso.'

'So, you know what you're doing? Lead her gently in by talking about Rosebay Willowherb, the company. Ask her to talk about it, and she will, because she loves doing what she does. Then ask how they take orders.'

'And she'll say over the phone. That's when I jump in and say which phone. She's not daft, that's when she'll know she's been rumbled. And that's when I start talking murder with its whole life sentence, or manslaughter with its judge's discretion sentence. I'll make it sound as though the first one to tell the truth gets the manslaughter charge, without actually saying that. I'll not say anything at this point about who the hell choked the life out of a twenty-something career woman who had everything to live for and didn't deserve to die.'

Grace stretched her arms and stood. 'Water?' She walked across to the fridge and took out two bottles.

'You keep chocolate in there as well?'

'No, water and peach tea. You want a peach tea instead?'

Harriet pulled a face. 'I'll stick with the water, thanks. Let's hope by tomorrow we're needing champagne.'

Grace's attention was distracted by the ping announcing an email, and she opened up the message from Paul. She forwarded it to Harriet's computer, then printed it off for closer study.

Harriet returned to her own desk to look at the report before printing it for her own file, and a minute later stood and ran back to Grace's office. Grace was leaving her office to go to Harriet.

'Have you seen...?' they said in unison.

37

Several things happened that day. The receipt found in the small pocket inside Shirley's bag for flowers delivered to Melanie Brookes' home was placed into an evidence bag.

Imogen North took a telephone call from DCI Grace Stamford, asking if she received a call on the afternoon of the second of May from Shirley Ledger wanting Juliet Vickers' telephone number, and she was surprised to find that they knew about it. 'I did,' she said, 'but please keep it to yourself because if Mr Vickers finds out I gave out that information, he'll sack me. She said she was a friend and she had lost contact with her.'

Grace smiled at the request not to tell Mr Vickers – it was highly likely that Imogen would be saying it herself, but in a court of law.

Shirley stared at the receipt that Harriet pushed across the table, then looked to Tim Nixon for help. He merely nodded, indicating she should comply.

'Do you recognise this receipt, Shirley?'

'Yes.'

'It was checked into evidence, and found in the bag you handed over when you were brought here. Do you remember signing for it?'

'Yes.'

'Where did you get it from?'

Shirley let out an anguished cry. 'From his fucking suit pocket that he left me to hang up.'

'You searched his pockets?'

'No, I picked it up off the floor where he'd dumped it, and decided it was due for cleaning. I checked his trouser pockets in case there was anything in them, then hung them on the hanger. Then I checked his coat pockets. That was in the inside pocket.' Tears were flowing freely down her cheeks.

'And you recognised the name and address where the flowers were to go?'

'Bloody Melanie. It's eleven years since my husband last bought me some flowers, and he was having a large bouquet delivered to her.'

'What happened next?'

'I put the receipt into my phone case cover, grabbed my phone and my bank card and did what I told you I did; I went for a drive around while I thought through my next move.'

Sam leaned forward. 'Can I clarify something, Mrs Ledger? Which phone did you take with you? The phone with the picture of your boys as the home screen, or the Rosebay Willowherb?'

Again Shirley looked at Tim Nixon, who once more indicated she should answer. 'Both,' she whispered.

Sam continued. 'And did you, at any point over the period you were missing, use the iPhone with the boys on it?'

'No.'

'Please remember you are still under caution, Mrs Ledger. Did you use the business iPhone with Rosebay Willowherb on it at any point during the first day of your disappearance, that is Thursday the second of May?'

Shirley let out an unearthly screech, stood up and slammed her hands down on the table. 'You fucking know I did, or you wouldn't be asking me these questions. But I wasn't the one who killed her, that was Juliet Vickers.'

Tim Nixon's mouth fell open.

Shirley's long statement confessing to luring Melanie Brookes to the small bridge where she and Juliet Vickers planned to 'sort her out' in order to convince her that sleeping with other people's husbands wouldn't be a good idea at any future point, helped Grace immensely when she finally joined Juliet Vickers and Penelope Tarbutt, her solicitor, the next morning.

'I'm sorry I didn't get back to you yesterday, Mrs Vickers, but we had a long and difficult day. I was also aware Ms Tarbutt was unavailable last night. I hope you weren't too uncomfortable in the cell, and you have been fed.'

Juliet Vickers' stare was icy. 'How dare you keep me here. And is it my fault you had a long and difficult day?'

'Yes, actually it is,' Grace said mildly. 'We had to deal with Shirley Ledger's realisation that we had so much evidence she had better cop to a manslaughter plea, and leave you to face the murder charge.'

Juliet swung around to face Penelope. 'Penny, for fuck's sake, get me out of here.'

'Juliet, sit down,' Penny Tarbutt said quietly. 'And keep your mouth shut unless I say it's okay to open it. You think you can do that?'

Juliet didn't deign to reply.

Grace continued. 'You went for an evening run with Melanie Brookes, one you organised whereby you accidentally bumped into her as she was leaving home. Or maybe you called at her home and asked her to accompany you as you fancied a run, but didn't want to be on your own at that time of night. You knew running was a big part of Melanie's life and she wouldn't say no. On the way back, she went into a Chinese takeaway and bought you both a meal. You then walked back as far as the bridge, eating the meal. At the bridge, Shirley appeared from the trees at the side, and you strangled her while Shirley looked on expecting you to eventually stop to let her recover. But she died, didn't she, Juliet.

'You then both got her down to the river, and threw her in, holding on to her bag to take home with you. As we speak, there is a team of officers at your parents' home, doing a remarkably thorough search. Did you ever intend Melanie to recover from that strangulation, Juliet? Or did you always intend she would die? She'd ruined your marriage, sending you back to sharing a house with your controlling parents – who, by the way, are going to be pretty pissed off with you. It's not a nice feeling having your house turned upside down.'

'Utter rubbish,' Juliet said, shrugging off Penny's restraining hand. 'It was Shirley who strangled her. I tried to make her let go, but she kept gripping tighter. I tried to revive Melanie, but it was obvious she was dead.'

'How did you meet Shirley in the first place?'

'I ordered one of their journals, and she came to my parents' house with samples of what they do. I chose what I wanted, and I told her why I was there, with my parents. I mentioned Melanie's name as being the tart Kevin had slept with, and he had been stupid enough to let me find out by Imogen North telling me. I left him immediately.'

'Did Shirley contact you to discuss the plan to frighten Melanie, after she'd found a receipt?'

Juliet suddenly realised that she was saying too much, and she turned to her solicitor. Penny simply ignored her.

'For the flowers? Yes. She did. Her words were, "let's give her a good hiding. We'll both feel better for it, and we can get on with our lives."'

Grace stood. 'Thank you, Mrs Vickers. I'm going to leave you with PC Harte now, who will take your statement. I will need to speak with you further before you're charged with this murder...'

Juliet stood. 'Charged with murder? But I didn't...'

Penny Tarbutt also stood. 'Sit down, Juliet,' she said wearily. 'Fucking sit down.'

Got them! Blaming each other for strangulation, but CPS advise both charged with murder. Result. Big thanks to both of you for our taxi drivers.

Doris read out the message to a sleepy Wendy as they sat in deck chairs in the back garden, the sun streaming down on them.

Wendy opened her eyes. 'Awesome! Did we do that?'

'Escalated it, I think. They would have eventually got to the point of thinking taxis, because Harriet was already working on alibis and lies, but your head is in taxis so we got there first because of that.'

'Happy to help,' Wendy said with a smile, and closed her eyes again. She didn't want to tell Doris how bad the pain was getting; it was easy to hide it behind closed eyes.

'I have to ring Rosie. She must be going through hell. We had to cancel their visit here, so maybe we can invite them over for the day before you head back to Sheffield and Bingo Jen.'

'You're going to the funerals?'

'Probably.'

'I'd like to go with you, if that's okay.'

'Of course it is. I'm dreading you going back home, if I'm honest. You've been a giant-sized rock for me throughout this. Ever since I got that letter from Rosie addressed to Harry, I've felt a bit adrift.'

'I know,' Wendy said, her eyes still closed. 'But as time goes on it'll fade into the distance. Don't lose touch with Hucknall, though. Promise me that.'

'I won't. They're going to need a lot of support. Some hard times are coming for the two little boys, they're not even twelve yet. And as you know, I've taken a real shine to Megan.'

The women slipped into their own thoughts and allowed the sun to use its healing warmth on their bodies.

'Wendy, you asleep?'

'Not yet. Give me five minutes.'

'You want a drink?'

'Water and a couple of paracetamol, please. Shall I get the drinks?'

'No, you stay there. And when you go home, you go to the doctors. These headaches aren't normal.'

Wendy's eyes remained closed. 'I will. It's a throbbing one today. I should have taken the tablets earlier, but I was a bit wobbly when I stood up, so I sat back down again. I'll be fine when I've swallowed them.'

Doris stood and walked towards the open kitchen door, Belle following at her heels. Doris stopped halfway and looked back. She was worried, and considered ringing her own doctor and asking for advice without Wendy knowing.

Doris continued to the kitchen, poured two glasses of water, and dropped the packet of tablets into her skirt pocket. She topped up Belle's water, and headed back down the garden, the little cat still following her.

She put the drinks down on the small table they had been using as a coffee table, and took the tablets out of her pocket, popping two of them into her hand. 'Is two enough, or do you want three?'

By the time the doctor, the police and the funeral director had left, the sun had sunk low in the sky. Doris had cried for ten minutes, holding on to Wendy's hand, before ringing for help; she hadn't wanted to believe the evidence of her own eyes, she had desperately wanted to hear Wendy speak just one more time. It wasn't to be.

The doctor had confirmed her medical records indicated a brain tumour was the cause of Wendy's problems, not mini-strokes as she had said to Doris at the beginning of the holiday. Wendy had known her time left was limited.

The conversation with Wendy's sister, Marjorie, had been one of the most difficult Doris had ever undertaken, and both women had cried until they were drained.

The day drew to a close. And once more, Doris picked up the phone. Three people in her life would help her get through this, and she needed to talk to each of them. She had something to tell them.

Wendy was gone.

EPILOGUE

C onnection had closed for the day, no employees were available for investigative work of any nature. Kat, Mouse and Luke had supported Doris as she again visited City Road Cemetery, this time to see Wendy laid to rest with her late husband.

Marjorie and Doris hugged each other; neither had known of the life-threatening tumour, and each felt glad that they hadn't known. Waiting for the end would have been so much worse than the way it did happen, sleeping quietly in the back garden of a beautiful cottage in Derbyshire, the sun's rays warm on Wendy's face. But knowing that didn't stop the tears.

The slightest thing left Doris with tears in her eyes; the journals they had started on their holiday around the celebrity graves, the sight of her own yellow raincoat, the photographs they had taken and shared, all turned Doris into a river of tears. She knew it would pass. She had been the same when Harry had died, but she had got through it.

Grace and Harriet had both sent condolence cards with

beautiful messages inside, something else that started the tears all over again, and Rosie had been on the phone constantly, checking that she was okay.

Rosie brought Megan to the cottage a few days after the funeral, and once the tears had subsided, Doris showed them her home. Megan was captivated by it. Doris had to explain that the reason she had children's books in the small bedroom was because Kat had a young daughter, Martha, who occasionally stayed over with Nanny Doris. The cot had been replaced by a single bed as Martha had outgrown her original sleeping accommodation; the cot was in the attic in case it was needed again.

'How are the twins?' Doris asked. 'You haven't brought them.'

'Resilient,' was Rosie's initial response. 'Dan's taken them fishing today, he's bonding with them, he says. They have to share a bedroom at ours, but that's no hardship. Over the next couple of years we'll be extending the kitchen and that will give us another bedroom above it, so we've explained this to them, and they're happy to be included in our lives. It's sad that they've had to see their mother dragged through the newspapers and television, but these memories will fade, they're still young.'

'And you?' Doris asked. 'How are you coping without Shirley?'

'I'm still struggling with it, if I'm honest. And because both of them are denying the actual act of murder, I don't know what to think. Would I have ever believed Shirley capable of it? Not on your life. I'm the more volatile one, but I guess the years of mental and physical abuse from Mark changed her. I don't know Juliet Vickers beyond her being a name in the order book, so I can't say with any degree of certainty who I actually believe killed Mel. When DCI Stamford told me each one was blaming the other, it sort of went over my head. I was trying to come to terms with a two-boy increase in my family, shuffling around of bedrooms so the boys had the slightly bigger one that Megan used to have...'

'Huh.' Megan was stroking Belle and tickling the cat's ears with some grass but didn't look up.

Rosie smiled. 'But whatever happens, Shirley isn't going to be coming home for a considerable amount of time, and I have to cushion the twins for as long as it takes.'

Imogen North transferred the switchboard to night mode, and picked up the two letters that needed posting. To her surprise, Kevin Vickers came down the open-plan stairs, and through to reception, stopping at her desk.

'Mr Vickers? You need something?'

'To give you this,' he said, and handed her an envelope.

'For posting?'

'Not unless you put your name and address on it. It's a hand delivery, Imogen, and it's to give you immediate notice, four weeks' pay and no reference.'

Imogen stared at him. 'You can't do that...'

'I think you'll find I can. You want some advice, young lady? If you ever manage to get another job as a receptionist somewhere, make sure your mouth doesn't give secrets and information away to all and sundry. Leave the post on the desk, and get out of the door.'

Trudy Dawson thought often of her visitor, and wondered how she was managing away from the two young boys she had loved so much. She couldn't begin to imagine how Shirley's life must be, living on remand and knowing prison life would be even harder in the future.

In July, Trudy had a minor catastrophe of her own when a

guest had a wardrobe collapse while he was trying to hang up his clothes. She moved the man into a different room, apologising profusely, but the second room was much nicer and bigger anyway, so the man considered it a win–win situation. Shirley, too, had loved this same room.

The following afternoon Trudy moved into the room that was no longer in use, armed with a hammer and a screwdriver, and slowly dismantled the wardrobe, eager to get it out of the room to make way for a new one. The backpack was down the back of the wardrobe, not visible until she moved two large pieces of wood. Her immediate thought was that someone had stored it on top of the wardrobe, and thought no more about it because it had fallen down the back.

She pulled it out and registered it was a Nike bag, and fairly new. There was a purse and a phone inside it; inside the purse were bank cards in the name of Melanie Brookes.

Trudy's doubts about Shirley's guilt disappeared in an instant, and she stared at the bag. She flicked the dust off it, and took out her phone to ring DCI Stamford. There was, unfortunately, only one person who could have put the bag there, and having the bag recovered from Oleander House would definitely seal Shirley's fate.

After a minute of deep thought, Trudy put away her own phone, stashed everything in the backpack and wrapped it in a large black rubbish bag. It would go in her wheelie bin the evening before the early morning bin collection; by Wednesday morning it would be gone. Shirley may be guilty, but Trudy had liked her, had felt sorry for her, and she was damned if she was going to be the one that put her away for life. Shirley was taking her chances with the jury, so be it.

·   ·   ·

Doris didn't return to work until August 2019. She had spoken several times over the summer to Grace Stamford, and Grace had reassured her that the police were confident of getting a double-murder conviction.

Doris wasn't sure how she felt about that.

THE END

ACKNOWLEDGEMENTS

Thanks are going to be flying around all over the place following my completion of this book. Primary thanks, as always, go to my publisher, Bloodhound Books. Fred and Betsy have backed me from the beginning (thirteen books ago!), and they, along with their amazing team of Alexina, Tara, Heather and the publicity team definitely deserve my gratitude.

I also have thanks to give to my long-suffering editor, Morgen Bailey, who constantly tries to get me to understand the concept of point of view. Never going to happen, Morgen, never going to happen, but my most grateful thanks for trying!

My love and gratitude go to my friend and partner in crime, Patricia Dixon. She has cheered me on from the sidelines, read the book at crucial stages, and made me promise not to kill Doris. Patricia knows me so well. Thanks, Dixon!

With every book I write I have readers to thank, and sometimes those thanks extend to them giving me permission to use their names, even if I turn them into a corpse. Shirley Ledger is a long, long-time friend and a huge fan of my work – Shirley, thank you. Megan Steer is a budding young author who

I was proud to include, and Melanie Brookes, you have a starring role!

Enid Hill was someone we met almost a year ago while on holiday in Corfu, and we became united by our Sheffield accents. I gave her one of my books to read, and within a short space of time of our arriving home, she had every one in paperback form, signed by me, and passed on in Marks and Spencer's café in Crystal Peaks. Sadly Enid died on 9 March 2020, but she would have loved her name being used in this book; she was a huge fan of Doris.

And baby Adeline is a real baby Adeline!

I have to thank my beta readers for their encouragement during this book's journey – Marnie Harrison, Sarah Hodgson, Tina Jackson and Alyson Read. Thank you for your thoughts, and I hope you enjoy the finished version as much as you enjoyed the first 50,000 words.

And now thanks are due to my ARC readers, who read the novel prior to publication day, and are ready and waiting to upload reviews on the day. Fantastic job, I am so grateful.

The idea for this book came from the book *Who's Buried Where in England* by Douglas Greenwood. Fascinating stuff, and I sent Doris and Wendy off on their holiday after identifying some graves that were fairly close to Bradwell, their starting point. They didn't reach the grave of Sylvia Plath, and I'm sorry about that, so I'll go and visit her for them.

My final thanks go to my readers who didn't want the Kat and Mouse series to end. This, although not part of the series, is my compromise!

Love from Sheffield,
    March 2020